The

FRENCH
GIFT

Also by Kirsty Manning

The Lost Jewels
The Song of the Jade Lily

The

FRENCH GIFT

GIFT

A NOVEL *of* WORLD WAR II PARIS

KIRSTY MANNING

wm

WILLIAM MORROW

An Imprint of HarperCollins*Publishers*

P.S.™ is a trademark of HarperCollins Publishers.

HarperCollins books may be purchased for educational, business, or sales promotional use. For information, please email the Special Markets Department at SPsales@harpercollins.com.

Originally published in Australia in 2021 by Allen & Unwin.

FIRST U.S. EDITION

Library of Congress Cataloging-in-Publication Data has been applied for.

ISBN 978-0-06-304556-9 (paperback)
ISBN 978-0-06-308232-8 (hardcover library edition)

21 22 23 24 25 BRR 10 9 8 7 6 5 4 3 2 1

For Jemima, who carries resilience and joy in her heart.

You are all kinds of wonderful.

The

FRENCH
GIFT

Chapter 1

MARGOT

The grand marble foyer was bursting with color and excited conversation. Politicians, artists, writers, socialites, and local French gentry sipped champagne and martinis, and greeted each other with kisses to each cheek, merry backslaps, and firm handshakes. A five-piece jazz band played in the corner, and the warm summer air was thick with expensive perfume, pollen, and a hint of cigar smoke.

In the simple uniform of a housemaid, Margot Bisset squeezed through the crowd, slipping past women in drop-waist sequinned gowns and sheer silk sheaths, and men in tailored tuxedos. Her job for this first part of the evening was to carry a cup of incense among the guests, filling the room with wafts of cloves and orange oil.

Her mistress, Madame Tilly Munro, had pushed the cup into her hand and purred, "So *exotic*, darling, *very* seductive. Just keep moving around the foyer until it runs out." Madame Munro's backless silk dress trailed along the floor behind her. "Oh, look, you've got a streak of gold paint across your cheek, how sweet." She pulled a handkerchief from her beaded purse and wiped the paint off Margot's face.

"*Merci*, Madame."

The older woman's voice dropped as she tugged Margot into a corner away from the guests. "About our little game tonight: it's very important you do exactly as I say."

Unease crawled up Margot's spine.

"*Vous comprenez?*"

Margot nodded, holding her breath.

"Good. Now, you need to hide yourself on the balcony over-looking the pool. Just before midnight, pull the revolver from behind the palm and shoot it into the air when the fireworks go off. It's loaded, so make sure you point the barrel well into the sky. We need the gun to be smoking when they find Peggy's body. Evidence!"

"Are you certain?" said Margot warily.

"Absolutely, darling. Now go! Set the mood for our guests. Isn't it heavenly?" Madame clapped her gloved hands before launching herself into a hug with a bemused Duke and Duchess of Windsor.

Margot took a moment to watch the former king of England and his demure wife take time to greet their hostess and the assortment of shiny guests gathering in her wake. She knew the Munros were supremely wealthy, but to so casually touch a former king . . .

As Margot walked around with the incense, she looked to where a vase of white lilies with golden stems stood in the middle of a circular table. Madame had insisted they be painted for the party.

No one loved an extravagant surprise more than Tilly Munro. For last year's Bastille Day party she'd drained the swimming pool and had it filled with Krug champagne. Who could forget the fountains that'd sprayed delighted guests with bubbles, coating their summer tans, dresses, and tuxedos with a sticky layer of good cheer?

Apparently, the only way to top such opulence was an unexpected death.

Early that morning, Madame Munro had summoned Margot to her chamber and, while she dressed, declared that someone would have to be murdered at the party. "Nobody ever remembers what we ate or drank—lobster or quail, Krug or Dom Pérignon. They only remember the fun times."

"But m-murder, Madame?" Margot stuttered. Had her employer gone completely mad?

"Don't be silly, darling." Madame leaned in toward the mirror and closed one eye to draw on some black liner. "I don't mean a *real* murder. Did you think . . . ?" She turned to look Margot up and down before continuing to apply her eye makeup. "It's a *faux* murder."

Margot blinked. "Who—?"

"Peggy Schramsburg." Madame's voice chilled a fraction, before she said brightly, "She doesn't know it yet. I'll tell her just before lunch. She's a good sport, though."

Margot wondered if *being a good sport* extended to being a fake murder victim.

"Do smile, Margot. You look sour otherwise and it's unbecoming for a young woman. Tonight's just a *game*, remember. It's going to be a scream."

Now, Margot swallowed and turned her attention back to the party guests—particularly Mademoiselle Schramsburg, who stood nearby. The willowy American heiress wore a scoop-necked emerald gown cut low at the back. Crystals on the shoulders and her belted waist caught the light, and her tight curls were set with a matching headpiece. She was chatting to a woman in a beaded blue dress. "These flowers look *magnificent*, much prettier than natural lilies, don't you think?" Mademoiselle selected two glasses of Krug from the coupes lined up with military precision and gave one to the other guest, her hand shaking slightly. The women clinked glasses before Mademoiselle stepped back to admire the spectacle unfolding in the foyer. "Trust Tilly to add that bit of extra magic to the evening," she said with a tightness to her voice, as everyone looked up to where the huge central chandelier had been replaced with a trapeze.

The jazz band played louder, and spotlights pointed to the ceiling. A birdlike woman was perched on her feet, swinging on the bar, dark hair gelled across her forehead like a bathing cap, green glitter twinkling above her eyelids. The trapeze was pulled higher, and the acrobat started to swing higher, garnering an appreciative whoop from the swelling crowd below.

No one was more astonished than Monsieur Ted Munro. He had just meandered into the foyer in his dashing white tux, tie undone, and walked across to find Madame Munro, who had extricated herself from the Windsors. "There you are, my love.

Can't fasten this jolly ti—" He stopped mid-step when the acrobat swung above him, arms dangling down; as she unfurled her nimble body, it became apparent that she was not wearing a leotard, but sequinned nipple tassels in the shape of stars.

"Shut your mouth, dear. It won't do to drool on your tux," Madame Munro murmured to her shocked husband.

The crowd whooped again, and Peggy Schramsburg touched the hostess on the arm as she pointed to the trapeze with a white-gloved hand. "Whatever will you think of next, Tilly? What a riot! I can't imagine what else you have planned for tonight's little soiree."

Madame gave her young guest a taut smile and said, "Oh, can't you?"

A tall dark man accompanied by a chic, tiny woman greeted the hosts. The man walked with his broad shoulders pulled back, the white tuxedo tailored to his frame. His hair was short and slicked back, and an unlit cigar dangled from his bottom lip. Margot recognized him at once: he was a business associate of Monsieur Munro and Peggy Schramsburg's former lover. An arrogant man—she'd heard him brag as he smoked by the pool on previous visits about both his romantic conquests and his direct line to the German chancellor. The woman by his side wore dusty-pink chiffon silk with layers that hugged her curves and a fox-fur stole draped around her shoulders. She smiled tightly as she took in the room—a smile that did not reach her dark eyes. Instead, she raised an eyebrow at the man by her side, as if there were a million other places she'd rather be.

"Herr Bloch, Coco—so glad you could join us," Madame crooned. "I was thinking you might not make it."

Beside her, Peggy went pale.

"Well," said Herr Bloch, "after your husband guaranteed me priority for supply of their cloth, it would be ungracious not to show my face. And Coco here has been such a darling host for the summer, I could hardly deny her a party. Mademoiselle Schramsburg." He stepped toward the American and lifted her limp hand to his lips. "Always a delight. You look splendid."

She stiffened as he kissed her hand, her eyes darting around the room, then she swallowed twice in quick succession, as if trying to suppress a cough. Margot poured a glass of water and passed it to the young American.

Herr Bloch and his companion stepped to the far side of the room to greet other guests.

Lingering at Mademoiselle's elbow in case she needed anything else, Margot moved her spiced incense to one side to stop it from billowing up her nose. Madame Munro had assured her that all the plans for the game were in hand. But with Mademoiselle looking so wan, maybe it would not proceed? It hardly seemed fair if she was out of sorts.

Or perhaps Peggy Schramsburg was a first-class actress.

Margot looked between the two glamorous women, one older and shrewd, the other seemingly doe-eyed and innocent as only the extremely rich could be.

The crowd roared and clapped as the acrobat looped over her trapeze to hang by one leg. Her sparkly breasts bounced around, and no one could keep their eyes off her.

Monsieur Munro wrapped an arm around his wife's waist and said to their American guest, "Take lessons from this one! Nobody throws a party like my Tilly. Just hope the stock market holds and that Herr Bloch keeps buying my cloth. I know he was a scoundrel to you, and you mark my words, the man will realize what a fool he's been as soon as you set sail. But business is business, right? The world needs to keep spinning." Monsieur Munro chuckled, kissed the top of his wife's wavy hair, and reached for some champagne.

Margot had assumed the American was jittery because of the murder game that had been thrust upon her. Now, she realized the pretty young woman's head was elsewhere. She was nervous about seeing her ex-lover. Her square jaw was clenched.

As they clinked glasses, the heiress stretched her pale neck toward the ceiling like a swan and seemed to gather herself. "Tilly, wherever did you find this magnificent performer?"

"Through Gabriel, one of our gardeners! Would you believe he used to be in a Parisian circus troupe?"

"Really!" gasped Mademoiselle, fluttering a hand to her chest.

"He's a dish, darling Peggy. But it never ends well if you mix with the staff. Nobody likes it when somebody steps outside their station."

Monsieur Munro interrupted. "Well, I don't care where you found her, Tilly, I like her!" He gawked up at the acrobat again, then winked at Mademoiselle before giving his wife another squeeze. Madame flinched slightly, and Margot couldn't work out if it was a reaction to her husband or the younger woman.

Thinking of Gabriel, Margot stared past the terrace and pool to where the terra-cotta roof of the gardening shed poked out from the circle of the bay hedge. Was he there now? She wanted her note delivered before service started. After this silly murder game was finished, she hoped he would join her for a glass of champagne on the cliff tops overlooking the sea. The staff were permitted a drink once their duties were done, a patriotic nod to the holiday. Usually Margot was too tired to partake, but Gabriel's mysterious years away from the village since they last saw each other at school—his tales of travel from Madrid to Istanbul with his circus troupe—fascinated her and left her wanting more.

She paused to breathe in the incense. For the first time, her future smelled of the joys of discovering faraway places.

The foyer was a dreamy haze of silk, perfume, fur shrugs, and sequins as the five-piece band started its next tune. Madame Munro nodded at Margot and gestured for her to keep circling the room. From the corner of her eye she spotted little Maxime Laurent trussed up in a miniature tuxedo—surely tailored by special request of Madame—greeting guests at the front door with a cheeky grin, dark curls slicked back with Brylcreem. To the women he handed out posies of rosemary, thyme, and lavender, which they threaded about their wrists with fine red, white, and blue ribbons. Each man was issued a boutonnière of tight buds that matched the posies.

Maxime was Gabriel's younger brother, and they lived with their father in the caretaker's cottage on the other side of the hedge. Margot was fond of the boy and often minded him when his father had to work after dark or on a weekend. Maxime loved picture books, so Margot would scavenge the secondhand bookstalls at the village markets for pretty bargains she could read with him.

She walked over to where he stood. His eyes grew large with

delight when he saw her, and he dropped the velvet pillow he was holding for the boutonnières and gave Margot a hug. "Ma-Ma."

"Maxime!" She knelt to pick up the pillow and gather the few remaining posies from the marble tiles. "You look *magnifique!*" She kissed him on both cheeks and gave him a hug.

The boy yawned and dropped his shoulders. "I'm sleepy. Will you take me home and read me a story?"

"I can't, little one. Not while I'm working." His face fell, and she pinched his cheek. "What a good job you've done." She glanced around and decided no one would miss him now that they were well into their second and third glasses of champagne. "You should run home."

"But . . . Madame—" He looked as if he might cry.

"Shush, Maxime." She squeezed his hands. Over his shoulder she saw Madame Munro grab another champagne coupe and do a few steps of the Charleston with one of the American writers from the village. Margot had often seen these writers at the café, craned over coffee in the morning and anise-flavored pastis in the late afternoon. They debated politics with the locals and each other, read each other's notes, and idled away the time drinking and scratching in their leather-bound journals. She thought of her own notebook upstairs—a treasured birthday gift from her mother—lying blank.

Margot ushered the child to the back door. "Go home, Maxime." She kissed the top of his head.

"Margot!" Madame's voice trilled across the room.

Margot stepped into the doorway to shield the child from view, then slipped her hand into her apron pocket and took out the note. "Can you give this to Gabriel? But please don't tell anyone else." She kissed his soft cheek; he smelled of cut grass and soap. "It's our secret."

"*Promis juré.*" He lifted his pudgy hand and proffered his little finger.

"I promise," she echoed.

The boy ran outside, passed the pool, and disappeared into the shadows, waving her note in his sweaty fist, leaving Margot holding the pillow. She tucked it into a bay window before resuming work.

The dazzling acrobat continued to spin overhead, and the evening air was thick with jazz and breezy conversation. Glamorous women clamored for the attention of scruffy writers and debonair politicians. Thousands of lights glittered over the sapphire water of the pool; the ocean just beyond the cliffs was an inky black. Margot sighed with nerves and a dizzy kind of happiness.

It had been one of those typical hot, dry Côte d'Azur days that run into each other throughout July, but the slap of the sharp summer mistral against her cheek was a reminder that a cool change was on its way.

❧

When it was nearly midnight, Margot did as instructed and hid herself behind the potted palm on the villa's balcony so she would have a clear view of Mademoiselle Schramsburg.

She checked the watch Madame Munro had lent her: 11:56 P.M.

Four minutes before the American heiress would glide onto the balcony swathed in silk and doused in House of Worth perfume, pat her curls, and—

Well, there was nothing to be done but wait.

Laughter and the clink of crystal flowed through the open doors, and gauze curtains billowed in the breeze. Usually she would tie them back, but Madame had instructed her to stay in position. It wasn't her place to disobey.

Instead she wriggled her legs to stop them from going numb and took in the scent of the hillside. The salty wind was brushing up the cliffs from the Mediterranean, and the grand avenue of cypress swayed. She was soothed by the trickle of fountains at each end of the pool.

11:58 P.M.

A whistle that sounded like no bird on this stretch of the coast made her catch her breath. When she looked to the garden, a shadow disappeared into the far bay hedge. He was there, waiting for her.

11:59 P.M.

The American stepped from the dining room onto the balcony and lit a cigarette. A gentleman in a white dinner jacket stepped out to join her: Herr Bloch. Or was it Monsieur Munro? Both were broad and dark—it was hard to tell from where she squatted, and he had his back to her.

She froze. This wasn't part of the plan.

The gentleman muttered something under his breath to the heiress, and Margot strained to hear. Then he grabbed Mademoiselle's forearm. "You shouldn't have—"

She snatched it away. "Stop. You won't get away with it."

The gentleman went inside, and Mademoiselle flicked her cigarette over the balcony. She put her hand to her long neck and stroked it. Her bare back was tense.

Margot expected Mademoiselle to turn and face her, but the American kept her eyes fixed firmly on the sea as if she were looking for something.

Margot reached for the gun behind the palm, steadied the cool barrel against her thumb, and held it skyward.

Bang!

Fireworks screamed into the sky and exploded in tiny silver stars as the beautiful heiress spluttered and fell to the ground. She writhed, silk sliding up her legs and pooling at her hips.

Blood seeped from the back of the American's head across the terra-cotta tiles. Margot froze as she felt warm liquid dribble down her face.

Bestselling novelist Joséphine Murant dies, aged 100

OBITUARY BY DR. CLÉMENT TAZI

La grande dame of French mysteries, Joséphine Murant, has died just one month after celebrating her hundredth birthday. Her thirty-nine novels have sold more than fifteen million copies worldwide and been translated into twenty languages. Perhaps her best-known title is *The Forgotten,* soon to be made into a Netflix series.

Murant admitted on publication of her debut novel, *Little Lost Child,* that her first completed manuscript had been rejected, stating in an interview in the literary journal *Réalités*: "My publishers knocked back my first attempt at a mystery. They said the plot was implausible. A good lesson for any writer to learn." She refused to be drawn further on the subject.

In her youth, Murant studied literature at Sorbonne University, then became a journalist and critic prior to World War II. Though she always denied being a formal part of the Resistance, during the Occupation she was convicted of working for clandestine newsletter *Liberté*, which had eight issues between mid-December 1940 and the end of March 1941. She was arrested and sent to Fresnes Prison in 1941, where she shared a cell with the infamous Margot Bisset. In

1942, Murant was tried by the Wehrmacht and sentenced to deportation and five years in prison; she and Bisset were sent to Anrath Prison in Germany, where they worked as forced labor at the notorious Phrix Rayon Factory. Records show Bisset died at the factory in a workplace accident.

On her release from prison in 1945, Murant initially returned to Paris, but she refused any further work as a critic, journalist, or social commentator and lived as a recluse. Still, she continued to write: she retreated to the world of fiction, producing thrillers that focus on social class and boast strong female protagonists. Her work has been described by many critics as the "forerunner to domestic noir." According to *New York Times* bestseller Nancy Popper, "Murant made the world realize that 'women in crime' is not a subgenre."

Forty years after meeting Margot Bisset, Murant purchased Villa Sanary on the Côte d'Azur: the luxury home where Bisset had worked as a maid prior to her arrest. It was also the site of the notorious 1939 murder of American heiress Peggy Schramsburg. The killer? Bisset.

Murant refused to be drawn on details of her incarceration and her friendship with Bisset, except once: during her *Réalités* interview, she commented with surprising vehemence that "Margot Bisset is innocent of any wrongdoing."

In her later years, Murant lived in peaceful seclusion in her Côte d'Azur villa, but she did not retire from writing until her final eighteen months, when failing eyesight and dementia made it impossible for her to continue. She told the BBC *Crime*

Writers series that "magnums of rosé, long cliff-top walks, and zero pesky children" were the key to her long life.

Murant is survived by her great-nephew, Raphaël Allard; his wife, Genevieve Black; and great-great-nephew, Hugo Allard.

Clément Tazi, a historian and documentary maker, is head curator at the Marseille Museum. In 2004, he interviewed Joséphine Murant as part of *Uncovering History* for the BBC.

Chapter 2

EVIE

From the back seat of their Uber, Evie Black and her son, Hugo Allard, watched the concrete towers on the outskirts of Nice give way to rolling hills in progressively steeper inclines, ribbons of vineyards, and charming pale stone villas with blue shutters. In Evie's lap lay the handwritten letter from Dr. Clément Tazi that had prompted this visit to the Côte d'Azur: a request for help with an exhibition.

With the increasing public interest in World War II history, I thought this retrospective might be a good opportunity to display—with the greatest respect—some of Joséphine Murant's artifacts and perhaps some working documents to tell the story behind Joséphine's conviction and wartime experience.

Forgive this intrusion, but the funding for this exhibition has been allocated for staging in fourteen months, so I am most keen to

16

meet with you. I would be most grateful for your participation in and support of this project.

When Joséphine was alive, Evie's husband, Raph, had loved to leave his trading office on a Thursday evening and slip down to the ragged coast and warm salty air with his family. When she died, he insisted on keeping up their relaxing weekend breaks. But then everything had changed, and a year had passed since their last visit.

Evie looked over at Hugo, who scrolled through his phone, oblivious to the lush blankets of lavender that stretched across the plains below and the olive groves that clung to the rocky terraces above. This would be Evie's last summer with her son before he went back to school for his final exams, the *grand bal* formal, and all the graduation rites of passage.

She returned her gaze to the letter's last line. *I wonder if it would not be too much of an intrusion to display Joséphine's unpublished manuscript.*

Evie ran her hands through her hair and scratched her head. Joséphine's publishers had asked her estate for this manuscript when she died, as it was guaranteed to be a bestseller. Unfortunately, nobody knew where it was or even if it still existed.

At the time, Raph had been handling all of Joséphine's estate matters. Then, just six months after his great-aunt's passing, he'd died suddenly of a brain aneurysm.

It had taken almost eighteen months for Evie to pick through the French probate and inheritance laws, and she was only now getting to the bottom of the paperwork. On top of that there were deadlines for her botanical illustrations, a business to run—her Saint-Germain shop, La Maison Rustique, which sold rare botanical books, illustrations, and manuscripts—and a grieving teenager to parent. She'd barely had time to catch her breath, let alone look for a missing manuscript, no matter how valuable.

Joséphine's will decreed her publishing profits went into the specially created Joséphine Murant Foundation. Another bestseller would bolster the kitty for the foundation for years to come, providing books for local schools and shelter for women who needed refuge. Surely Joséphine would have wanted that. Still, something niggled at Evie. If there *were* an unpublished manuscript, why hadn't Joséphine published it? The author had been formidably compos mentis until dementia addled her brain. If Joséphine Murant had wanted it done, it would have been.

Of course, before Evie could make any decisions about the manuscript, she had to find it.

She traced her fingers over Dr. Tazi's letter. *Thick stock—old school*, she thought, as she wondered what the curator was like.

Joséphine's will left Raph and his family Villa Sanary, the Paris apartment, and the contents of both properties. The directions were peak enigmatic Joséphine: *I trust you to love these places as I have done.* The remainder of the will contained instructions for the foundation and general operational notes for the villa and apartment. These stipulated that certain staff were to remain employed for life, allocated the olive oil harvest among the neighbors (apparently a touchy subject), and provided a maintenance to-do list that Raph had been halfway through: the bay hedge needed sections replanted to plug holes, all the squeaky windows in the villa were to be replaced, along with parquetry and wallpaper in the Paris apartment, et cetera. *I trust you to care for these properties and everything within for the next generation.*

Evie and Hugo had inherited all of this, along with foundation board positions, and Evie had resolved to tick a few more items off the list this summer. The exhibition was just the push she needed. And if there was an unpublished manuscript, surely it would be buried in Joséphine's library somewhere among her papers.

Evie wound down the window to breathe in the sea air as they drove through pockets of villages selling just-baked loaves and baguettes. Pretty bottles of rosé were lined up in shop windows, pink and white roses spilling from buckets on the footpath. Her mouth salivated at the neat rows of tarte Tatin—the local apple tart—canelés, crème brûlée, and croissants in a tiny patisserie, and again at the food truck selling paper-thin crêpes folded into triangles that oozed warm nutty cheese and a sprinkling of local spices or Nutella.

They'd returned here only once since Raph died. Evie knew she was being churlish, but it irritated her to imagine all those happy holidaymakers walking around the pretty seaside villages arm in arm, laughing and taking selfies of their sunburned noses, clad in caftans and espadrilles. Quaffing rosé and filling their faces with warm salty bread and local olive oil, fat baby tomatoes, stuffed vine leaves, and freshly grilled fish. She and Raph were once these shiny, happy people carrying Hugo in a sling, then a pram. Picking through *brocantes* and vintage linen at the markets, stopping for a glass of bubbles midmorning for no reason other than it was the holidays, and they were young and in love.

But she'd missed this place, its prettiness and charm. Before she'd met Raph, the Côte d'Azur had been a postcard destination. A cliché, like Paris. But she loved Paris—and she loved Raph. So why not the Côte d'Azur?

Soon she and Hugo would be at the first village in the foothills, where Raph had always asked the driver to pull over as he ran to the nearest boulangerie, then jumped back in holding three brown paper bags of warm fougasse. They'd torn the bread apart, filling the car with steam and the scent of herbes de Provence.

She looked at her beautiful boy, almost eighteen, with his ever-present AirPods poking out from his curls. He was hunched over and peering into his phone, scrolling with his thumb in what seemed like one endless movement. He smelled of antiperspirant and shampoo—better than the usual alternative—and she had to stop herself from reaching out to brush away the lock of hair flopping over his face as she used to do when he was tiny.

Evie had been completely unprepared for how much she missed Hugo's baby snuggles. His drunken sailor toddles. His screwy face when he kicked a goal in the youth soccer league. All these versions of Hugo had passed, just like Raph. Now she lived with a thoughtful, curious teenager, who tottered into manhood like a foal finding its feet one day and simmered like a raging dragon the next. Over dinner he'd launch into philosophical debates ranging from the injustice of the war in Syria to why burping at the table shouldn't be considered rude as such conventions were only recent social constructs. Evie loved these conversations.

But some days it took all her energy to cajole Hugo out of his darkened room. Finding his father dead on the bathroom floor had understandably taken its toll. He could withdraw and become sullen, or sad, at moments he'd expected to share with his father—after winning a game, or at a restaurant. His counselor assured Evie that the grief and trauma were normal and would lessen with time, love, and consistent therapy.

She hoped this summer break might give him—give them both—the breathing space they needed to pause and heal before her son charged off into the world.

As they approached the village, Evie asked their driver, "Can we pull over for a minute, please? I just want to grab something from the boulangerie."

The car stopped, and Hugo looked up from his screen to give his mother a quizzical look. "What's going on?" They could have driven into a war zone, and this teenager would not have noticed.

"That." Evie pointed to the boulangerie and jumped out of the car.

Two minutes later, she was handing a paper bag to the grateful driver, then another to an inscrutable Hugo. The car filled with the scent of rosemary, thyme, and oregano as they ripped apart the still-warm bread and stuffed it into their mouths.

"I remember these," said Hugo softly.

Evie nodded, trying not to choke as the bread stuck in her throat. "Of course," she said through a mouthful.

"I miss him. I miss Dad." Hugo stared at her with his father's dark eyes and blinked quickly to stop tears from spilling out.

"Me too." Evie held her son's gaze and squeezed his knee with her spare hand.

"Dad loved it here. The food 'n' stuff." Evie marveled at how her son had such an Australian casualness to his voice even though he'd only ever been a visitor to her homeland.

"He loved these." She waved the last of her fougasse in the air with an upbeat smile that masked the tightness in her chest. Hugo finished his bread and wiped his eyes with his palms. As he tapped at his phone to play music, Evie rested her head on his broad shoulder, lowered her voice, and whispered, "And he loved you, kiddo. More than anything."

Hugo shoved two white buds back into his ears. "Whatever."

Evie felt his shoulder tense, and she lifted her cheek to study him as he gazed out the window, a twitching leg the only sign he was listening to music. Who could blame this child for feeling lost?

She tried to comfort herself with the views of rocky coastline out one window and the gentle dance of foothills, vineyards, olive groves, and villas that fell past the other as they whizzed through village after village. Eventually they passed the front gateposts of Villa Sanary, and the car slowed to crunch over the gravel while they inched along a driveway of olive trees underplanted with lavender. The combination of gray and blue always made her heart soar; she was pleased to see it unchanged and thriving.

The caretakers, Monsieur and Madame Laurent, had clearly been keeping up their excellent work. This place was precious to the old married couple too. In fact, the villa had been Maxime Laurent's employer—his home—all his life. He'd met his English rose when she'd holidayed here with her family.

As the drive widened to the terrace, Villa Sanary revealed herself: soaring stone walls pink-hued in the afternoon light, cobalt shutters, and an assortment of silvery succulents and pencil pines in terra-cotta pots.

The Laurents rushed down the front steps, each grabbing a car door, then tugging Hugo and Evie into the sunlight.

"Bonjour, Evie, Hugo, so pleased to see you both," the Englishwoman murmured in her thick Yorkshire accent as she hugged Evie. She was soft and smelled of rosewater. Her gray hair was looped back into a loose chignon, and she wore the same blue pinafore she always did.

Monsieur Laurent, who always looked delighted, was almost giddy as he shook Hugo's hand and continued to pump it up and down. "Hugo. So tall! Lucky Madame Laurent cooked some extra focaccia today. How's the soccer? Your mother sent us a photo of your team after the final." He let go of Hugo's hand and grasped the boy's shoulders. "So big! What has this mother been feeding you?" He walked over to Evie and kissed both cheeks. "*Ma chérie!* We're so glad you're here for the summer."

"There's a chicken on the rotisserie, with potatoes underneath—just the way you like it, Hugo." Madame Laurent rubbed her hands together.

"Sounds wonderful, thank you," said Hugo, sheepishly plucking out his earbuds and discreetly tucking them into his pocket before kissing Madame Laurent on both cheeks. "You both look well. How's the veggie patch doing this year? Last year you guys could have fed the village if you had to!"

The Laurents smiled at each other, delighted that this lovely young man had remembered their passion.

Evie had to stop herself from appearing gobsmacked. Hugo

could be polite; it was as though he saved it up for other people. She knew this was standard practice for teenagers, but that didn't make it hurt any less.

Madame Laurent threaded her arm through Hugo's and led him inside. "Come, I've made a lemon poppyseed cake for you. You can have it with some iced tea out by the pool. It's hot, m'lad!"

The four of them walked through the foyer across terra-cotta tiles, past the wrought-iron spiral staircase, and out to the back terrace, where the pool lay sparkling in the afternoon sun.

Madame Laurent and Hugo shared a look. "My favorite spot!" he said. "Might have to take a dip."

"You seem to spend most of your time in the pool, if I remember, *mes amis*." Monsieur Laurent grinned before he ducked off toward the kitchen. "*Excusez-moi*."

As Hugo, Evie, and Madame Laurent settled into cane chairs, the British woman clapped her hands. "I'm so pleased you've come." She paused. "Sorry, I know you've been busy, and it's not the same without our lovely Raph." She patted Evie's forearm. "We'll do our best to make it special. This is your home! Monsieur Laurent has been edging the lawn for weeks, and giving the tomatoes a little extra water. It's been wonderful"—she leaned in conspiratorially— "because when he's busy with the garden, that keeps him out of my hair in the kitchen." She chuckled.

"I was going to offer my services to Monsieur Laurent," said Hugo, "but it looks like he's got it under control!"

"He would still love your help, young man," said Madame Laurent as her husband appeared with a silver tray holding a cake and four glasses of iced tea.

The ice clinked when he put the tray on the table, and for the first time Evie noticed a tremor in the old man's hands, a thinning of his hair, and a stoop to his back. With a shock, she tried to estimate his age—between eighty and ninety? He'd always been spritely and robust. And Madame Laurent hadn't aged a day: with her ruddy cheeks, stocky build, and elegant bun, she seemed to be an eternal sixty-five, although she had to be older. Her grandchildren were grown, one working in the vineyards in Burgundy, the other a budding Hollywood actress.

Evie surveyed the perfectly manicured garden and lawns. "The place looks *magnifique*." She glanced at her son, who was enthusiastically cutting up the poppyseed cake and handing it around on blue china plates.

They chatted about Hugo's studies—he preferred physics to chemistry, Baudelaire to Rumi, and didn't get that Brit, Shakespeare, at all. The conversation rolled from school to the rare orchid manuscript Evie had just sold to a collector in Amsterdam, to the new biodynamic brew Monsieur Laurent had devised for his roses.

"Smell!" Madame Laurent lifted the vase of blush-pink and white roses up to Evie's nose, and she agreed their scent was wonderful.

The four of them continued to catch up and share anecdotes while butterflies fluttered about their heads and the sun slowly sank.

"So, this letter from the museum," said Madame Laurent, folding her hands in her lap. "Is Dr. Tazi still planning to come by tomorrow and go through Joséphine's work?"

Evie smiled to herself, still charmed by the handwritten letter. "Yes, as far as I know. We've had a brief phone chat. He's very keen to curate an exhibition that will inspire budding writers, please her fans, and also honor her story. As I understand it, he'll combine the more personal items from her postwar life and career with archival material from the war."

"I remember him, you know, from that BBC documentary. He was *very handsome*." Madame Laurent's cheeks matched the blush of the roses, and Evie was touched. She made a note to watch the documentary before their appointment tomorrow. Dr. Tazi had emailed the link, but between the shop business and rare-book appointments before she'd left Paris, Evie hadn't yet had a chance to see it.

"There's something else," she said to the Laurents. "Dr. Tazi has asked if he can display Joséphine's first manuscript, the one that never got published. I know Raph looked into it a while ago, but I'm not sure what he found. Did she ever mention anything about that to you?"

"No," said Madame Laurent, while her husband shook his head. "And I never asked. Never crossed my mind. When it came to her work, we only really talked about the books she was writing. Sometimes she'd give me a few chapters here and there to read, and ask my opinion on a certain character. To be honest, I preferred to read them when they were properly cooked—was a bit hard with her notes and scribbles all over the page to work out what was going on. I can't recall seeing an old manuscript, but I never looked. If there *is* one, it'd most likely be in her library, where all her manuscripts and drafts are stacked."

"That's what I thought. I'll have a look in there with Dr. Tazi tomorrow."

Monsieur Laurent beamed good-naturedly and tucked into another piece of cake, while Madame Laurent reached over to squeeze Evie's hand. "Everything is in order, I assure you. I haven't moved a thing. Not my place."

"Of course, thank you both," she said quietly. "I wish I'd known her better." She glanced at the gnarled branches of the apple trees in the orchard and longed to lean against their trunks, hidden among the long grass, her botanical sketchbook in hand. "You're the ones who knew her best, besides Raph."

"*Oui*," said Monsieur Laurent. "But Joséphine liked to keep to herself. Apart from your family, there were few visitors. Only once a year, in May—the month before each new novel came out—she would invite journalists here. They were free to wander the garden and take afternoon tea. Madame Laurent would make this cake, or a chestnut chocolate," he added proudly.

"Yes, yes," said his wife, swatting her hand to shush her beloved. "They'd wander around chatting with each other, poking their curious little faces up at all the windows until their allocated fifteen minutes with Joséphine. Although it was much shorter if they overstepped—the publicist ensured they only asked about her books and writing process! Sometimes you'd get the odd fan trying their luck, showing up at the front door. They got short shrift, I can promise you!" The housekeeper sat back in her chair and laughed, while Monsieur Laurent wrestled with a curl of vine that had strayed from the stone wall, bending it back and forth to break off the stem.

Hugo raised his eyebrows at Evie as if to say, *Wow, Aunt Joséphine really was next level!* He knew she was famous, but of course, her kind of fame existed in a different world from the one the family occupied. To Hugo, Joséphine was simply a much-loved wrinkly great-great-aunt.

Madame Laurent took a sip of her iced tea and said, "The journalists would come here in their three-piece suits, carrying notebooks, their faces hopeful and earnest, and line up as though they were to meet royalty"—she patted her forehead with a blue hankie—"which she was in a way, I suppose. But apart from this house, she lived simply. Toast and an egg in the morning. Maybe pasta or a piece of fish for lunch—if I could convince her. Onion soup for dinner. Ate like a sparrow near the end. No guests, meals served at the same times, and she never wanted me to fuss over her." The housekeeper lowered her voice. "Once Monsieur Laurent took a tray with some soup and tea up to her room, and she hissed at him to leave, insisting he never serve her again. He was shocked, of course. Joséphine always had a soft spot for him—never a sharp word." She smiled warmly at her husband. "I took it she was upset because she was in a nightdress and felt immodest. But when I thought about it more, well, I believe she threw you out because you took tea instead of rosé."

Monsieur Laurent laughed. "Right you are. A rosé a day!"

"Spoken like a true local," said Evie.

"Anyway, where was I?" Madame Laurent dabbed at her neck. "Yes, the journalists would line up, asking where she got her inspiration from and this and that. Not unreasonable, when you think she bought this villa. She was constantly pestered about her friendship with Margot Bisset—it must have driven her mad! They wanted to know all the gory details about the murder of that poor American girl, Peggy Schramsburg. I suppose they assumed Margot would have spilled the beans in prison and that's why our Joséphine wrote crime books. Can't say I blame them for connecting the dots—plenty of inspiration for murder mysteries in prison, I should think." Madame Laurent chuckled. "It also very much peeved Joséphine when they asked why she wrote mysteries, as though they were frivolous, when she used to be a journalist and could have written about the war."

Evie had read most of Joséphine's novels, but the one that resonated most was *Little Lost Child*, a mystery in which desperate parents scour the Continent looking for their kidnapped child. The novel contained a raw tenderness that had kept Evie up reading right through the night. She'd found she couldn't put it down—the mother's suffering was so visceral. But Evie had never summoned the courage to ask Joséphine about her work.

⁂

A few minutes later, when Madame Laurent had taken the tray back to the kitchen, Evie glanced across to where Hugo was disappearing into the garden with Monsieur Laurent as if they were being swallowed up by the pale-pink roses, Joséphine's favorites.

Evie found herself wondering, for the hundredth time, if it was fair to show the unpolished work of an author to the public. She thought of the unfinished paintings in her sketchbooks, of all the hard work she put in to make an image seem light and effortless on the page. The hybrid Himalayan poppy that needed a second layer of blue wash. The juvenile *Hedera helix* that needed more veins and light on the foliage, and would need to be redone from scratch. The too-heavy hand on the outline of her geranium, where it seemed her frustration had seeped into the thick paper stock.

Evie considered Madame Laurent's comment about journalists hounding Joséphine for details of the murderer Margot Bisset. Their friendship must have had a great impact on Joséphine. Why else had she bought Villa Sanary and started writing about murder? Yet she had never discussed that portion of her life, and perhaps she'd had good reason to keep it from public scrutiny. The war had surely scarred more than her face and hands.

Just how much of her story—her life—was it appropriate to exhibit?

Leaning toward the vase of summer roses, Evie drew their scent into her lungs. Perhaps she was overthinking this. Joséphine must have kept everything for a reason; otherwise, surely she would have destroyed it all or left instructions to that effect in her will.

She had endured darkness and horror, and she'd been reclusive, but she had also reached for optimism and dignity, and fashioned a rich life from harrowing circumstances. Evie recalled the joy on her face when the Laurents presented a platter of fresh radishes and carrots from the garden with handmade aioli, or a perfectly grilled flounder, or a bouquet of roses. Joséphine had been delighted by Hugo, and she'd savored the precious time they had all spent together at Villa Sanary.

Evie sliced another piece of cake, scooped a large forkful into her mouth, and gazed at the pool. As she brushed the crumbs from her lips, she took a deep breath and resolved to clear her head with a swim before her meeting with Dr. Tazi tomorrow.

She knew that Joséphine's life and work should be celebrated. But first, she needed to learn more about who the famous author had been.

Chapter 3

Right on time for their meeting, Dr. Clément Tazi roared up the driveway in a vintage blue Mercedes sports car. As he got out, dressed in black jeans and a white linen shirt, Evie was embarrassed to admit to herself that this French museum curator was far younger, more relaxed, and more crumpled than she'd imagined from his formal letter of introduction. She felt a jab of curiosity. Madame Laurent was damn right: Clément Tazi was handsome. Sexy, even. Evie's gut reaction was a little discombobulating.

Fidgeting, she plucked a needle from a rosemary bush, crushed it between her thumb and forefinger, and took a whiff to calm herself with the woody scent. She still hadn't watched the BBC documentary, and she'd been expecting a man well over fifty, dressed in a tweed coat with leather arm patches. Because who else still wrote letters?

"Bonjour!" she called as she walked across the gravel to shake his hand. She was surprised at his firm grip and how hard and callused his hand felt against hers. Again, she was struck by the contrast with her expectations.

She preferred strong hands that bore the signs of hard work. Perhaps it was her country roots: she was descended from a line who had worked the land, grown golden grains, and split apart fleece with their thumbs as they classified sheep. But she had fallen in love with an office worker—she winced, appalled at herself, then pushed Raph from her mind.

"Pleased to meet you, Dr. Tazi."

"Clément, please. I appreciate your taking the time to meet me and show me the villa, Madame Black."

"Genevieve, but please call me Evie. Australians love shortening their names."

When Clément smiled, tiny laugh lines appeared around his eyes. His face was tanned, weathered, but open as he studied Evie.

They stood there for a beat, perhaps two. Uncomfortably warm, she glanced at a rogue shoot of ivy scurrying up the wall of the villa and disappearing into a crack on the second story.

Following her gaze, Clément pointed at the villa. "Joséphine Murant had wonderful taste."

"She did." Evie ran her eyes over to the far pink stone walls covered with clematis and jasmine and noticed how nature made the villa sing. "I can imagine what she felt when she bought it all those years ago. Every time I pull up that drive with the pale gravel, the olive trees and lavender, I start to feel more relaxed. It's a safe little enclave here, far from the city. See the windows and shutters on the top floor? We just replaced them. Joséphine even specified the exact blue in her will."

"It's charming. But Mademoiselle Murant didn't buy this villa because of its appearance, did she?"

"I guess not. She must have had quite the connection with Margot Bisset."

"Did Mademoiselle Murant ever mention her?"

"Not much. Just that Margot grew up here along the Côte d'Azur and had fond memories of sunny days, herbed bread, salt and sea, and all the fresh fish you could ever want."

"That's the Riviera for you. All the clichés, but within those is beauty—even just in the summer air." He smiled.

Evie did the same, enjoying the combination of salty sea breeze and wild herbs, enough to clear her nose. "Shall we go inside?" She ushered him through and out to the terrace, where Madame Laurent greeted the museum curator like an old friend, with tea and a still-warm lemon and rosemary cake.

As Clément and Evie enjoyed these refreshments, he explained he'd only recently been appointed head curator of the museum, and he wanted to shake things up. "My doctorate was in modern European history, specifically World War II. Twenty-five years ago, most students were still fixated on the ancients. I've always wanted more than just tenure and research papers—I want to show people history. For them to feel it."

"So, museums."

"So, museums!" He grinned. "I don't think people want to walk through a gallery looking at old bones and pieces of jewelry any-more. Attention spans are shorter, and they can find most things on the web. What's the point of going? I took my nephew the other day—he's six—and do you know what he said? 'Uncle, too much old stuff.' He's right, of course." Clément finished his iced tea. "We need to take people away from stuff—and stuffiness. A sliver of time that we've preserved. We need to give them stories."

"Is that why you started making documentaries?" asked Evie.

"At first, back almost twenty years ago, it was, how do you say in English . . . a side hustle?" He blushed slightly, and she was charmed. "But I found video footage and spoken word injected life into our walls, reaching out to audiences who may never step inside a museum."

"So, you're like the David Attenborough of history?"

"Hardly." His cheekbones bloomed redder. "I'm hopeless in the wild, away from coffee, and most of my subjects are dead. It's more like unraveling a mystery—poking about to find forgotten pockets of history. Joséphine Murant was, and remains, such an enigma."

"Is that a kind way of saying she could be a little prickly?"

He raised his eyebrows and opened his palm in a diplomatic gesture. A dark curl fell across his face, and he brushed it away. "I'm not sure how to answer that. You know, at the Marseille Museum it would take me over a century to display everything we have in storage. There is so much more hidden away than on display."

Evie gave the curator a curious look. "I'm not sure what that has to do with Joséphine?"

He took a breath. "Well, that was my impression of her too—so much more hidden away than was on display. She was a master of her craft, a survivor of the Nazis, a Resistance fighter, a brilliant journalist. All that is on the public record. But in the many interviews with her I've read—and the one I conducted—only once did she reveal anything deeply personal, when she defended Margot Bisset. Well, she spoke of her penchant for rosé, and everything here on the Côte d'Azur, but that's hardly a scoop."

Evie had a hazy recollection of Raph mentioning, years ago, that documentary makers had requested background information about his grandmother Lulu and great-aunt Joséphine. Back then, Hugo had been a colicky toddler, and Raph's trading desk was just getting started; he was working eighteen-hour shifts, while Evie had just bought her shop. Raph had politely answered basic questions for the documentary and left it at that.

"I know a little about her childhood," said Evie. "Joséphine loved to read well after her bedtime, and would debate anyone at the dinner table night after night. Her father gave her a franc if she could concisely argue her point and convince him by the time he got to the bottom of his glass of pinot noir. Her favorite foods were duck confit and lobster, tarte Tatin for dessert. She was always playing dress-up in her mother's closet, parading around in silk and sequins, draped with fur coats and boas. Mucked about with cold creams and her mother's lipsticks—apparently she achieved the perfect pout at twelve!" Evie paused, not quite sure where all of that had come from.

"You know much more than a little," said Clément. "Thank you for sharing those details."

"No worries. I wish I knew more. She had a rather fractious relationship with her sister, Lulu, I'm afraid. Lulu was rather conservative . . . er, she could be difficult." Evie didn't want to speak ill of Joséphine's long-dead sister, but the woman had been rather limited. "I understand Lulu was rather toxic. She used to start every sentence with 'The problem is' or 'The trouble is.' Apparently she found fault with everything Joséphine did."

Clément nodded. "I gathered as much." He changed the topic. "Did you get a chance to watch the documentary?"

Embarrassed, Evie shook her head.

"I'm sorry, you've been busy, and I'm asking a lot. But I have it here." He pulled out his laptop and moved his glass so he could balance it on the table. "Don't worry, I'm not going to show you the whole thing. There's just this one bit . . ." He clicked the file open and scrolled through. "Here."

Joséphine's scarred face took up the screen, angled so the camera focused on her preferred side. She had a silk scarf over her hair and tied under her chin—her trademark—and wore fuchsia lipstick and a green fur stole. Evie was startled: she'd never seen Joséphine in makeup, and it was rare to see her out of brogues and woolen slacks. But her sparkling eyes and flirty manner surprised Evie the most. Joséphine had always come across as modest, yet here she was, an octogenarian flirting with the camera—or was it the cameraman?

Evie shyly glanced at Clément. Reminding herself to be professional, she returned her gaze to the screen as Joséphine started to speak.

My first novel, Little Lost Child, *came about after I read an article in* Le Monde *about a stolen child. The mother was wrongly convicted of the kidnapping and subsequent murder and was sent to prison.*

Off camera, the interviewer's warm voice—clearly Clément's—

asked, *That's a huge topic for your first book. What prompted you to write about crime, and this one in particular?*

Evie sat up straighter; she'd always wondered about this, but it had felt a little too invasive to ask Joséphine. She leaned toward the screen.

Joséphine stiffened, emitted a dry laugh, then took a sip of water. *That's your first mistake. You assume a crime book is about the crime.*

The camera panned to Clément, who looked perplexed. *Then what's it about?*

Joséphine: *Justice. Through character and motive. It's a jigsaw of misdirected longing and deception. You have to hook the reader enough to take them into dark places before delivering some kind of justice.*

Clément: *So, you said the inspiration comes from real-life news stories. Is there anything of your own life experiences in your books? I know you went to—*

Joséphine raised her hand. *Prison. Germany. The war. Yes, yes, I know where you are going with this. An author perhaps writes some particular traits—or anxieties—into her characters. But I've written twenty-four books now, and I bet anyone who knows me couldn't put a finger on which novel has the most of me in it.* She shot Clément a cheeky look. *It would be a mistake to conflate Joséphine Murant with the characters in my books.*

Refusing to be put off, he tried a different tack. *But your books always start with a murder. They're so . . . visceral.*

Beside her, Evie thought she saw Clément give the faintest shiver.

Joséphine responded with an arched eyebrow, clearly enjoying the exchange. *Crime novels always start with a murder. As for being visceral, murder is horrific. And a reality. To pretend otherwise is actually a crime—if you'll forgive my pun! If you want pleasantries, read something else. I want to plunge readers into immediate and inconsolable shock. They need to feel rage and despair. To linger in some dark places. Trust me, the dark makes the light shine all the brighter.*

"So true!" said Evie, her gaze returning to Clément. He was certainly a disarming interviewer. She'd always wondered why Joséphine had agreed to participate in this documentary when she had rejected all similar offers. What was it about Clément that convinced Joséphine to participate? Surely it couldn't have just been sex appeal.

He switched off the laptop before slipping it back into his satchel and pulling out a manila folder. "I've brought you a sample of interviews she gave over the years—I'll leave them with you. But there's one in particular I want you to look at." He pointed to an article with a photo of a shy young Joséphine Murant awkwardly holding up a copy of *Little Lost Child.* "See here." He tapped a sentence highlighted in green. "In the cult literary journal *Réalités*, she said to the young journalist Albert Remon that she'd written another manuscript, and it was rejected. Did Joséphine ever mention anything about that?"

"No, but her publishers have made us aware of it. I understand it's a big deal that there may be an unpublished Joséphine Murant book floating about. And I imagine it isn't *that* unusual to have a few failed attempts at a novel before you get one published. I read an article last week in *Le Monde* about a debut author on the bestseller list." Evie paused to scratch her nose as she thought. "She wrote three full manuscripts before the fourth was picked up. Three! Imagine those babies just sitting in a lonely file on your laptop, rejected and returned." Evie looked at Clément. "Would you trash them, or keep them?"

"Keep! It'd be hard to throw away all that effort. And I guess maybe when I *did* get subsequent novels published, I'd realize that my early attempts *were* probably rubbish. If I were as famous as Joséphine and had a reputation to protect, I wouldn't let substandard work go into the world. Why disappoint readers like that?"

"Still, it would be worth a fortune," said Evie. "Not that the royalties would come to us," she added quickly, hoping he didn't think she was after a quick buck. "Everything in her estate goes to her foundation, then on to her selected charities."

"I'm aware. Remember, I had to get clearance from the lawyers and the foundation to mount this exhibition. Thanks for pushing that through."

"Of course, she deserves to be honored."

"Yes, the manuscript would be worth a fortune," said Clément, his face composed, "but that's not why *I'm* interested. My role is to find the stories, preserve artifacts for future generations, and showcase stories for this one. The past can teach us how women like Joséphine lived—and survived. What kept her going during her internment? Communities and friendships really matter in tough times. Her connection with Bisset is important. What does it mean? Also, including an unpublished manuscript in the exhibition would show the evolution of a writer. We can study how she reinvented herself after the war and kept on pushing. So, I wonder if we might look for some of her earlier attempts among her notes?"

"Let's see what we find," said Evie, still feeling protective.

"Thanks. I've contacted her publishers, but they need your permission as executor to release private correspondence."

"Understood." Evie stood up. "Right, well, if you've finished your tea, let's see what we can find in the library."

Chapter 4

Madame Laurent unlocked the door to Joséphine's library and led them inside. "I always keep this locked. Occasionally we get a fan turning up and wandering around the garden. They're mostly harmless, but you never know." The housekeeper looked embarrassed. "I should have unlocked all the rooms when you arrived, Evie. I just feel safer—Joséphine's life's work is in this room." The older woman's blue eyes grew misty.

"I understand," Evie said reassuringly, as she felt a surge of guilt. She'd always assumed Raph would sort out Joséphine's papers. They'd talked about whether the material should be donated to a library or museum, or put on display at her publishing house. Then he'd died, and the probate cycle had started all over again. It was hard to believe that Evie, the dreamy young backpacker who'd traveled to Paris on a whim, was now charged with unpacking the substantial estate of the family into which she'd married. She had to protect the papers of a French national treasure.

"Here," said Clément as he took two pairs of white archivist's gloves out of their packaging and handed one to Evie.

"Thank you." The cotton cooled her skin in a pleasantly familiar way; she wore similar gloves most days in her shop when she worked with rare illustrations and botanical manuscripts. "This library is beautiful—I haven't spent much time in here." She twisted her head to take in the floor-to-ceiling bookshelves and ancient wooden beams propping up a white cathedral ceiling. The desk overlooked a rose garden, with a conservatory beyond.

She walked to the sunny end of the room, noting the contemporary sisal rug and overstuffed linen sofas in a soft denim blue. She wanted to plop onto one immediately with a book; maybe she would, once her meeting with Clément was over. The books were divided into classics and philosophy, then mostly crime by the looks of it, in French and English.

"As I said, Joséphine had impeccable taste," said Clément, running his hands over the small cherrywood desk, then pulling back a curved Louis chair.

"I love this desk." Evie traced her fingers over a whorl.

"She brought this with her from Paris," said Madame Laurent. "Along with her typewriter. Never switched to a word processor or computer. Used to get this machine serviced every July before she started a new manuscript."

"Funny," said Clément, "she didn't strike me as superstitious when I met her. But I guess every writer—every artist—has her secret follies and rituals."

"Don't we all?" said Evie with an awkward laugh. Madame Laurent and Clément looked at her; neither spoke. Her cheeks grew hot.

Clément cleared his throat. "I know we're here to look through her papers, but now that I'm standing in this room, I wonder if we could perhaps photograph it, then put the desk, chair, and typewriter on display in the museum. You know, show people where and how she wrote."

"Great idea," said Evie, turning to the housekeeper. "Do you know if she kept anything else on her desk apart from the type-writer? A vase?"

"Notes or notebooks?" Clément asked with a hopeful inflection.

"Well, Joséphine had a thing for herbs. Always had a vaseful at her elbow while she worked, of fresh rosemary, lavender, and thyme. Said it kept her alert. Just picked them right off the cliffs over there." She pointed out the window. "They reminded her of her childhood."

"We'll have to put a little vase on the desk," said Evie with affection.

"And in answer to your question, Dr. Tazi, Joséphine did make notes by hand, but mostly on the drafts. You'll find them all cataloged and in boxes on that back bookshelf." Madame Laurent proudly pointed to a shelf of cardboard archive boxes in a neat row. "All in order by year of publication. Just as Joséphine left it."

"Perfect. *Merci.*" Clément lifted up his leather bag. "Mind if I bring out my gear?"

"Please," said Evie. "Use Joséphine's desk." She stepped back to give him space as he unpacked a woolen felt roll and spread it across the table, then beside it placed a loupe magnifying glass and some clear glassine envelopes used for storage of fragile papers and photographs. Next he produced a small document camera, a notebook, and a pen, and arranged them neatly on the desk.

Evie admired the methodical way he'd unpacked his tools. It showed that he truly felt a reverence for Joséphine's process and her craft as a writer, as well as his obvious curiosity about her history. Then Evie eyed his camera, the latest model. "Nice," she murmured, and he shot her a grin.

Until today, Evie had seen this exhibition as a necessary task—like taxes, probate, foundation guidelines, and pelvic floor exercises. She needed to seize this opportunity to honor Joséphine, and Raph would have wanted her to—of that she was certain. But now she realized that she shared professional similarities with Clément, and the task ahead—to identify documents suitable for exhibition and find the missing manuscript, if indeed it still existed—had just got a lot more interesting.

Madame Laurent smiled and turned her attention to Clément. "Now, I got to thinking about your question on Joséphine's notes and notebooks. As I said, she made notes on the manuscript pages with a fountain pen. Retyped draft after draft—sometimes up to six times per book, before it went off to her publishers in Paris and they put it on the computer."

"Yes, I remember this from when I interviewed her publishers. They even offered to buy her a computer and deliver it with someone from Paris to show her how to use it, but she refused!"

"Sounds like our Joséphine," said Evie.

"So," said Madame Laurent, "she had no need of a notebook. Went straight from her head to the page. But there was a book she pulled out from time to time . . ." The housekeeper scrunched up her nose. "One of those French philosophy books—never had much truck for them myself. A paperback. Dog-eared as all get-out. I never saw her writing in it, but it was full of notes by the looks of it, and almost falling apart. Kept in that bottom drawer." She pointed to the desk.

Evie exchanged a look of excitement with Clément, then she went to the desk and bent to open the drawer. A dusty copy of Gaston Leroux's classic *Le Fantôme de l'Opéra* sat inside.

She closed her eyes and took a deep breath. Her years of dealing with old and rare manuscripts had taught her she needed to concentrate at times like this. There was no photograph, no facsimile, that could replicate seeing a rare botanical illustration for the first time: the fold of a page to hide a mistake, overpainting, erasures, notes in the spine, and nuances of color and texture could all be missed in photographs. This job required patience and focus, elusive qualities in an era when almost all information could be gained at the end of a cursor.

"A French classic," said Clément beside her. "I wonder why she chose it. Perhaps the mystery element . . . *The Mystery of the Yellow Room*, an earlier novel by Leroux, was considered to be the first locked-box crime book. Pre–Agatha Christie."

"Who knows?"

Joséphine had obviously kept this paperback close for a significant portion of her life; its story might tell them something of hers. Perhaps it was an inspiration, or served as some kind of creative muse. But it was in a delicate condition: the cover mottled and curling at the edges, the spine folded and peeling from years of being bent open. The cheap thin paper stock had turned brown and brittle.

"I don't have a book pad with me," said Evie, realizing that if she lifted the volume up and opened it in the middle, it might split apart. She needed a padded cradle so it could be opened gently on an angle.

"I can come back with one. Let's just leave the book where it is, but have a quick peek to see if she wrote her name inside, or any dates or clues as to when she might have bought or been given it." Clément pulled out his phone and shone its light into the drawer so they could better see the book. He took his loupe from the desktop with his other hand and passed them both to Evie before taking out his notebook and pen.

"Thank you," said Evie as she gripped the tools and leaned in for a closer look. "There are watermark stains across the cover and down the front here, suggesting some of these pages are fused together."

"I see." Clément nodded as he took down the title and made some notes.

Evie felt an adrenaline rush kick in as she handled the old book—it was like staring into the crevices of a person's life. "Okay, I'm going to lift the front cover," she said before she carefully prized it open. A folded piece of paper sat between the cover and the title page, and she wiggled it out. "There!" She placed the paper on the felt and slowly unfolded it to reveal a handwritten letter in French. She translated as she read:

December 13, 1940

Dear Joséphine,

When I last visited you at Fresnes, the chief warden said I could bring you a book. Consider this your Christmas present.

You are lumped in his tiny mind with the prostitutes, dilettantes, tax avoiders, and petty thieves, I'm afraid. When I said you had an education and you used to work at Le Monde, *the warden just shrugged. "Ne rien savoir faire de ses dix doigts," were his exact words, I'm very sorry to say. While it's true you were not so blessed with coordination, you are by no means as useless as he suggests.*

I know you'll go mad without something to read and somewhere to record your thoughts. Notebooks are strictly forbidden, so I hope this little care parcel sees you through until this ridiculous prison sentence or war (whichever ends first) blows over.

Bises,
Mama xx

"Neither of Joséphine's parents survived the war," said Madame Laurent. "She never spoke of them—though that's not unusual. My parents never spoke of the war. Perhaps that's why she kept this book close."

"Perhaps," said Evie, as she turned from the letter to the book, desperate now for a closer examination. She lifted the title page, then the subsequent page, noticing the stiffness; if she turned too many more, she ran the risk of the pages detaching from the spine. She half lifted one more and shone the phone flashlight onto handwritten notes that took up the better part of the page. There was a tiny sunflower doodle in the margin, with dotted ink for the seeds. Although the ink was smudged, the cursive letters were still discernible. "Look!"

The three of them brought their heads together over the paperback.

Fresnes Prison
January 1941

My trial starts tomorrow. The charges are "possession of prohibited items" (ink, paper, stencils) and the production and distribution of Gaullist tracts. They can prove nothing. They only have the franc notes. I could have gotten them anywhere. All day I have been pacing my tiny cell—four steps—spurred by rage.

I'm surprised at my fury, my energy. It's as if I've kept it tucked under my pillow, simmering until my trial. Now it feels like a ball of fire I could throw at anyone who approaches me.

The fatigue doesn't help. At night I pull the thin blanket over my head, so my breath warms me like an oven. But every hour, the guards burst into my cell and prod me to check I'm still alive. There's been a problem with suicide, apparently. Though for the life of me, I can't work out why.

When I run my fingers along the concrete walls, the dripping water has turned to ice, and my bed is sodden by evening. My pail is left unemptied and uncovered for days. The window does not open, and our single meal is some thin soup, with salty sardines on a Sunday. Who needs the Ritz?

Today, though, brought a reprieve from the pacing. A new cellmate: Margot. She has dark skin, glossy brown hair—the type that will mat within the week, I wager—and flashing dark eyes. Her hands are broad and scarred. When she introduced herself, "Margot Bisset from Sanary," she held her hand out to shake mine with such warmth that I couldn't help smiling.

Margot Bisset from Sanary. Charged with murder.

"Well, I never," said Madame Laurent. "Never looked at it myself—that would have been prying. I just thought it was a favorite book that she'd left comments in—that she was sentimental about, you know? No wonder she kept it close."

"Indeed," said Clément, his voice awed.

"In her own words," said Evie, feeling teary. "She sounds so vibrant, so upbeat, in those *awful* conditions." She set down the loupe and passed the phone to Clément, who switched off its light. "I can't risk turning any more pages all the way. Most are stuck together. Can I please use one of those glassine envelopes?"

"Of course," said Clément. He passed one to Evie, who labeled it with a date and title before slipping the letter inside. "Looks like we have our first item for the exhibition." His voice was so exuberant, he almost sang. "I think we should leave the book in the drawer, undisturbed, until we can get it to a restorer. I have several contacts—"

Evie jumped in. "I'd like to give it to my colleague, Gilles Lavigne, at my shop La Maison Rustique. He's one of the best manuscript and botanical illustrator conservators in Paris. Lectures at the Sorbonne. People fly him around the world to give his opinion on a binding, or to analyze and repair parchment and ink. Hopefully he'll be able to unstick the pages and preserve the stock."

She looked at Clément and realized she was putting him on the spot—he was a museum curator with a roll call of experts. But this was personal: she didn't want Joséphine's innermost thoughts read by just anyone. It felt right to keep the paperback close until they knew exactly what they were looking at.

To her relief, Clément was gracious. "Of course! It is your book. If you like, the museum will arrange secure transport and pay for the restoration and facsimile. We don't have to decide now what we do with it."

"You're right. First, we need to focus on preservation. Then we can find out if there's anything else in there. But even if it's just this one entry, how extraordinary! Reading that page, I felt like Joséphine was right here in the room with us. Her energy just buzzed off the page."

"And it starts to answer those questions journalists were hounding her about for years."

Evie realized they were leaning extremely close to each other.

Madame Laurent coughed and said, "Did you know my husband also knew Margot Bisset? The maid used to babysit him, and he has fond memories of her singing him nursery rhymes, taking him around the markets, and buying him a palmier or ice cream. The lass had endless patience and was quick to laugh. Quite the softie, by the sounds of it. My husband couldn't believe his ears when his beloved Ma-Ma—as he called her then—was bundled off to jail. Heartbroken he was, according to his father. Sobbed into his pillow every night for weeks."

Clément gave a sympathetic nod, encouraging her to go on.

"Madame Bisset, Margot's mother, was so upset. Her family had been in service to this villa for generations. Monsieur Bisset had died young, apparently, so she needed to work. She got the boot, as you can imagine, when her daughter killed that rich American—can't have the staff knocking off people."

"Huh!" said Evie, fascinated. "I never knew. Well, Monsieur Laurent is a good judge of character, so there must have been something to this Margot Bisset if he liked her. Still"—Evie winced—"it's impossible to stay here without thinking about the murder. It used to spook me in the early days. Raph teased me about it once, when a shutter was flapping about in the wind one night and I jumped up to put the latch on. He said it was the dead girl's ghost trying to climb in the window."

Evie smiled to herself as she remembered him getting on top of her and tickling her all over when she slipped back under the feather duvet. The tickling had turned to a slow caress as he slid her nightie up her thighs.

"You all right?" asked Madame Laurent. "Looks like you *have* seen a ghost. But I can assure you, there are no ghosts in *this* house!"

"Only secrets in paperbacks," said Evie, forcing a smile.

"She kept her cards close to her chest, that one." Madame Laurent shook her head. "Can't have been easy in a Nazi prison. She never spoke of it, of course. Few did. My father was just the same—different army, same horror."

"My dad always said the same about his father. My *jadde* Karim was never the same after he returned with de Gaulle's forces from

North Africa . . . used to wake up screaming and shouting in the middle of the night. Sometimes they'd have to change his nightshirt two or three times because it was so drenched in sweat. Severe nerves, they called it." Clément's deep voice had grown heavy.

Evie understood at once what had drawn Joséphine to Clément and why she'd trusted him with her story—well, part of it. "How awful. Who knows what they all witnessed?"

Madame Laurent nodded sagely. "Oh, I agree with that. Joséphine was no stranger to darkness. Her books are terrifying. Where on earth she got her ideas from—all that gore! Well, it ain't natural, is it? To think like that."

Evie said, "I'm not sure I even understand anymore what *natural* means. Maybe it's best to let your imagination roam free. To get it all out onto the page." She thought of her watercolors and of the botanical illustrations in her shop, each of them a painstakingly accurate—and sometimes more vivid and beautiful—depiction of the real plant. "I agree Joséphine's novels are scary as hell, but in real life she was . . ." Evie fished for the right word. "In real life, Joséphine was *content*."

Clément rubbed his hands together and looked from his notebook to the Leroux paperback. "It seems to me that if we are to get to the heart of Joséphine's story of prison and war, then we need to find out more about Margot Bisset."

"Agreed," said Evie. "Let's research her case."

"I can look into that," replied Clément.

She eyed the archive boxes along the far wall of the library. "Thanks. But for now, we should get busy. If the unpublished manuscript survived, surely it's in this room."

Madame Laurent went off to make her plum jam, and Clément and Evie spent the next two hours sorting through piles of manuscripts. "I can't believe she typed out so many fresh drafts," said Clément, shaking his head as the pile he was working on threatened to topple over. He'd made thirty-nine neat stacks, one per novel, that took up much of the library. "It will be great to get some of these on display." He laughed as he held up a page smothered in red ink.

"No sign of the early manuscript?" asked Evie, and he shook his head. "Oh well, I'll scour the villa from top to bottom. Madame Laurent will help, I'm sure." Evie didn't want to burst his bubble just yet and say she thought the manuscript had probably been destroyed. If it had been stashed somewhere else, surely Madame Laurent would have found it by now. Then Evie remembered that the villa wasn't the only possibility. "We own the apartment Joséphine lived in before the war—we rent it out." Evie paused, feeling a pang of guilt about the neglected maintenance list.

"Do you think we could have a look there?"

"Maybe . . . It's an Airbnb, and it's pretty booked over the summer. But we should be able to get in one morning when the cleaners come. It's not very big, more a studio. I'll check with the concierge and get back to you. I have to be honest, we lived there for five years and it's tiny. If anything was there, I'm pretty sure we'd have found it. We installed so much storage! And we took everything with us when we left. I'll go through

Raph's paperwork in the archive boxes we have at home, though I doubt it's there."

Clément looked despondent. "Well, might be worth a look anyway."

Evie pointed to the drawer with the Leroux tucked inside. "You never know, there might be something in that paperback that tells us where it is. The first page suggests she used it as a make-do diary."

"Maybe." Clément's tone suggested he was unconvinced. "I'm more interested in her diary—if it is a diary—because it might give a firsthand insight into her war experience. There are so few first-person accounts, so it would be a breakthrough. We'd get to know her in her own words."

"We'll let Gilles do his work, then we can take a look." Evie decided it was best to focus on what they could exhibit. "I have something exciting for you." She reached into her handbag and placed a green silk jewel box on the desk. "This is Joséphine's Legion of Honour medal." Evie wanted Clément to see her as organized and professional, even though she'd just fished it out of a box of Raph's stuff she still hadn't gotten around to sorting.

"Thank you," Clément said solemnly as he opened it. "I've never actually seen one, let alone held one." He studied the medal for a moment. "It really is an honor. May I?" He picked up his phone.

"Of course."

After he'd taken a few photos, Clément handed the medal box back to Evie. "I'll make sure that when our team collects these items, we bring the proper storage material. This will need a secure

Perspex container." He jotted down more notes. "So now we have the accolades—the ending, if you like. I'm hoping we can discover the beginning and middle of her story. And I get the feeling there's a lot more to it than we realize."

*

That evening, as Evie relaxed on the terrace beside the shimmering pool with a glass of wine, she recalled a family visit to the villa. She and Raph had sat beside Joséphine in these same chairs, enjoying a celebratory dinner after the Legion of Honour ceremony. It had been a typical midsummer evening, the air thick with sea spray, humidity, and the heady smell of roses.

Joséphine wore a blue cashmere jumper that softened her dark eyes, and her head was wrapped in a triangle of silk knotted under her chin. Evie had never seen the old woman without the bright scarf, which provided a distraction from the mottled scars that wove across her nose and cheeks, and clawed their way down her neck and hands. Over the years these scars had thickened and hardened like old sea ropes, a daily reminder of an incident during her imprisonment. She had never spoken of it. Whatever had happened, it had not hardened her heart, nor her sense of humor.

Evie nearly choked on her lobster tail when Joséphine declared, "I said to my old rat of a publisher before he left today that I was higher on the bestseller list than that *andouille* Brit, James Archibald. They must pay me equally for my next book! And do you know what? My publisher looked bewildered. 'But you don't have *children*,' he argued. 'What would you spend it on?'" Joséphine paused, then said with tenderness, "But I do have a family. I have you."

"And we're so glad to have you," said Raph warmly. "That man is an idiot."

Evie nodded firmly, too outraged to speak.

"Yes, an idiot," said Joséphine. "He *implied* I wasn't a proper woman because I've never had a child. Worse, that I was greedy and selfish because I asked to be paid what I was worth. That's one advantage of old age—I care less and less what people think of me with each passing year." Her voice lowered. "To think of where I came from. What a mouse I was." She took a slug of champagne, and her feisty demeanor sagged as though all the air had gone out of her. She suddenly looked like a frail old lady.

"Come on, Aunt Joséphine," said Raph, picking up the medal box that sat between platters of lobster tails, grilled asparagus, and stuffed peppers, "you were given France's highest honor today."

"Pfft, I write a racy yarn. That is all." She shrugged with typical French nonchalance. "I have not found a cure for cancer, nor helped solve world hunger. My feats are minuscule."

Raph shot Evie a frustrated look. "But the Resistance—"

"Resistance, Resistance," Joséphine hummed. "Always people ask me about this, for half a century. France has found her feet, and the stories of the people who did truly great things deserve to be told. They must!" She topped up the champagne flutes. "Those people were the most courageous I ever knew. But I am not the one to tell their story. It is not mine."

Chapter 5

JOSÉPHINE

Raphaël and his lovely Australian wife had come to Villa Sanary to celebrate Joséphine's Legion of Honour award. After the ceremony at the local town hall, the three of them were sitting on the terrace with canapés and champagne when Raph proposed a toast. "To the great Joséphine Murant, commander of the Ordre des Arts et des Lettres."

Evie leaned over the table to read the certificate and congratulatory letter that had come with the award. She brushed her curls behind one ear and looked at Joséphine as she spoke softly. "It says here your award is for your literary contributions to France, as well as *your commitment, loyalty, and bravery* during the war."

"A double honor!" said Raph proudly. "That's our Joséphine." Then he cleared his throat and said, in a gentle voice, "We know about the books, but . . . look, I'd like to hear about the war in your words. Not learn about it from history books and award ceremonies. I can't imagine the horror, but I think I should try. It's an important part of who you are . . . who *we* are."

"Raph!" Evie shot her husband a warning look, and he ducked his head, sheepish. "Joséphine, I'm sorry, it's fine if you don't want to talk," said Evie.

"No need to apologize, honestly." She gave Evie a grateful smile. Raph's wife was very kind. This freckled young woman with flat vowels was broad and strong, steady and unflappable. Raphaël was lucky to have found her. He'd told Joséphine that he had bumped into Evie running for the Métro on a rainy day and offered her his umbrella. But Joséphine had noticed that it was Evie who often shepherded and sheltered Raph.

To Joséphine's relief, the conversation was interrupted by Madame Laurent's appearance with three bowls of steaming bouillabaisse. Over the soup, paired with a fragrant rosé, Raphaël and Evie raised the topic of Joséphine coming to live with them in Paris. "Just as a trial," Evie assured her as she reached for her hand.

Joséphine gently withdrew her hand and reminded herself that they meant well. "*Non, merci.* My home is here. You're welcome to join me at any time, for however long you please. This is your home too, Raphaël. But I have no business with Paris now."

The confused couple tried to protest, but she closed her eyes and held up a hand to still them. She belonged with this house and would be here until the end.

Raphaël slurped his soup and nodded. "Okay. But our offer still stands. And we can't move down here, Aunt Joséphine, you know that."

There was an uncomfortable silence before Evie deftly changed the subject, and soon they were talking about the spectacle of the ceremony.

Out of the blue, Raph asked, "How did it feel to be called a hero?"

Joséphine swallowed, as she had up onstage during the ceremony when the sun was beating in her eyes. She could see how others viewed her: a hero, a recluse, modest about her wartime past. What to do about such unwanted adulation? Her survival owed more to luck than merit. The web of secrets, subterfuge, and deceit that had led Joséphine from Paris to prison and then the factory had been refashioned into a heroic tale, told at elegant dinner parties and award ceremonies around France. Meanwhile, she gritted her teeth and accepted the awards on behalf of all the truly brave people who had been alongside her during the war, to ensure *their* lives would never be forgotten.

Joséphine's stomach roiled at any suggestion she was noble. She had survived—that was all.

"It's very flattering to be called a hero," she said finally. "But undeserved, I assure you."

She studied Raph and Evie. They made a handsome pair, with matching curls—his blond, hers dark—and athletic builds. But where Raph's eyes were almost black, Evie's were blue, and with shadows underneath, unsurprising when she was surely up half the night feeding Hugo.

Joséphine reached for Evie's hand and held it, then she took Raph's. She noticed the couple give each other bemused looks, but they didn't pull back. Her unease slipped away, for now. She was sitting by the pool with two of the people who mattered most to her in the world, and there was nowhere she would rather be.

Before the ceremony, she'd helped bathe the baby. Evie had gathered Hugo out of the bath, little sausage arms and legs poking and kicking with a giddy glee, before wrapping him in a towel and placing him in Joséphine's lap. "Forgot his romper," said Evie. "Back in a sec!" She dashed out of the bathroom, and Joséphine was holding Hugo tight when he looked up at her with the timeless dark brown pools of his eyes. Innocent. Ageless. He gave her a gummy smile and poked her cheek. She kissed his pink cheek in return, breathing his soapy milkiness deep into her lungs and wishing she could hold it there forever.

How could she tell Raph and Evie that Hugo's clumsy poke meant more than any medal? That the way he tipped his head and laughed straight from his belly was everything? She spent most days trying to forget the war, the horror of prison. But this pudgy child sent her back there with each giggle and fart. Because, if not for Hugo, then what was it all for?

Joséphine spent her days roaming the cliff tops along the Côte d'Azur. If she went farther afield, she would see her name on billboards at Métro stations and airports. Literary festivals begged her to appear as a keynote speaker. In the early days, she'd gone; decades ago, crime and mystery writers were not the authors du jour, and as such her talks had been fortunately confined to small, drafty halls with a smattering of enthusiasts. She'd liked her fellow panelists: clever, witty, relaxed. Their darkest thoughts were on the page for all to read, and when they returned to their hotel rooms, they no doubt slept soundly. Not so Joséphine.

When people asked her why she wrote mysteries, she usually gave some glib answer. A crime novel, like a prison sentence, always starts with the crime and then explores the subsequent questions: Who did it, why did they do it, and how were they brought to justice? Her readers loved to be pulled into a web of deception, with complex timelines and motives. Her novels were full of lies, wrong turns, red herrings. Also ghosts of lives past. Faces that haunted her . . . just like the book she kept by her side.

It was inexplicable to her—a woman who sought an anonymous, quiet life—that she had become a literary phenomenon. Now there was talk of a documentary by an enthusiastic young historian, Clément . . . something.

People had tried over the years to draw parallels between her life and her novels. And she understood that readers often conflated the lives of authors with their work. Her trial was on the public record, along with Fresnes Prison. Anrath. Dark, airless cells.

It wasn't lost on her—or her publishers—that with a renewed interest in World War II, her literary stocks rose. The world was running out of time to interview anyone who was there. She was considered something of a war hero. A survivor. An enigma.

It was a trap.

Joséphine Murant had survived in name, that was all. She was not the brave, starry-eyed woman who had stuffed pro–de Gaulle five-franc notes in her garter, or shepherded airmen through the backstreets of Paris in the dead of night. But to refuse the accolades would be to insult the legacy of those who had died. Brave people she had shared a life with. It was too painful to think of them all by name.

She released Evie's and Raph's hands and ran her fingers over the medal, a gift from the nation so many had given their lives to save. These people lived in her heart, though most of her life since then had been spent alone. The first months after the war had been consumed by seeking work. Her scarred red face meant people usually steered clear of her—certainly few invitations eventuated. In time, she made the occasional romantic connection with a man, but perhaps because she was so self-conscious about her damaged face—and her tender heart—it was easier to be alone. There would be no children from her womb; years of starvation and missed periods had affected her fertility.

After a time, fleeting connections and odd jobs were not enough. She needed something else to paper over the void. Crime fiction seemed to come naturally. She knew darkness and horror better than almost anyone—devoting her days to blood and trauma felt more real than anything else. Unexpectedly, doors in her life kept opening, and she muddled through as best she could, slamming each one behind her as she went.

Joséphine plowed her writing profits into charities. Women's shelters. Public schools. Success begat success. "This is not for me," she told herself each night when her head hit the pillow. People depended on her to survive; giving away most of her profits was her penance for survival.

She looked from lovely Raph to Evie, who each met her gaze fondly. Shaking as she reached for the wine bottle, she knocked her glass off the table. It shattered and scattered like diamonds across the terra-cotta tiles.

"Had enough?" asked Raph with a tentative smile. "Perhaps we should call it a night." He grabbed the bottle and placed it beside him, then picked up the medal box and snapped it shut.

"Perhaps you're right," said Joséphine, ignoring her slight slur. She drank too much, that was true. Why not? Rosé at lunch, aperitifs by the pool, champagne and more rosé with dinner. Her doctor insisted she cut back, but not abstain—he was from Sanary, after all! She wanted to laugh and cry at herself, to shake out the turbulence that quaked just under her wrinkled, scarred skin.

She unsteadily rose to her feet, leaned forward, and took the medal box from the table. Raph jumped up and grabbed an arm, Evie the other.

"Let's get you upstairs," said Evie softly.

Joséphine rested her head on Evie's shoulder as she studied her nephew and thought of his son swaddled upstairs. "This medal is yours." She pushed it into Raph's hand. "Take it. It is as much your story as mine."

Chapter 6

EVIE

It was an unremarkable gray Parisian morning. While Evie waited for Gilles to come in to work, she sat at her chestnut table drinking black coffee and dabbing at the leftover flakes of her croissant with her finger as she turned the pages of *Le Monde*.

This had been her morning ritual ever since she'd bought La Maison Rustique seventeen years ago. She took comfort in the dappled light that fell through the shop windows, the lifetime of scratches and grooves etched into her antique table, and the warmth of the floor-to-ceiling wooden bookshelves grouped by subject: *Horticulture, Conception de Jardin, Fruits, Légumes . . .*

Evie was trying to focus on her newspaper, but she kept eyeing the small wooden archive box sitting at the far end of the table that held Joséphine's book. After her meeting with Clément, she'd taken a week to search the villa for the missing manuscript, undertaking a bit of late spring-cleaning as she went. She'd returned to Paris by train last night to talk to Gilles about preserving the Leroux and separating the pages. The book had been delivered to her shop this morning in an archive box by Clément's museum transport team. Gilles had agreed to come in and have a look, promising that if he couldn't take care of it, then he had a colleague at the Louvre who could.

Evie swallowed the last of her coffee and sat back in her chair, taking a moment to enjoy the shaft of light falling through the front window. Outside, Paris was starting her day. Potted plants and round tables were placed on the footpath, umbrellas popped up in front of cafés. Queues gathered outside tiny boulangeries. As the street filled with traffic and pedestrians, Evie cocooned herself in the wooden walls of her shop, as she had for seventeen years.

A decade ago, when the business was still getting on its feet, Hugo would give her a goodbye kiss and a delighted squeeze as he donned his backpack and joined his rowdy classmates in the cobbled streets to kick a soccer ball and race off to elementary school. Raph would leave at the same time, adjusting the collar of his tailored sports jacket, grabbing his briefcase off the hook on the wall, and pausing for a quick peck on the lips before he raced to catch the subway to his day-trading office at the Bourse. Evie sighed as she wondered how long she'd be able to recall Raph's just-shaved cheek pressed against hers, the way the edges of his eyes turned up a little when he smiled, his wavy sandy hair brushing his collar.

Her next thought was of Clément Tazi. As they'd worked together in Joséphine's library, he'd been methodical in the cataloging, reverential and curious. Occasionally, among the rustle and crinkle of papers, he'd looked up to ask questions of Evie: about her Australian childhood, Hugo's final-year subject choices, how she'd come to have her shop, and watercolorists and botanical illustrators she admired. They shared an easy banter as they knelt and shuffled across the thick carpet, stopping to chuckle at some of the more outlandish margin notes on Joséphine's drafts. When Clément laughed he threw his head back, his eyes almost disappearing—and just to see him do this, Evie found herself telling lighthearted anecdotes about Hugo's childhood, boorish clients, and her shop.

She hadn't felt a flicker of interest toward any man since Raph. Her well-meaning girlfriends, Camille and Nina, had tried to set her up: Nina's fellow partner at her law firm (too boring—Evie nearly fell asleep during a monologue about the first-growth burgundy, or was it bordeaux?), the cute new head coach at Camille's local soccer club (too foppish, like a prancing colt), and the lanky cellist in one of Paris's finest touring quartets (wickedly funny, but placed an insipid hand on Evie's thigh halfway through their second glass of chardonnay).

Not to be put off, the same friends had decided casual sex might help, so they'd set her up on a dating app for over-forties.

"It's just sex—*mon dieu,* are all Australians so conservative?" asked Camille as they shared a bottle of pinot gris at her chic new apartment overlooking the Luxembourg Gardens. She'd divorced for the second time last year and was currently seeing three men, one of whom was in his twenties. Mind you, with her cropped bob, balayage, and impeccable skin, Camille could pass for a woman a decade younger. "Don't worry, it's just for Paris," she said as she downloaded the app on to Evie's phone. "You won't be connected with a lonely corn farmer in Minnesota, just locals." Evie was pretty sure they didn't grow corn in Minnesota, but she let it pass. "See!" Camille held the phone out. "All loaded."

But just looking at the little blue icon made Evie uncomfortable. Not least because she wasn't *good* at technology—she was frightened she'd conjure a serial killer into their lives with an accidental swipe right.

Nina and Camille were absolutely correct, though: she couldn't sit at this table brooding and eating croissants forever. Her French girlfriends would be horrified at her daily pastry intake. She reached for her phone and texted them both: *Lots to catch up on. Drinks tonight?*

Oui. Olivier's at 8, responded Camille.

There was nothing from Nina, but that wasn't unusual; she was probably prepping for court.

Evie looked again at the wooden archive box. She was itching to peek inside, but she would need to wait until Gilles worked his magic. Instead, she'd make a start on some other work. She moved her plate and coffee cup to the shop counter and lifted a larger sealed archive box onto the center table. There had been an online inquiry for one of her rare antique books, and she needed to check all was in order before the potential buyer came in for his appointment tomorrow. She slipped on her archivist's gloves and was soothed by the feel of the cotton. Affixed to the front of the box was a typed A4 sheet:

Orchids of Australia: the complete edition drawn in natural color / by W. H. Nicholls with descriptive text; edited by D. L. Jones and T. B. Muir.

Followed by some notes:

His paintings of Australian orchids. 476 color plates, 500 pages. Binding has been repaired, otherwise in excellent condition. (Many copies of this book have had the binding repaired because the book was too large and heavy for the binding the printer used.)

1,000USD

She studied an exquisite illustration of a blue spider orchid. The collector would be pleased—the cerulean hadn't faded with the decades. Certainly, the blue was so bright the pigment must have been made with lapis lazuli from Afghanistan.

Her heart did a little flip: piecing together the provenance of a botanical book was as much fun for her as analyzing the composition. It was both an art and a science, with just the faintest stroke of magic.

She flipped through the remaining pages, then closed the book using both hands and carefully placed it back in the archive box. She gulped when she saw the sale price, perhaps a little too hefty. Gilles had gently chided her over the phone yesterday. *It's as if you don't want to part with these rare books, Evie.* Well, perhaps she didn't want to part with this particular book because it reminded her of her Australian childhood.

The shop door opened, and Gilles shuffled in, smoothing his

gray hair mussed up by the morning wind, booming, "Bonjour, Evie," before his eyes fell on the book and he started to smile. "So, you are going to sell it after all." He bent down, picked up the mail from the floor, and dropped it on the end of the table.

"I don't really have a choice." She shrugged. "I have to pay those bills—you taught me that! The shop has to pay for itself."

"I admire your pragmatism. Is that for me?" He pointed at the museum's locked box and clapped with excitement. "I'll work on it all morning, and I'll know what needs to be done within a few hours. Then we can talk time frames." He rubbed his hands together. "Come have lunch with me today. Olivier has a mullet entrée on at the moment with Puy lentils and garlic confit that you must try. He's been asking after you."

"Your husband is kind. As are you. Thank you, dear Gilles. I don't know what I'd do without you. Especially since . . . well."

Gilles nodded, blue eyes filled with warmth and affection.

She kissed his cheek quickly and added, "I have to go upstairs and do some invoicing. I'll leave the orchid book here in its container. Take the center table for Joséphine's book." Evie was desperate to stay and see what he found, but hovering over his shoulder would just annoy him. She took a step toward the old man and placed a hand on his forearm. "And, Gilles, I really appreciate you coming in to help out. When I bought the shop, I didn't realize you came with it."

Gilles reddened and tugged at his waistband to lift up his perpetually sagging trousers. "Of course, I enjoy it. I love the books"—he took in the shelves—"and you and young Hugo. How is the boy, by the way? I haven't seen him in months. Still at the villa?"

"He's with Simon for the day," she replied in a voice that sounded much lighter than she felt. Simon was Nina's eldest child—she had a chaotic household of six. "He doesn't say much. And when he's around, he's glued to his phone."

"Sounds like a normal teenager. My nephews are the same."

"Perhaps." But it wasn't normal for a boy to find his father's dead body on the bathroom floor.

She didn't know if she'd ever be able to right this wrong. The counseling was definitely helping, but he needed time to find his own path through the heavy fog that sometimes seeped in and threatened to smother his days. She'd spent the past year and a half stepping beside him on some of those days and calling him through on others. But mostly, he preferred to navigate his sadness on his own.

"Thanks again, Gilles. I'll leave you here for the morning. Just give me a yell if you need any help." She winked. They both knew he would be lucky if anyone walked in the front door. Though it was a Saint-Germain institution, the shop was appointment only. Collectors from Singapore to Boston and Dublin sought out her catalog and thought nothing of making a trip specifically to view a rare manuscript.

Gilles had opened La Maison Rustique four decades ago, and it now sat tucked between the pastel and gilded tearooms of Ladurée and an achingly cool start-up menswear label that had electronic music on rotation from 10:00 A.M. She glanced at her watch and estimated she had thirty minutes before the beats shook their shared walls. Pinching the top of her nose at the anticipated headache, she wondered when she had become such a tired old witch. She liked music. Liked dancing, even. It was just that nightclub music was distracting when she was trying to work. Maybe she'd pop in and have a chat with the boys later today about keeping it down a bit. Actually, no, she wouldn't—she'd just come across as tired and grumpy.

What was it Hugo had hissed at her the night before they'd left for Villa Sanary, when she had simply queried why his chemistry assignment was late again? *Why are you always on my case? You're ruining my life. I can't wait to—* He'd stopped himself, then stomped into his bedroom and slammed the door.

His words had stung, but she was the adult in the room and had to stand strong, like a mast remaining upright while their ship bobbed around in a storm. Even when the insults flew, and the teenage rage became almost too much to bear, she held firm. Then—when the door was slammed—she'd creep into her room and cry into a pillow, so Hugo would never know how much watching him struggle hurt her. She needed to find a way to help her beautiful boy reach calmer waters; she just wasn't sure how.

Gilles furrowed his bushy brows. "Are you okay, Evie? Can I—?"

"I'm fine." She nodded at him, swiping the mail off the table and tucking it under an arm as she trudged upstairs.

When she opened the door to her apartment, a cool breeze struck her face. She looked to where she'd left a sash window open, the linen curtains flapping about in a tangle with the breeze. She hurried over to pull the window shut but lingered to take in the scent of warm bread from the boulangerie next door, chiding herself for eating a croissant when it had barely touched the sides of her appetite.

She moved to the old chestnut desk in the corner of the living room and sat down, allowing the mail to spill across the surface. As she leaned back in the chair, a knot pressed into her lower back, and she tugged out one of Raph's old scarves that had been wedged in the leather seat. How long had it been hidden there?

Most of his stuff had been donated to the nearest thrift shop last year—Evie's therapist had insisted she needed to *let go*. The rest of it, mostly property titles and yellowing piles of family paperwork, was in archive boxes on top of her wardrobe that hadn't been touched since they'd moved to this apartment from the studio apartment when Hugo was born.

Evie grabbed Raph's scarf and yanked it from the crease in the chair. Without thinking, she lifted it to her nose and inhaled. *Raphaël.* She closed her eyes and was picking through the Clignancourt markets looking for blue-and-white dinner plates, oak dining chairs, and antique white linen to cover their duvet. Stopping for champagne and oysters with a vinegar and wasabi dressing at a tiny hole-in-the-wall, and devouring steaming piles of *moules frites* with a sharp pinot gris when their Saturday market-hopping was done.

She wrapped the scarf around her neck, picked up the letter opener, and started sorting the bills into piles. Then she opened her laptop and began the mind-numbing task of plugging in account numbers, wiring funds, and settling debts. She sent a text to the manager of her Montmartre apartment to see when she could get in for a look. Though she doubted the manuscript was there, she'd promised Clément she would try. This morning she'd go through Raph's paperwork—she seriously doubted anything would be there either, but one last look couldn't hurt.

Sometimes she wondered what Raph would think of her new-found life-admin superpower. When he was alive, her desk was scattered with paint samples, glasses of water, botanical manuscripts, and some of her own doodles and sketches. A few winters ago, their gas had been turned off! Not because they couldn't afford to pay—Raph's stockbroking gig ensured they were more than comfortable, and La Maison Rustique proudly held its own—but because Evie had used the bill as a bookmark, then reshelved the novel.

Every time Raph had asked her about bills and budgets—pleaded to take over the household payments—she'd batted him away with a kiss even though she hated all forms of life admin. She *intended* to be that woman who got the school forms in and paid her taxes in a timely manner. She *intended* to get more organized and then lead the glossy life expected of a stockbroker's wife and sixth arrondissement *maman*.

Evie had wanted this life, chased it. She'd had a shiny road laid out in front of her, paved with privilege straight from the door of her private girls' school. All she had to do was work hard, tick the boxes, and stay the course.

Growing up, she'd adored the freedom of riding her pony in broad paddocks fringed with eucalyptus and wattle trees. The yellow acacia buds glowed in the sunshine as she galloped across the cracked earth, leaving whirlwinds of dust in her wake. She'd tether her horse to a log and eat her Vegemite sandwich, lying on the prickly brown grass and looking up at the wide blue sky, dreaming about all the places she would go when she was old enough.

At university, Evie discovered delicious subjects that had always been sold to her as "soft" by her reptilian school career adviser: philosophy, metaphysics, fine arts, life drawing, botanical illustration, history of biology. Her law degree became a rambling arts degree with no fixed major. Three years later, she emerged with short shaggy hair, a decent pair of walking boots, and no idea where they would take her.

So, she had decided to put her stilted schoolgirl French to use and got a job at the most darling botanical bookshop in Paris: La Maison Rustique. Under Gilles's careful tutelage she learned more about botanical art, and soon she was taking night classes. She learned to study a manuscript—*as quirky and individual as any child*, he'd quipped as he patiently showed her how to study a print, the shape of the outlines, the watercolors.

She came to see orchids and roses through the eyes of the illustrator, the dip of a petal, the dab of light. With time, Gilles showed her she was not just studying the plant but also the way the illustration unfolded. The heavy strokes, the delicate etches—each revealed a nervousness, a passion, a doubt, a love. "It's never about the vellum or the ink, or the scarcity of the flower. It's about eyes that see not just beauty, but the shadows and the rot too. It's a *commitment* to sit down and craft a manuscript like this. To place the flowers in the right order so they create a rhythm to the book: the pitter-patter of tiny orchids, spiky stamen, and pointed petals up front, slowing to a more languorous stretch of roses with their soft, fur-like petals."

A knock at her apartment door.

"Come in," she called.

"A word, if I may?" said Gilles as he opened the door. "Your book is going to take some work."

Her face fell. It had been silly to expect results immediately: she knew better. But she'd hoped to have something to tell Clément.

"I'm not going to prize any pages apart, not today. I'll secure the spine and put it in a holder, then go page by page. Now, are you going to join me for lunch?"

She stared at the mess on her desk. How had three hours passed? "I'm going to keep looking through Raph's boxes for anything that might help with the exhibition."

"Well, okay. If you insist. But make sure you eat."

"I will. And I'm going out with Camille and Nina tonight for a drink after dinner, so I'll see Olivier then."

Gilles laughed. "Well, in that case you really need to make sure you have a proper meal. Line your stomach before you meet those two!"

As Gilles headed down the stairs, she shot a text to Clément. *Going to apartment tomorrow, will keep you posted.*

Her phone pinged in response. *Thanks for letting me know. Cataloging the manuscripts here—your Joséphine had a fiery way with a margin note.* He attached a pic of a page with French swear words scrawled down the margin and angry lines zigzagging through chunks of text that were obviously not going through to the next draft.

It was incredible to Evie how an inanimate page of typeset letters could zing to life with handwritten annotations. Joséphine's scrawl was more legible than some of the blurred words of the inky Leroux, even though her handwriting had been much neater when she was in Fresnes, before her hands were scarred. Evie forwarded the page to Gilles, thinking it might help him decipher some of the text, when it came to that. First, they needed to separate the pages.

She turned back to Raph's boxes sitting on her desk and continued her search for anything that might be of interest to Clément.

Evie had known very little about the great Joséphine Murant when she married Raph. Only the statements embossed in gold letters across each of her novels:

FRANCE'S FAVORITE CRIME WRITER

GENRE-BENDING THRILLER

NEW YORK TIMES INTERNATIONAL BESTSELLER

When Evie and Raph were newlyweds, she'd read some of Joséphine's novels: *The Forgotten, Little Lost Child,* and *Hide and Seek.* If she was honest, they terrified her: kidnappings, murders, broken families, and broken dreams, all described in horrific detail. She would never understand how people got their kicks from gorging on fictional misfortunes. But they did—fifteen million people, according to Joséphine's royalty statements.

Evie took no joy in death, fictional or otherwise, and had found herself wincing as she sat up in bed reading late one night. "Your great-aunt is a full-fledged psychopath," she'd said, nudging her bare-chested husband.

"Hmm, you think?" said Raph absentmindedly as he continued to read the stock report on his laptop.

"Of course! I mean, three people have been slaughtered in as many pages. I'm going to need to see a shrink at the end of this novel just so I don't get PTSD."

"So, stop reading it then. Nobody's forcing you!" He grinned at her.

"That's the thing, I can't stop. It's like *The Silence of the Lambs* meets *The Great Gatsby*."

He shut his laptop and kissed her on the lips. "You wait until you meet Joséphine next weekend. Now . . ." He lifted the book from her fingertips, whipped off his glasses, and placed both on his bedside table, along with his computer. As he rolled over, Evie clambered on top of him and buried her nose in his chest, rubbing a cheek against his muscles and taking his sandalwood aftershave deep into her lungs.

As Evie focused back on the here and now, she rubbed her eyes. The *goosh-goosh* of the electronic beats next door poured in her window and pounded her brain. She could feel the beginnings of a headache and jumped up to close the window, but not before a gust of wind blasted into her apartment. The original letter from the museum fluttered on her desk. She slammed the window shut, picked up the paper, and again reflected on her meeting with Clément Tazi. She was surprised at how much she was looking forward to the next one.

❦

Over dinner with Hugo, Evie showed him a photo of the first page of the Leroux diary.

"Cool! It talks about that murderer, Margot." He flicked through pics they'd taken in Villa Sanary's library. "Does Joséphine spill any details?"

"You've been watching too much Netflix." Evie sighed and took a sip of her burgundy. "Well, we've only seen one page—who knows, maybe there will be some revelations about the murder."

"Yeah, look what Joséphine did for a living! So, any sign of that missing manuscript?"

"Nothing." Evie noticed there was no offer to help her go through boxes. Typical teenager. "I looked everywhere here today. Even the attic. Nothing. I'm going to the old apartment tomorrow—though we took everything when we left. Still, it's a good excuse to check the place is still in good shape."

"Anything with Papa's stuff?"

"Zip. There was her medal, but I've already loaned that to Clément." She rubbed her eyes. "At least we've got the old Leroux, and it does look like a diary of her time in prison during the war. I'm in two minds about it. Should we use it?"

"Definitely," Hugo said between mouthfuls of spaghetti. "Everyone reads Anne Frank's diary in elementary school. And there are so many new books coming out about World War II. For school we're reading about a tattooist in a concentration camp. Auschwitz. I had no idea . . . All of them are brutal, and the authors are brave. Aunt Joséphine was in the Resistance, right?"

"Allegedly. She denied it in court. Said nothing."

"That's so cool. I'd believe it—she didn't give anything much away." Another mouthful. Bolognese sauce dripped onto his soccer jersey, and he wiped it up with his finger, then licked it.

"Manners! You don't think it's too . . ." Evie tried to gather her thoughts.

"Too what?" He lifted a finger, obviously planning to run it along the rim of the bowl and collect the last of the sauce.

"Don't even think about it, kiddo! So, you don't think it's too intrusive? I mean, she rarely spoke to me or your papa about the war. She didn't discuss it in interviews. She was a storyteller—if she'd *wanted* this part of her story told, surely she would have done it herself?"

Hugo wiped his mouth with a napkin and pushed his bowl away as he leaned back in his chair. "I think you should help this museum dude. Is it that Joséphine didn't want her story told, or that nobody ever asked the right questions? I mean, there's not much history written by women, is there? Not that I've seen, anyway. The page you've shown me—that's her own words. I felt like I was right there in her prison hellhole. And that's just the first page! Then there's the murderer, Margot."

"That's your Netflix projection." Evie shook her head. "I swear, what you kids watch these days."

"Is *nothing* compared to what Joséphine lived through, I'll bet. She would have seen some shit—"

"Language!" Evie smiled to herself as she swallowed some pasta. Hugo's history teacher had said in their last parent–teacher interview that Hugo had written a brilliant piece on the gender wage gap.

"Besides," his voice softened, "I'm not sure that covering things up . . . It's not always for the best. Adults always tell us to mind our own business, but if you—" He paused and closed his eyes.

Evie sat perfectly still, scared that any sudden move, even a blink, would cause him to clam up. She waited for her son to finish. Held her breath.

But Hugo just picked up his fork and started tracing a pattern on the bowl, while one leg knocked against the table. The conversation was over.

"Okay," she said, "I'll keep looking for this manuscript. We'll go back for the rest of the summer—if that's okay with you? Can you miss one soccer camp? Will Simon cope without you?" There were so many children in Nina's house that they never minded Hugo bunking in for a night or a week, so he stayed there whenever she went to conferences.

"Sure. Guess so." She was probably imagining it, but was there just the faintest twitch of a smile in the corners of his mouth?

As she looked at the young man trying to use his knife to scrape up the last of the sauce, she got butterflies. Lately, dinnertime talk had often been about college majors and gap years. The Joséphine Murant exhibition was scheduled for fourteen months—it could be one last project for them to work on together before Hugo went out into the world. And their summer at Villa Sanary was just the circuit breaker they needed.

Hugo was now clearing the table, clattering the cutlery and plates on top of one another exactly as she asked him *not* to do every night. When he stacked the last plate, he looked up at her under his long eyelashes and said, "It's the right thing to do. Papa—he'd be all for it."

⁓

Evie met Nina and Camille for a martini at Olivier's chic new Left Bank bistro overlooking the Seine. Outside, lovers walked along the paths arm in arm, stopping to pick through tables of antique books, admire watercolors set on easels, and watch the local graffiti artist re-create a da Vinci in colored chalk. Across the black velvet strip of water, the Eiffel Tower twinkled like a Christmas tree.

The women sat up at the marble bar, eating whatever plates Olivier sent out from the kitchen. Over tuna ceviche, oysters with a miso dressing, and fresh, squeaky burrata, they swapped news, traded tales of their teenage sons—who'd met on the first day of nursery—and joked they couldn't wait until the boys slammed their bedroom doors once and for all as they left at the end of the year.

They ordered a second round of cocktails, and Camille told them about the model who'd snorted so much coke in her hotel room she hadn't turned up to the YSL shoot Camille was supposed to be styling that day.

Nina sighed and said, "Who does coke anymore? I thought these girls were into wellness."

"Maybe she imbibed it with her green juice." Camille rolled her eyes and flicked her perfect hair off her face.

"And her probiotics," scoffed Nina, taking a gulp of her martini. "I have news. I think we're going to move to a bigger apartment. I said to Dan it's either that, or I'm getting my own!"

"Good for you," said Camille, as they clinked glasses. She turned to study Evie. "You got a bit of a tan this past week—the Riviera suits you. Come shopping with me! I'll get you some pretty things to go with your glowy vibe."

"I—" Evie started to protest. She hadn't been shopping for ages.

"C'mon. It'll be fun." Camille picked up the ends of Evie's hair. "And I'll take you to Marco and get this mane sorted. I love these curls—don't you dare try to tame them—but let's . . . enhance. Because you, my friend, are perfect. So, tell!"

Evie enjoyed the sharp tang of her martini as she updated her friends on the exhibition, the missing manuscript, and the diary entry. "It's a puzzle. Joséphine the Resistance fighter and prisoner of war on one hand, Margot Bisset the murderer and former maid on the other. We have no idea how they fit together, just that they do, somehow."

"So will you publish whatever you find?" said Nina quickly, always alert to legal issues. "That's a minefield."

"Yes. No. Maybe." Evie shrugged. "Hard to know before we see the full diary. Clément's doing some research into Margot's backstory."

"I'll help you," said Nina graciously. "I'm already doing the stuff for the foundation."

"*Clément!*" Camille interrupted with a raised eyebrow. "First-name basis with the museum curator, are we? Do tell."

Evie's cheeks grew hot, and she looked across to where a DJ was spinning Sultan + Shepard in the far corner, then back at her friends. "I like him," she said, not wanting to give much away. "We have a lot in common. He's kind, very professional. Quirky."

"Oh my God! Stop, woman! You sound as if you're in a retirement home commercial. What's next—bridge?"

"Camille! She *likes* him. Look at that grin." Nina elbowed Camille and turned to Evie. "You deserve someone great," she said softly.

"It's nothing, it's work. Then there's Hugo . . ."

"Who is doing *much* better, by the way. Even Simon commented on it over his coffee this morning. It's great to see. Besides, they're off traveling soon. What're you going to do with all that spare time?"

Evie laughed. "Great. So you guys think I'm officially boring. Um, I'm going to put on an exhibition. Ramp up the botanical illustrations. Maybe fly home to Oz and see some friends and family."

"Can I move into your apartment while you're gone? I'll tidy it—and permit Dan over for conjugal visits twice a week."

"Only twice!" Camille said with a chuckle. "I don't believe that. You guys are rabbits. Look at how many kids you have. That's just boasting."

As Nina spluttered an objection, Camille and Evie exchanged a look over the top of their martini glasses. Mothers of only children, they were awed by how their clever friend juggled working at one of Paris's top commercial law firms, keeping a steady marriage to Dan, mothering four children, and heading school committees for anyone who asked. But it wasn't just Nina's to-do list that was impressive: it was her attitude. She made time for everyone.

Evie smiled, grateful for her friends. "Yes, you can stay in my apartment, Nina. Yes, you can take me shopping, Camille." She was probably going to regret the latter, but a freshen-up couldn't hurt. Camille had introduced her to skin serums a year ago, and now she had one for every feeling: vitamin C for perky, hyaluronic acid for calm concentration, and a blend of herbs and oils for when she couldn't sleep.

"Cheers, ladies," said Nina, beaming. "And I agree with Camille—you look great, Evie. Relaxed. It's lovely to see."

"Thanks, I feel good." The trip to the Côte d'Azur had done her wonders. She wasn't sure when she would see Clément again, and she was no closer to finding the manuscript, but she realized she was going to lean in to all the possibilities and see what happened. She hadn't felt this free since her backpacking days.

Her phone vibrated, and she pulled it from her purse. "Sorry, better check. Hugo!" She knew they'd understand.

But it wasn't Hugo—it was Clément.

"Judging by that coy look," said Camille, "it's definitely not your son!"

"No," Evie said with a grin as she read the message.

Thanks for the update today. Been doing some digging on Margot Bisset. Article attached. Looking forward to seeing you again when you get back down to CDA. C.

Murdering Maid to Be Executed

Margot Bisset, assistant housekeeper to British citizens Madame Mathilda and Monsieur Edward Munro of Mayfair, London, at their Côte d'Azur estate, Villa Sanary, has unanimously been found guilty by the jury today in Marseille Courthouse and sentenced to be executed for first-degree murder. She will be transferred to Fresnes Prison immediately and will remain there until her execution date is set by the court.

Due to current European political circumstances, the defendant's former employers provided written testimony for the trial. Their solicitor, Monsieur Jacques Caron, spoke on their behalf outside the court. "It is over. Mademoiselle Schramsburg's family will be relieved and have sent a telegram to thank the courts for upholding justice. Our thoughts and prayers are with the Schramsburg family at this difficult time.

"As for the guilty party, Margot Bisset, may God have mercy on her soul when she is executed."

Lawyers for Bisset have stated that there will be no appeal.

Chapter 7

MARGOT

Margot sat in the dock beside the bench, nursing her head in her hands as she was sentenced. She tried to swallow, but her throat was knotted. Her white cotton shirt was clammy against her skin, and her swollen feet ached in the heeled shoes her lawyer had given her to wear to court so she "wouldn't look like a jealous, desperate killer" in old boots.

The courtroom broke into a merry cheer at the sentence of execution, and the jurors all stood to stretch their legs, shake hands, and pat each other on the back. It had been a long, drawn-out trial. Delayed at first when the Munros were unable to travel from Britain, then again by the Occupation, which saw political trials take precedence. When her case finally came to trial, Margot found she had only the government-issued lawyer for support.

Margot had grown thin from the strain. The agony of not being believed. Her hair was lank and stringy, and she couldn't remember when she had last brushed her teeth. She spent every night alone in her cell, running over the events, remembering each tiny detail about the party . . . right down to the salmon canapés and the row of covered buttons down the back of Peggy Schramsburg's plunging dress.

No one visited, except her mother once a month with a fresh baguette and a large wedge of Comté she couldn't afford. Each month, Margot assured Vivienne that it was a mistake . . . that she'd be released soon. But as seasons passed and the following summer rolled around, it became clear that not only did no one believe Margot, no one cared. Justice, it seemed, was a luxury preserved for the wealthy.

Margot had been certain the Munros would back her up—but they denied any suggestion of a murder game. No one else except Peggy Schramsburg knew about the game. It was Margot's word against her employers'.

Who would believe Margot when all the evidence suggested otherwise? She had been caught with a smoking gun in her hand. A dead body at her feet.

The night Margot was arrested, she'd overheard Madame Munro say to the police, "We planned a party game, of course—a general amusement. Charades at midnight. But I *always* have games at my parties and no one has ever *died*." Madame Munro put a hand on her heart. "I feel *dreadful*. One of my own staff!"

"Darling Peggy was a ball of nerves. No doubt she was rehearsing on the balcony. Heaven knows what got into Margot—but I *promise you*: there was never any mention of murder."

The Munros had lied. What were they hiding?

Margot had gone over and over the details of the murder game. First to the policeman who arrested her. Then again to his senior officer the next day. And so it went, for days, weeks, then over a year. Her legal representation had changed twice, and none of her lawyers had believed her. Just like the police, her lawyers encouraged her to plead guilty right from the start.

Smoking gun.

Dead body.

The only person who believed in Margot's innocence was her mother. Each day, Vivienne had sat in court dressed in her Sunday best, bag clasped on her knees, expression thunderous—she would never forgive Madame Munro for failing to protect Margot. Her face had pinched in pain when the charges were laid out. Today she looked so thin, so frail, it seemed she might not be able to get to her feet unassisted. She sat alone in the gallery, crying and clasping her crimson rosary beads, while the crowds gossiped and chattered as they clambered past her knees to leave the courthouse and get on with the business of their lives.

Margot mouthed, "I love you," to her mother before a wall of police blocked her view.

Margot was still sitting in the dock beside the bench, head hung low, trying with all her might to swallow her tears as everyone else was funneled from the courtroom. When it was empty, she was roughly hoisted to her feet by her elbows, handcuffed, and bundled into a police van with the day's murderers, rapists, and petty thieves.

She burned with rage at the betrayal by the Munros. Where were they now? No doubt ensconced at their town house back in

Britain . . . cooking up another game. The Munros should be in prison, not her. It was *their* game. Their party.

Her hands were cuffed so she could not hang on to anything as the police van sped over cobblestones and whipped around corners without any care for the prisoners. With each knock and bump, Margot was jolted out of her shocked state. As her cheek slammed against cold metal and her jaw ached, her fury blazed hotter.

She huddled close to the wall of the van, hoping it would prevent more knocks. She closed her eyes and remembered the morning of the Bastille Day party.

⁂

As an employer, Tilly Munro was as changeable as the mistral that blew down from the foothills and threatened to bend in two the olive trees and pencil pines dotted along the cliffs. But as a hostess, she was charming, warm, and utterly convincing when it came to getting what she wanted. This year, she wanted her Bastille Day party to be the talk of not just the Côte d'Azur, but Paris and the whole of Europe too.

"It's La Fête Nationale, darling Margot!" Madame Munro called as Margot entered her chamber. She sat at her dressing table sweeping rouge across her cheeks, swathed in a navy silk dressing gown, with diamond-and-pearl pendants dripping from her ears. "Who wants to stand around for hours singing 'La Marseillaise'? It's a dreadfully boring way to celebrate. Things will remain steady in France, thank God!"

Margot swallowed. She sometimes read Monsieur Munro's

newspapers as she tidied the library, and recently she'd found out that the Germans had enlisted nearly a million soldiers for military maneuvers. She didn't know exactly what that meant, but she knew it wasn't good. Her papa had fought against German soldiers, and his nightly screams after he'd returned from the war still rang in her ears. It was her earliest memory.

Marc Bisset had arrived home an empty and broken man. He'd wasted away for several years—nursed by a stoic, doting Vivienne—until he died of consumption: a carcass with ruined lungs crumpled on a straw mattress.

If Madame noticed Margot's hesitation, she ignored it and continued to rant. "Herr Bloch insists this is just a hitch. You'll see, this nonsensical standoff will pass quickly and the German economy will fly. It would be *such a shame* not to have a piece of that. The Windsors agree—they took tea with Hitler, after all. Heard it straight from the horse's mouth that all will be well. They insist he's a shy gem, misunderstood." Madame held up two different earrings. "The diamonds, or the diamond drops with sapphires?"

"The blue matches your eyes, Madame. You were talking about Hitler and Germany?"

"Oh, never mind *that*. Nobody wants to talk boring politics tonight. We need to celebrate! It's summer. I always throw the party of the season. That's why we need something really big this year. A distraction. So, I've decided that someone needs to be murdered tonight!" She waved her hands in excitement. "Nobody ever remembers what we ate or drank—lobster or quail, Krug or Dom Pérignon. They only remember the fun times."

"But m-murder, Madame?" Margot stuttered. Had her employer gone completely mad?

She was relieved to hear this wasn't the case, but she still frowned as Madame explained the plan.

"Stop *worrying*, Margot. And don't tell Vivienne—she most definitely would not approve." Madame winked at Margot, who pictured her hardy mother bent over the laundry boilers downstairs washing endless sheets and towels for guests, pressing table linen, and generally making sure Villa Sanary ran seamlessly through summer.

Vivienne found Madame's extravagance loathsome, and silently Margot sometimes agreed. The money spent on a quarter of the champagne tipped into the pool last year would have kept the local village school going for years. Still, there were few jobs in the village that paid the full year for service, even though the Munros only visited the Côte d'Azur for summer. And Margot's family had been in service to the Munros for three generations.

"I'm not sure I understand, Madame. How do you fake a murder? Won't people be ter—"

Madame interjected, fanning out her hands like stars for maximum effect. "Terrified! That's the whole *point*, darling. I want tonight to be unforgettable."

"But how are you going to make this . . . believable?"

Her employer was applying mascara now, and she turned and batted her lashes. "A lady doesn't give away all her secrets! What I *will* tell you is that I've arranged for the gendarmerie to arrive."

Margot's eyes widened.

"Oh, don't be shocked. Monsieur Munro asked Commissioner

Moreau as a personal favor. They will show up, declare Peggy Schramsburg dead, and proceed to interview all the guests. Just like an Agatha Christie!" She gave a delighted clap. Margot took a deep breath and exhaled while Madame brushed her face with a shimmery translucent powder to set her makeup. "Trust me, Margot. You'll never forget this party." She stood up, snapping the gold compact case closed. "Now be a *darling* and go pick armfuls of the blush-pink roses for our centerpiece. That *dishy* new gardener brought in buckets of the white roses, even though I clearly said pink, pink, pink!" She waved her hands in the air as if she were conducting an orchestra. "He's a bit on the slow side, but we can't be blessed with everything, can we?" She chortled. "The Lord giveth and the Lord taketh away and all that . . ." Madame sighed and looked out her window to where Gabriel's silhouette was disappearing past the orchard.

Margot's stomach groaned as she remembered how much she had to do, and how little she'd had to eat. "Madame, can I please pick the roses after I go to the village for Chef? All the kitchen staff are busy preparing for your party." She deliberately brightened her tone. "It smells delicious!"

"I'm sure! Yes, you may go to the village for Chef." Madame's voice hardened a fraction. "But *don't* forget my roses. Promise?"

"Promise. *Merci*, Madame." Margot quickly backed out of the room before she was tasked with yet another errand.

"Honestly, Margot. *You*, my darling, are the only one I trust around here to do things properly."

❧

That night, the Munros were quick to see Margot taken away like one of Madame's last-season silk dresses she no longer had a use for.

Peggy was bleeding from the single, dark bullet hole in the side of her skull, hidden by her curls. Margot was crouched beside her, trying to revive her, when guests spilling out onto the balcony to watch the fireworks found Margot with the still-smoking gun in her right hand.

More guests crowded onto the balcony, drawn by the screams of women melded with fireworks. Some recoiled in horror. A doctor pushed his way through the shocked crowd, knelt, and felt for a pulse. Peggy Schramsburg was dead, he declared, glaring at the gun still in Margot's hand.

She was terrified and confused. Was she about to be shot too? Was the killer still out there in the garden? She rested her dizzy head against the wall, the stone cooling her cheek. She had to make them all see what had really happened.

Two policemen arrived and barged onto the balcony, pushing guests aside to get to the victim. The Munros were mortified and tried to soothe their guests as they ushered the women onto velvet sofas in the drawing room. They demanded immediate action: their maid *must* be taken into custody at once. *"Look, she still has the gun in her hand!"* Margot was truly scared now: Madame Munro had assured her Monsieur Munro had let them in on the game. Had the police been waiting nearby at the villa? Who had called them?

But mostly: Why didn't the police believe Margot when they knew about the murder game?

"But the game . . ." Margot pleaded. "I fired the gun into . . ."

She was arrested on the spot.

She stood on the balcony with her hands cuffed behind her back, flanked by two policemen. The one interrogating her and taking her statement had been to the village elementary school with her. She tried to recall his name. Jean-Marc? Jean-Paul? His blue eyes pleaded with her to pay attention and answer the questions, and he spoke her name at first as if they were friends. Comforting. Cajoling. But what to say?

The two men spoke to each other about her, offering indirect advice. *Perhaps it was an accident, and Margot did not mean to kill the American. It would be easier—make the judges more lenient—if she were to plead manslaughter.*

Several gentlemen stood across the doorway so the maid could not leave the balcony. A line of white tuxedos.

Half a dozen more police arrived and swarmed onto the balcony, now looking for evidence among shattered champagne coupes, linen napkins, and discarded salmon canapés. The gun had already been taken from her by the first policeman.

"It will be easier for you if you confess," the blue-eyed inspector said to Margot, his voice hardened now, his eyes full of doubt.

Her brain throbbed with sadness, fear, and confusion as she tried to unpack the moments that had led to Mademoiselle's death. There had been a plan—the police needed to see that Margot's involvement was just part of a game. But how? Wouldn't the Munros tell them?

Out by the pool she could see Gabriel, with Maxime tucked over his shoulder, wailing and confused, calling, "M-M-Ma—" The poor child should be in bed; it was so late. The young man tried to console his tiny brother, patting his back, but Maxime would not be hushed.

From where she was standing on the balcony, Margot saw Gabriel pass an envelope to a lanky policeman. The gardener pointed up to where Margot stood, then turned and carried his weeping brother into the shadows, with the child looking back over his shoulder.

As Margot was marched from Villa Sanary, tugged with her hands behind her back, she stumbled downstairs. Guests pressed themselves against the walls to avoid her, their faces turned away in revulsion.

When the first policeman placed his hand on her head to steer her into the car, Margot caught a glimpse of Vivienne kneeling on the gravel driveway in her black uniform. Screaming, pleading. "*Ma fille est innocente!* My daughter is innocent!"

Chapter 8

Margot was marched in handcuffs through Fresnes Prison along concrete corridors lined with black railings. She had no idea if she was on the first floor or the fifth, as the long rows of cross-barred cells all looked the same. She'd never been to sea, but it felt as if she were deep in the bowels of a ship. From behind the barred wooden doors came guttural moans and high-pitched screams. Cream walls were stained with blood and urine, and pockmarked below knee height from the frustrated kicks of prison-issue boots. Fetid barnyard smells seeped from under every door.

The lines of tiny windows and neat blackened stones on the exterior of the prison had given no indication of the desperation within. Her shoulders slumped further as she traveled deeper. Eventually, they reached the last cell in a corridor. The older warden nodded at his younger counterpart, who returned in the direction they'd come.

"This cell is yours," the older warden said so softly he might have been passing her a toy. "Mademoiselle Murant is . . ." He shook his head and failed to suppress a smile. "Well, you'll see." He pulled a key from his chain and turned the lock.

The door swung open to reveal a dark-haired young woman with an impish smile and unkempt hair. She was clutching at her gray prison pinafore and pacing the room in the sunlight from two high windows.

Margot held her breath. The woman looked a little mad.

"Mademoiselle Murant, meet your new cellmate: Mademoiselle Bisset." The guard removed her handcuffs.

"Joséphine." The woman stepped toward Margot and held out a hand to shake. Joséphine looked to be about her age, but the woman had a wiliness about her; her body was tense as though she might pounce like a fox at any moment. She both intrigued Margot and made her a little uneasy.

"Margot Bisset from Sanary," she responded shyly as she took Joséphine's hand, blushing as the woman felt her calluses. Joséphine's hand was soft, thin, and cold. Margot wondered to what work these hands had been turned, concluding that they had done nothing. Joséphine was almost certainly wealthy—she had the hands of Mademoiselle Schramsburg and Madame Munro. Margot twitched and pushed images of those glamorous women from her mind.

The warden glanced over his shoulder and passed Joséphine a small box of chocolates from inside his jacket. "*Bonne année*, Mademoiselle Murant," he said warmly. "May this year bring you *la liberté et la victoire*."

The exchange touched Margot. Nearly six months had passed since France had rolled over to Germany, and there was talk of Slovakia and Hungary joining with Italy, Germany, and now Japan. The world outside these prison walls was shifting, borders changing. Yet Margot knew almost nothing of these countries; her only thoughts were for her mother.

Had Vivienne found somewhere safe to live in the village? Was someone looking after her? At the prison where Margot had been held during the trial, she'd asked for a pen and paper to write to her mother, but her requests had been forgotten or ignored. In a crowded holding prison, who had time to cater to a lowly country maid?

"I hope so too," said Joséphine, returning the guard's warmth, "for all our sakes, Monsieur Masson." Margot must have looked shocked, because Joséphine laughed lightly as she accompanied the warden to the door. "Go, *mon ami*. A happy new year to you and your beautiful family! Thank your good wife for these chocolates." She clutched the box to her chest. "My new friend here and I will have quite the party tonight. Pity you couldn't smuggle in the champagne too." Joséphine was drawling like a Gallic Scarlett O'Hara. "Now go, get out of here and leave us ladies to get acquainted." She shooed the bemused warden from the cell, reminding him to lock the door. As it swung closed and the lock clicked, Joséphine turned on her heel and smoothed out her pinafore.

Margot's spirits lifted. Perhaps this warden might be able to help Margot get a letter to Vivienne? She would ask Joséphine, when the moment was right.

Joséphine pulled the lid off the chocolates and offered the box to Margot, who took one. "What's your charge?" Joséphine asked as lightly as one might inquire about a preference for tea or coffee.

"Murder. I was sentenced to death, but the judge has suspended the execution. The Boches insisted on this, perhaps because they have too many people to execute! So now I am serving life."

Joséphine blinked, then reached out to take Margot's chin gently between her thumb and forefinger, moving Margot's head from side to side as though she were a scientist studying a specimen. "Who'd you kill, pretty Margot from Sanary?"

"Nobody! It's all a mista—"

"Huh! That's the standard chorus around here." Joséphine chuckled as she dropped her hand and resumed her pacing. "You've got to do better than that, sweet girl. You're a convicted murderer. Those blushing cheeks and wide brown eyes will be no help to you in here. Some of our neighbors will beat that innocence right out of you in the exercise yard if they get a whiff of it. Don't let them smell your fear." She pointed at Margot's worn boots. "I guess your family couldn't afford proper representation."

Margot blushed and tried to pull her pinafore down to cover her boots.

"That wasn't an accusation, by the way. It's not a crime to be poor."

Who was this woman who seemed to read the truth of Margot's life just by looking at her? She didn't answer; she just walked over to sink into her bed, before immediately springing up.

"Sorry, I should have warned you, our mattresses are soaked through. Not sure which is worse: when the walls drip with water, or when it freezes so we have a thin sheet of ice to snuggle against all through the night. My side is drier, so you can share the bed with me if you like—top and tail."

Margot marveled at Joséphine's Parisian confidence. They were similar in height and build, both with brown hair a touch darker than mousy, yet her cellmate's energy lit up the room.

"What's *your* charge?" asked Margot.

"A misdemeanor. My charge sheet says I'm a Gaullist with a penchant for paper and ink." Joséphine's brown eyes flashed with amusement. "*Apparently* I wrote something naughty on some five-franc notes. The Boches didn't take kindly to my comments. They think I'm anti-German—arrested me and another journalist."

"You're a journalist?" Margot whispered with a mix of awe and fear. She grabbed the metal frame of her bed to steady herself as she recalled the headlines:

THE MURDERING MAID

KILLER SERVANT

BASTILLE KILLER

Margot wondered who had made them up. They sounded like titles of the crime novels she had often pulled out to read by candlelight while little Maxime slept. Her stomach clenched as she thought of the boy's peaceful sleeping face peeping out from her blanket. Then his look of confusion—furrowed brow, tear-filled eyes watching Margot when the police led her out of Villa Sanary in handcuffs.

Joséphine interrupted her ruminations. "So, my sweet *murderer*"—Margot winced—"if you are going to share my bed, we must trust each other. I've never slept beside a killer before," she teased in that husky Hollywood voice.

"I'm not—" Margot took in the gray walls, the endless *drip-drip* of water, and the wretched smell of feces, and wondered if the guillotine might have been better. She'd been moved to a new prison because French jails all over were apparently overcrowded with new political prisoners alongside the convicted criminals. Now it seemed she'd gone straight to hell. She pressed her palms to her eyes and wept, in loud, shuddery sobs so intense she started to wheeze.

"There, there, Margot. *Très désolée*. I'm sorry you ended up in this hellhole. I'm sorry your bed is wet, and I'm sorry for the stink." Joséphine wrapped Margot in a strong hug. This only made Margot cry harder, but her new cellmate held her tight until it eased. When Margot lifted her head from Joséphine's shoulder, there was a damp spot. "Pfft, my sweet, it will dry. Now, sit on my bed. I promise I won't bite—skinny girls aren't my thing!"

Margot hiccuped through a sob and wiped her nose with the back of her hand. What had she become? Her mother would be . . . She giggled. How ridiculous her life was! She was a convicted murderer—it was hardly likely she could disappoint Vivienne anymore!

"Thank you. You are kind. It's just the journey, I'm sure."

"You're right. I mean, this room's just peachy. You wait till you smell dinner! Turnip soup, or onion—not French onion soup, mind. Romanian, probably."

And so the two started to banter and slowly get to know each other as the evening shadows darkened the high windows.

Chapter 9

JOSÉPHINE

Joséphine Murant sat tucked into the corner of a cozy Montmartre bistro. She huddled around the table with half a dozen other members of the Société Charles Perrault: a passionate group of disheveled students, cravat-wearing museum curators, a lawyer, a former political secretary, journalists, and the energetic octogenarian Jean-Benoît Dubois, publisher of *La Fontaine*. As J.B. was by far the eldest, and the only one with a printing press, they all respectfully left him the last slice of baguette.

To anyone observing, this group was preparing a collection of lighthearted fairy tales for children. *Contes de ma mère l'Oye, Tales of Mother Goose*—just a little something to lift their spirits during the Occupation. Innocuous and frivolous.

Joséphine brushed bread crumbs from the red-checked tablecloth, took a sip of red wine, and called for a refill of water before she returned to her note-taking. Beside her, the open fire blazed—so if any Boches entered the restaurant, anything *not* a fairy tale could be tossed into the flames.

The Société Charles Perrault had been meeting here on different days every month to write and distribute pamphlets, propaganda, and a newsletter, and to exchange information from London radio broadcasts. It had started out printing pro–de Gaulle posters and plastering them all over Métro stations, telephone boxes, urinals, and alleys. Next had been a newsletter: *Liberté*.

What began as a group of passionate loyalists had grown to recruit specialist code makers, engineers, hikers, pilots—anyone who could solve a specific problem. Its scope had expanded so quickly it felt like an octopus insinuating its tentacles into every forbidden area of Paris.

Parisians had reached out from the shadows and asked their network to shelter downed British pilots and smuggle them to the Free Zone, then on to Barcelona where they would be rescued by the British consulate. The people of Paris also tried to think of ways to get food coupons to the elderly, sick, and disabled who were trapped in apartments and unable to flee to the Free Zone—or too scared to walk the streets lest they be preyed upon or arrested by Boches.

Joséphine had summoned the group today, as she had new intelligence. She looked at Albert Remon, her former colleague and cadet journalist. "I met with your . . . friend last week for lunch. The architect you introduced me to." She couldn't recall what they had eaten; no doubt some brown soup with flotsam, the only *spécial du jour* available to impoverished Parisians. Her cheeks grew hot as she pictured dessert: herself and the architect tangled up in her sheets.

"And?" said the impatient student Timothée Parsons.

"And he has a friend—"

Timothée groaned and pushed back his chair. Joséphine wanted to kick the insolent boy's shins under the table, but she composed herself. Being a petulant brat didn't mean he wasn't dedicated to saving his country.

So, she took a deep breath and started again. "His friend is a town planner who has maps. Munitions factories. Underground bunkers, power stations, sewer tunnels, and warehouses . . ." Her words tripped over themselves as she listed on her fingers all the things her delicious lover had outlined.

It was Jean-Benoît who spoke. "*If* we could get a copy of these maps, I could print them, and we could pass them on to the Allies."

Joséphine's skin grew cold. Had she done the right thing? Slapping a poster on Métro tiles was one thing, but targeting sites to attack—or bomb—was quite another. One misstep, and hundreds would be killed. She imagined bereft mothers holding burned children beside inconsolable fathers. Would her actions mean the ruin of thousands of innocent lives?

Louis Martin, a gentle lawyer, spoke up. "When can we meet this contact?" As if sensing her hesitation, he said softly, "This is a good thing, Joséphine. Intelligence changes weekly, supply lines have been cut. But one day we *will* walk the streets of Paris again. Freely. The plane trees will sprout new limbs. I dream of buying my children a cone of raspberry sorbet as we parade down the

Champs-Élysées, then gathering with friends at the Rodin. Perhaps I'll get my job back." He lifted a leg to show her the worn soles of his boots, and her heart sank; he had always prided himself on his dapper woolen suits, silk cravats, and vests. "My bootmaker in Saint-Germain is first on the list," he joked.

"Mine too," said Albert. He lifted his own worn boots and waggled them in the air. Everyone at the table smiled, and the tension hovering in their corner was broken.

The waiter lit the center candle and set down a plate of salmon terrine, a Puy lentil salad, and some aged goat's cheese along with a fresh basket of baguette.

"We didn't order—" young Albert started to protest. No Frenchman could afford this food; it was strictly reserved for the Boches.

"It's from Chef. He wants to thank you for your . . . patronage." The pale-faced waiter shrugged as he walked away. Joséphine felt sorry for the boy—he was so thin and sallow, it looked like he hadn't eaten in weeks. She'd give the chef a little extra, so the waiter had something to take home.

She swallowed—she'd not had a proper meal since she'd lost her job at the newspaper. Judging by everyone licking their lips, nobody else had either. Not since the Germans had started requisitioning virtually everything and sending it back to their homeland.

Before they dived in, they agreed on a time and location for Jean-Benoît to meet the architect's contact. Then Louis the lawyer called for another carafe of red wine, and for the next hour her little group buried their woes and fears. They made a toast to Timothée, who was to leave Paris and cross the demarcation line—again. They laughed, teased, discussed philosophy, and dissected literature.

"To Charles Perrault," said Jean-Benoît, raising his glass.

"To Charles Perrault," they all cheered, and clinked in reply.

෴

On her way out of the restaurant, Joséphine pushed handfuls of five-franc notes into the chef's pocket. "For you, and the boy." She nodded at the waiter, who looked almost asleep on his feet. But at least he still had a job. More than most.

The chef started to protest, before he noticed *Vive de Gaulle* in red ink stamped on the currency. "Mademoiselle, I shall spend these *carefully*." He winked before pushing her out the door.

Joséphine wrapped her old cashmere scarf tightly around her neck and buttoned up her coat, grateful for this long-ago gift from her mother. She could not even afford socks. It was a ten-minute walk to her Montmartre apartment through slush, mud, and autumn leaves. Shop displays—usually brimming with new-season blooms and bright colors—were pathetically empty. Bookshops displayed what was on permitted reading lists. Cake shops were bare, with only stodgy Black Forest and chestnut logs plonked in their windows to tempt a few francs from the greedy Boches.

When she reached her apartment, she tried to tiptoe past the concierge without disturbing her—but was betrayed by the pitter-patter of little paws. "Bonaparte." She picked up the small bulldog and kissed his nose before rubbing her cheek against his soft fur.

"Mademoiselle Murant," said Madame Thomas, the concierge, as she stomped from her chambers in a blue silk dressing gown and towel about her head, with arms outstretched to rescue her precious pet.

Joséphine handed over the dog, said *bonne nuit* to Madame Thomas, and ran up the staircase to her apartment. Once inside, she padlocked the door and added the chain.

Soon she was lying in bed with only moonlight for company, agitated and rolling from side to side as she wondered about the maps. The town planner contact was to meet Jean-Benoît in the next two days, the soonest they could arrange it.

❧

Three months into the Occupation, she'd met the architect quite by accident at a bar just around the corner from her apartment. The bar was small, dim, and crowded with Parisians who liked their liquor straight up with a shot of jazz. The Boches preferred the shinier, cleaner version nearby where the prostitutes kept their makeup fresh and layered themselves with expensive perfume and designer clothes.

On this evening, a Thursday, Joséphine hadn't wanted to sit around in her apartment fretting about her lack of employment. She'd pulled on her favorite peacock-blue dress and wrapped a scarlet feather boa across her shoulders to match her lipstick. She paused at the mirror to blow herself a kiss and check for smudges, and admired the way the bias-cut silk hugged her curves. Good things always happened when she wore her favorite blue dress.

The architect was at the bar, his white tuxedo slightly disheveled, smoking a cigarette with her ex-colleague at *Le Monde,* Albert Remon. She strode up to the bar and greeted them. "Ah, Joséphine," said Albert, kissing her on both cheeks and giving her arm an affectionate squeeze.

He introduced her to his handsome friend in the white tux, who took Joséphine's hand and kissed it. "*Enchanté,*" he murmured.

She was usually impervious to admiring glances, but tonight something flickered in her belly. She ordered herself a martini with a twist of lemon even though she could barely afford it, and paid using a five-franc note she pulled from her garter because she had no coins in her purse. She'd tucked herself between the bar and Albert, in the shadows where nobody could see her.

Albert tapped his eyebrow at the barman while he explained to the architect, "He's one of us."

As she slid her dress up her leg to get the note, the architect grabbed one and held it under the light. "*Vive de Gaulle,*" he read.

"Joséphine never stops," said Albert with collegiate pride. "Works like a fiend during the day, dances all night. I don't know where she gets the energy!" He beamed at her, but she noticed dark rings looped under his eyes. He was starting to look middle-aged, even though he was younger than Joséphine. The hunger and stress of working in clandestine conditions—never knowing who to trust—added to the relentless publishing program of *Liberté* were taking their toll. "Speaking of which, I must go. Early start tomorrow." He sighed as he picked up his hat and coat from the bar beside him. "Tomorrow, Joséphine." He nodded before shaking the hand of the architect and leaving them alone.

As Albert made his way toward the door, the architect smiled at Joséphine and pointed to her glass. "Another?"

"Yes, if you'll join me."

"It would be my honor," he said with admiration.

She slid her dress up again to grab some more notes—notes she was too proud to admit she could ill afford to part with. But the architect beat her to it and paid the barman.

When he smiled, his eyes almost disappeared and pleasant wrinkles formed at the corners. His skin was tanned, almost leathery, and his gaze ran over her body, taking in her dress and watching as she slid the silk back down her leg. "The blue suits you."

"It's my favorite." She shrugged, even though her tummy was tingling.

The architect leaned against the bar on an elbow, took a slug of his whisky, and waved a note in the air. "So tell me, Mademoiselle Joséphine Murant, why are you out roaming the streets in that magnificent dress with a stockingful of cash?"

⁂

Eventually she drifted off to sleep, her brain whirring with maps, goat's cheese, and the handsome architect hungrily tugging off her blue silk dress, garter, stockings, and brassiere so they lay in a pool on the wooden floor. He'd pressed her hard up against the desk, where she'd arched her back and wrapped her legs around him so tight he'd gasped, before he'd tossed her onto the bed and lain beside her. He'd softly kissed her breasts, her neck, her cheek, her lips, while stroking up her thighs. Then, when they could both no longer stand it, he'd pressed against her. They'd clung to each other, bit at soft skin, squeezed, and scratched.

Joséphine turned under her blanket, still dreaming of the architect. She could smell his cologne, an arty mix of spices and musk. Just as she was trying once more to recall his pink lips touching her breast, her door splintered as it was thrown open and two Gestapo officers dragged her from her bed, then her apartment, in her nightdress.

Chapter 10

Joséphine blinked and wiggled her feet. She had been standing with an interrogation light shining in her face. Hours had become days; she was sure of it.

A trio of French policemen stood silently in the corner. She scowled. *Traitors.* They refused to meet her eyes.

The older German officer, who'd dragged her from her bed by her hair, had confirmed he was Gestapo as he circled her in the interrogation cell. First, with large goose steps. Now, staccato. He was agitated.

Brahms played at full volume, making her dizzy. She'd always enjoyed the romantic layered texture of his music, especially the C minor quartet. But for the rest of her life she would associate Brahms's merry vigor with fear and anger.

Soldiers shouted questions, while a familiar *tap-tap* in the corner told her a typist was recording everything.

"No, I do not know anything about *Liberté*."

"No, I do not know of a . . . Timothée . . . who?" She fumbled over the name; she needed it to appear unfamiliar.

"Where did you get this five-franc note?" The Gestapo officer held up the money with the red stamped letters *Vive de Gaulle*. It must have been in her purse.

"I catch the Métro—perhaps I've accidentally picked up something there. There's so much rubbish about now with Germans in town!"

She closed her eyes to escape the hot glare of the lights. Her nightdress clung to her back. The music climbed to a crescendo, and her weary brain tried to recall the architect. She hoped that thoughts of happier times would distract her from this hell. He came to her in pieces: hands gripping her hair as he kissed her with such intensity he shook; lips on her neck, her collarbone; a nip of her breast.

The Brahms pounded; the soldiers yelled more questions, and she tried to ignore them. Her mind reached for the face of the architect. His torso pressed against hers. Fingers dragging along curves. Legs tangled in white sheets.

No one could have prepared her for this interrogation. The relentless questions, the heat. Dehydration. Forbidden from sitting down. Her legs had gone numb, and she was swaying. She was dizzy. Needed water.

She tried, again, to picture the architect's face. His square jaw.

She giggled as she imagined relaying this story to her family when the war was over. *I survived interrogation. Didn't spill a drop of information.*

She wouldn't tell them about the humiliation, and how she was terrified she'd never see their faces again. That when her body was about to give up, she took her mind elsewhere.

Over the years, the architect's handsome face would fade, and she would be left with the raw horror that burned like bile in her throat. The heat. Sweat. Bloody Brahms! And there would be nothing she could do to make the music—the torture—disappear.

A stomp of a heavy boot. She wondered what it would take to elicit a slap. *Non, non, non*, she answered. The questions went in circles. Her only outings were for a literary club. She'd lost her job as a journalist. She lived off savings, for now.

All the while she was grateful that every copy of *Liberté* published since September and the names of more than two hundred Resistance fighters and notes from Louis the lawyer were safe.

She promised herself she would never contact the architect, even if she was released that day. She wouldn't put him at risk.

Non, non, non.

It was as if someone else were speaking. She answered slowly, calmly. She tried to give the impression of being a bit bewildered. A misunderstanding.

The only evidence they had against her was the five-franc note, and she could have picked that up anywhere. Surely she would get three months in prison, at the most. It was a minor misdemeanor. Three months and a smack over the knuckles—that was a tiny price to pay for the freedom of her group. Her country.

She remained outwardly calm, but if the Gestapo officer had stepped closer and put a hand to her chest, he would have felt a heart beating furiously and known that Joséphine Murant would not be tamed.

The footsteps stopped. The light turned off.

Joséphine was felled to her knees with a kick.

"*Halte!* Charge her. Take her to Fresnes Prison." The Gestapo officer stomped out the steel door and slammed it shut.

Chapter 11

EVIE

VILLA SANARY, PRESENT DAY

Evie leaned against the kitchen island and sipped her coffee while Hugo sat at the oversized table with Monsieur Laurent, polishing off his second croissant. Madame Laurent was busy in the kitchen preparing a chicken curry for dinner.

Evie and Hugo had stayed in Paris for a week, sorting through Raph's paperwork and storage boxes for any hint of Joséphine's first manuscript. All she'd come up with were tax returns and handfuls of Paris Saint-Germain ticket stubs. Gilles was making good progress on the Leroux paperback and had promised to send some images very soon. She'd also negotiated the sale of the Australian orchids manuscript to a collector in Singapore; she would be sad to see this one go—the spidery lines of blue had woven their way into her heart.

Evie planned to enjoy the rest of her summer here at the villa with Hugo as she worked with Clément. The sun was starting to rise, and it bathed the conservatory in a pink hue. The day was going to be a hot one. Evie studied the soft rosy haze and took a deep breath as she thought about her early years with her dad out in the paddocks, where the relentless Australian sun beat down on parched, cracked soil. A glance at the grandfather clock in the corner told her it would be 6:00 P.M. back home. Her dad would be in his favorite chair on the veranda, having showered away the dust, a whisky in hand, studying the stock reports.

"Ready?" Monsieur Laurent had kindly offered to drive Evie to the museum for her meeting with Clément.

"Smells good," said Hugo, who swung around the kitchen island to see what Madame Laurent was cooking in her wok. "You spoil us."

"Not at all. I love having people to cook for. This big old house needs filling up. *You* need filling up, Hugo—look at those long limbs."

"Madame Laurent, you do look after us," said Evie. "We are so lucky to have you in our lives. Hopefully I'll be back in time for curry." She breathed in the spicy scent. "I'll text if I'm running late. Clément says he has a stack of stuff to show me." She pulled a blue cashmere scarf from her bag and wrapped it around her neck and shoulders.

She was looking forward to seeing Clément. In fact, she'd changed her shirt twice and taken an extra few minutes to put on mascara, blush, and a dab of the highlighter Camille had forced her to buy at great cost last week in Galeries Lafayette. Her friend had whipped off the lid at the counter and gently stabbed Evie in the corners of each eye, then painted stripes down her nose and across her cheekbones before blending them with an index finger. "See, it will add light here, here, and here. You look dewy and delicious. Wear your yellow Isabel Marant silk shirt, and I guarantee he'll be peeling you out of it by the day's end."

"Camille! I'm not . . . We're working together. The exhibition—"

"Pfft." Her friend batted away her protests. "You're not the first to meet a lover through work. I met my first husband on a shoot, remember? Besides, it's not like you have a huge social life, so where else are you going to meet anyone? You refuse to try online dating." Camille dabbed some gloss onto her lips. "Just make sure you wear a good silk bra and matching knickers. Make an effort, Evie. You're gorgeous. Enjoy it."

❧

"Thanks for agreeing to meet at my office," said Clément as he plucked some files off her seat and added them to a pile in the corner. He waved at them. "This is for an exhibition later next year, after the Joséphine Murant."

"It must be relentless." Evie smiled as she looked out the floor-to-ceiling sash windows across the bay. Fishing boats, yachts, and luxury cruisers huddled together, bumping against the docks.

Clément followed her gaze. "My great-grandfather worked on one of those trawlers for thirty years after he immigrated."

"Where was he from?"

"Casablanca. Migrated after the war. He was in the Battle of Verdun in 1916."

Evie shivered and looked from the boats to Clément. He carried trauma and displacement in his blood. She remembered him telling her and Madame Laurent that his grandfather—his *jadde*—had fought for the de Gaulle forces in North Africa. Suffered severe nerves. His research into Joséphine Murant clearly touched on something quite personal.

"Do you fish?" asked Evie, who suddenly longed to sit out by the ocean. Stripy umbrellas dotted the footpaths, luring holiday-makers and locals to sit and enjoy the region's rosé and specialty bouillabaisse.

"Me?" He seemed surprised. "I used to throw a line off the end of those docks with my *jadde*. But now my fish experience is limited strictly to eating. What about you? Do you fish?"

"Never! I grew up hundreds of miles from the sea. Raph took me a few times when we stayed down here, but it's not really my thing. I prefer my fish cooked too!" She grinned. "Sorry, I interrupted you. You were about to talk about the Joséphine Murant exhibition."

"I didn't mean *the* Joséphine Murant, like it's just another exhibition. It's not, I promise you. It's just that we have to schedule these exhibits years in advance. The next booking is a series of botanical illustrations. That's why I wanted you to come in here—otherwise I'd have come to you, of course."

Evie smiled, touched by his consideration.

Clément started to open a folder across the desk. "First, an update on Margot Bisset's conviction." He tapped the folder. "These are copies of all the witness statements. There is a typed statement from your Monsieur Laurent's brother, Gabriel." Clément lifted it up and read it aloud. "*Margot Bisset handed a letter to my baby brother, Maxime, with instructions he pass it to me. He did at about*

10:00 P.M. *I believe she wanted my forgiveness and help.* It seems your Mr. Laurent was there the night of the murder."

Evie rubbed her forehead. "But he was just a little boy," she said protectively. "It had nothing to do with Maxime."

"I know. But the note was pretty clear." He held up the evidence.

Cher Gabriel,

Meet me behind the hedge half an hour after the fireworks have finished. I'll bring champagne, from Chef, and perhaps some leftover caviar.

There may be a commotion on the balcony during the fireworks. Don't panic if you hear a gunshot. Or see police. I may be a few minutes late. Please wait!

It's all a game. A terrible trick. I'll be relieved when it is over.

I will explain what I have done when we meet. Don't tell anyone.

Margot

"That's ridiculous. Surely nobody believes this scribbly non-sense. Look, it starts *Cher Gabriel*—with affection . . ." Evie had no idea why she suddenly felt compelled to defend the notorious Margot Bisset. Perhaps because, as an Australian, Evie had an instinctive need to defend the underdog—and because Monsieur Laurent couldn't have been completely wrong about Margot, could he?

"The jury believed it! Also, it says on this page"—Clément produced another piece of paper from the folder—"that according to the detective's report, Margot's fingerprints were all over the gun that killed Peggy Schramsburg."

"Gun?" Evie glanced at the charge sheet.

Premeditated murder
Sentence: Execution

"But why?" Evie asked. "What would a maid hope to gain . . . ?
Was she *blackmailing* this Peggy Schramsburg?"

"Who knows? I've asked for the coroner's report to check
whether Peggy actually died of a gunshot wound. These newspaper
articles suggest she did, but it may take some time to clarify."

HEIRESS MURDERED

SHOT AT POINT-BLANK RANGE

MURDERING MAID

"I feel like we're in the middle of one of Joséphine's novels,
with all this talk of murder and guns." Evie winced. "Except this
isn't a guessing game. A real person died. Also, if Margot didn't
kill Peggy, then who did?"

"Well, it's speculation at this point." He looked serious, and
Evie wanted to see him smile again.

"Let's leave this for now," she suggested, then turned to survey
the piles of folders on the carpet. She presumed each pile and
color represented a different exhibition or collection. "If you put
that folder down, will you find it again? Seems like you've got a
lot going on here." She gestured around his office, sensing a fellow
procrastinator when it came to admin.

"I have a system!" he protested with a chuckle. "Come on,

come with me. I'll take you to these illustrations. Then we shall have lunch."

"Sounds like a plan," said Evie, who right at that minute wished Gilles was there to join them. He and Clément were kindred spirits, charming leftovers from a previous century. She stood up and tugged on her scarf, then followed Clément through a rabbit warren of fluorescent-lit back corridors and poky stairwells.

"Here we are." He tapped the electronic lock with his security pass.

Years of accompanying Gilles to auction rooms and specialist reading rooms had prepared her for the cellar-like conditions of museum reading rooms. But the chill was a small price to pay for the thrill of seeing a rare botanical manuscript for the first time. Outside, the sun would be climbing and the cobbled streets baking, and the ocean glinting. Not here, where it was all dim lights, velvet table covers, and cotton gloves.

Evie took out her notebook and loupe magnifying glass. "May I?"

"Of course!" Clément passed her a pair of archival gloves.

She opened the first herbal and sucked in a breath. "I've seen a copy of Cesi's *Botanical Manuscripts* at the rare-book fair in Antwerp, but nothing compares to seeing the original." She studied where the museum binders were stitched onto separate paper guards so she could open the book without bending the original parchment.

"This one was made in 1620, for the newly established Academy of Sciences in Rome." He gestured to the gold inscription on the front page.

Evie flicked through the pages, pointing out the precision of the artist. There were starry ferns and bryophytes, mustard- and lime-colored mosses and liverworts. She turned a page back and forth, feeling the soft crick of the centuries-old vellum and admiring the brightness of the ink. A double-page spread of moss was so vivid, she almost believed she'd feel the cool, tufty softness if she pressed her cheek to the page.

Gilles's sage advice as she'd worked on her own watercolors over the years came flooding back. *People rarely read the scientific annotations in the margins—always look to what is written in the creases, Evie.*

She paused, thinking of the Leroux volume now locked up at her shop with him, Joséphine's prison diary recorded almost entirely in the margins. Would it reveal her secrets, and those of Margot Bisset? Evie hoped Gilles would be able to separate all the fused pages so none of Joséphine's words would be lost.

She thought about all the hard work she and Gilles put in to chase the provenance of a botanical manuscript, analyzing composition. Clément seemed to enjoy the hunt as much as she did.

She leaned closer to the 1620 manuscript and ran her finger along a blade of grass. Did the artist paint this in the field, in the bowels of a ship, or in a quiet room by candlelight? It could be difficult to establish the provenance: how and where things were made. A manuscript could both whisper secrets and conceal them. A glance at the vellum could take you back five hundred years, but under what conditions was it painted? How did it change hands the first time?

How many hands had been over these pages?

Evie's head shot up, and she rested her loupe on the table. She looked at Clément. "I understand now why you want to see Joséphine's working manuscripts. Especially the missing manuscript. It's not so different, is it?"

When his eyes met hers, she sensed that he understood her perfectly. "Very true, Evie," he said. Their eyes locked, and she found herself holding her breath until he broke the contact. "Let's go have some lunch! I know a place that does the freshest coquilles Saint Jacques with just salt, butter, and white wine. And while we are there, I'm hoping I can convince you to take a daytrip to Suresnes with me. There's a memorial I think you should see."

Evie hesitated. Was this a work thing, or was he asking her on a date? Part of her wanted it to be a date—but there was Hugo. And she didn't want to complicate a professional relationship.

Besides, what could a war memorial in Suresnes have to do with an exhibition about Joséphine Murant? Could it somehow be linked to her diary? The missing manuscript? Perhaps Joséphine had told Clément more than he let on.

Chapter 12

JOSÉPHINE

FRESNES PRISON, JANUARY 1941

Joséphine studied Margot-from-Sanary sitting on the cot bed weeping, and thought, *She doesn't much have the look of a murderer.* This was their first night sharing their tiny, stinking cell. She offered her pretty new cellmate another chocolate from the box the kind French guard had given her.

"When does your trial start?" asked Margot.

"Who knows?" said Joséphine as she bit into a chocolate. "They tell me it could be months. A year. Lucky I've got this place to stay!" She licked the soft middle, suddenly feeling churlish. Joséphine found it hard to imagine spending the rest of her life within these damp stone walls with just rotten straw mattresses and an overflowing slop bucket. She counted her blessings that she was in for a minor misdemeanor, so her sentence would be months, not years.

Knowing there was nothing she could say to console Margot,

Joséphine passed her another chocolate. "Ah, caramel, my favorite," she said as Margot tentatively took it.

Joséphine pulled her Leroux paperback out from under her mattress and started to write.

"Are you writing in a . . . a book?" her cellmate exclaimed as she curled up at the other end of the mattress. Just beside her on the floor was the slop pail and a little enamel jug for drinking water.

"It's my diary. Mama gave it to me—she's unwell."

"I'm sorry to hear."

"*Merci.* I write so my family will know what a treat this place was!" She gave a wan smile. "And also to get my story right. You know, practice." Joséphine studied the younger girl with her full cheeks. "You remind me of my little sister, Lulu. She's strong, like you. As a girl, there was no tree she couldn't climb, and she beat all the boys in our arrondissement when they played soccer in the street."

"Did you play?" asked Margot with obvious surprise.

"Sometimes . . . mostly as goalkeeper, out of the way! But Lulu, she was a tiny poppet, but fierce. She'd dribble the ball right past everyone and score." Joséphine smiled at the memory.

"Where's your Lulu now?"

"With Mama and Papa at their apartment in Paris. Mama had scarlet fever as a child, and her heart was weakened. Now with the Occupation, it's hard for her to see her doctor. Mama doesn't want to make a fuss. So Lulu moved in to care for her—and Papa. She's a great cook, nobody makes duck confit like my sister. And she pickles her own cherries and vegetables. Fortunately they have a larder full of her preserves and confitures, enough to last a couple of winters. She's so clever—if it were left to me, we'd all starve. I have trouble poaching an egg."

Margot's eyes widened as if she didn't quite believe her cellmate.

"It's true! When I was at the newspaper, we'd work late, then go to a bar and a cheap little restaurant on the Left Bank—or I'd cleverly invite myself to dinner at someone's house."

"You must have dined with Lulu a lot. You must miss her."

Joséphine's eyes started to fill. "It's . . . complicated. My sister, she supports the Occupation. Vichy. She *despises* me for supporting de Gaulle. Thinks people like me make trouble for everyone and just prolong the inevitable."

"I'm sure she doesn't *despise* you—"

"Oh, she most certainly does," Joséphine said softly. "Lulu blames me for Mama's broken heart. She will never forgive me for resisting the Boches. Or for being stupid enough to get arrested. *Never.*"

"I'm sure you didn't mean—"

"It doesn't matter. Lulu hates me and has sworn never to speak to me again. It's not only France that's broken, it's my family." She paused to wipe away a tear. "I'd *never* forgive myself if Lulu was arrested, or hurt by the Boches. Everything I do, it is for her. For Mama and Papa too. I miss them all so much. I've caused them such worry. This arrest, my mama can barely take it. If it weren't for Lulu . . ." She shook her head.

"Your sister sounds very strong."

"She is. I miss my family. It's agony not knowing when I'll see them again. *If* I'll see them again." Her voice started to break.

"It is." Margot nodded, her eyes filled with pain. "I miss my mother."

Joséphine sighed, her heart aching for Margot. How could this sweet young woman be a murderer?

Chapter 13

EVIE

At ten in the morning, Evie and Hugo met Clément for their visit to the Mémorial de la France Combattante: the Memorial to Fighting France.

"Bonjour, Hugo. So glad you could join us." Clément glanced sideways at Evie as he shook her son's hand, before kissing her on both cheeks.

"I thought this was something Hugo should see," she replied a little too quickly, while Clément's beard pressed against her cheek. "You said it was important," she added, trying to keep her voice even. If Clément found it awkward that she'd roped her son into joining them, he was gracious enough not to show it.

She was glad she'd worn her sneakers as they wound their way up a wide path through the magnificent park carved into the side of Mont-Valérien. They walked past dark towering pines and stubbier yew trees, maples, elms, and grand oaks. Children wobbled bicycles and made way for cyclists in Lycra who moved in a peloton. Families lay on the lawns, reading, picnicking. A young couple lay with their Dr. Martens entwined, kissing as though their lives depended on it.

"Don't stare," hissed Hugo, striding up the path past her toward the entrance to the fort.

"Joy of teenagers," Evie said with a weak laugh, hoping Clément didn't notice her embarrassment.

"Hugo's great."

"Hmm. This park is incredible—I can't believe I've lived in Paris for twenty years and never made the forty-minute train trip out here." She and Hugo had returned to Paris for a few days and caught the train out together.

"The chapel I want you both to see is up near the fort, but in medieval times this was a popular path for pilgrims as they made their way to the hermitage at the top."

"What a beautiful place to absolve sins." Evie plucked a reddening leaf from a nearby tree. She turned the leaf over, studying the veins, the way the green rippled into the red. "*Cornus sanguinea.*"

"Sounds fancy."

"Not really." She pulled a face. "This is your good old garden-variety dogwood. And that big one over there is a sessile oak."

Evie unzipped her purse and slipped the leaf inside as they approached the arched entrance to the fort. She collected leaves all the time and pressed them into her notebooks to draw, but she wasn't sure it was quite the done thing to steal a leaf from a sacred site.

They passed through the entrance and stepped into a huge

courtyard paved in pink stone, with a cobblestone path leading to an enormous pink cross set against the far end of the fort. The wall on either side of the cross was studded with sixteen gigantic bronze sculpture reliefs.

Hugo stood beside Evie, their shoulders almost touching. She could hear him swallow as he tried to make sense of what they were seeing: a man struggling to free himself from octopus tentacles, two hands offered up in hope, another yanking a life from chains, more hands tearing at barbed wire lacing a tortured heart, a proud raptor, a soldier dressed as a phoenix, a lion, a furious snake.

Hugo was transfixed by the phoenix sculpture. He ran his fingers over the feathers before photographing it from every angle, documenting the destruction and transformation. Resistance. "Each of these reliefs represents one of the sixteen battles or events that people fought for France from 1939 to 1945. The bodies of Resistance fighters are in the crypt." He pointed to a small gold door tucked under the cross.

Goose Bumps rose on Evie's skin as she read the plaques describing the battles of the air force, the Resistance fighters in the woods, and the soldiers along the Rhine, in the mountains overlooking Italy, Algiers, and as far off as Norway. As they stepped along and observed the sculptures, Hugo snapped more photos with his phone. Evie reached out to trace a finger along the barbed wire; the bronze was icy, despite the warm day.

Hugo wandered ahead.

Clément looked at Hugo's disappearing back and said, "I used to come up here when I was doing my thesis. Some days I'd sit in front of one of these and imagine myself in the front line in Libya." He touched a star flanked by two forearms. "Other days I tried to imagine myself in the depths of winter along the Rhine." He stepped closer to look at the relief depicting water pouring into the soil—the river looked almost fluid. "But the truth is, I can't imagine. You know how I told you about my grandfather's night terrors? Well, they informed everything I studied. You see, I was raised by my grandparents. My parents . . ." He shrugged. "They weren't exactly neglectful so much as absent. They were archaeologists. Always in Egypt. Iran. Israel. Anywhere but home." His voice softened. "But they loved their work, and it was important work. Inspiring work. Now here I am doing almost the same thing: chasing stories of dead people. Working with relics, articles, statues. Trying to give a voice to those without one."

"This place is why you became a historian."

"One of the reasons. I want to understand war. Why it keeps happening. How people pick themselves up and recover." Softer again, he added, "Or not."

Evie shivered. She'd come here looking for Joséphine Murant's story, to find the story of Raph and Hugo's family. But, of course, the search was personal for Clément too.

She looked around for Hugo.

"He's already gone through to the chapel. C'mon." Clément took her hand, firm and tender, and she clasped his in return. She wanted to stand in the sun for a moment more and enjoy the sensation, but he led her to the door of the crypt, where sixteen tombs lay covered with the tricolor flag.

"I can't go in," said Evie, shaking her head.

Clément's grasp was gentle. "I understand. I just wanted you to see it."

Still holding her hand, he led her to the little white chapel, and they stepped inside. Hugo was already there, snapping photos of graffiti scratched into the wall. Clément let go of Evie's hand as they entered.

When they reached Hugo near the far wall where the altar once stood, he quickly wiped his eyes and turned away. Evie put a hand on her son's shoulder as he said in a tight voice, "This is where they locked up the Resistance fighters before they were marched outside and shot."

"One thousand and ten, according to German records," said Clément. "But now they think it's quadruple that." He pointed to where half a dozen hand-whittled coffins were clustered on a plinth. "They placed the bodies in simple coffins and buried them in mass graves anonymously under the cover of darkness, in cemeteries all over France. So, families never knew where their loved ones ended up. And no one could mark a site, so it couldn't become a symbol of Resistance solidarity. A martyr prevention program, if you like."

Evie thought of how she and Hugo went to visit Raph's gravesite. They'd bring flowers, sit at the headstone—sometimes she'd pour a glass of good pinot—and talk about everything and nothing. She didn't think Raph could hear them; she certainly wasn't woo-woo about spirits and an afterlife. It was just comforting, in a strange way, to know he would always be in that spot. Closure, she guessed some would call it. Except her heart would always be full of Raph.

She held her breath as she gazed at the coffins. Standing in the chapel made Joséphine's story come alive for her—and that of others too. For the first time, Evie felt she fully understood why Clément wanted an exhibition. Why a research paper wouldn't suffice. He wanted people to *feel* the price of war.

"What are those?" Hugo asked, pointing to the dozen shredded telegraph poles.

"Those," said Clément, swallowing quickly, "are execution posts. The prisoners were tied up against them—blindfolded, if they wanted to be—and shot by a unit of forty soldiers. Their comrades, the next ones to be shot, would be lined up to watch before it was their turn."

"Fucking hell!" said Hugo.

Evie didn't have the energy to glare at him for swearing in a chapel. She stepped over to read the graffiti and tried to imagine what it must have felt like to be locked in this tiny chapel—a place of worship—to await the march to execution.

October 2, 1942
I kiss all: my dear René, my children Geneviève, Louis, Gilbert, Hélène, my mother, Gustave, André.
Long live France
Died for France long live the Soviet Union
Long live the Communist Party

It struck Evie that all the messages were proof of an honorable life, love, or *liberté*. She couldn't see any hateful comments or calls for revenge. *Long live . . .* She read the lines over and over, until she felt dizzy. These were Resistance fighters about to die, and their final thoughts were for the future. For a life beyond the war. For their families and loved ones. For their country.

The magnitude of their bravery made her shiver, along with the cold. She was stepping away, heading outside, when she saw two names etched side by side that stopped her in her tracks.

Timothée Parsons, 1942
Louis Martin, March 1942

Timothée Martin was the name of the crusading detective in Joséphine Murant's first three novels. He was brave, fierce, and modest, and he didn't stop until the criminal was jailed. Evie called Hugo and Clément over, and pointed out the names. "Do you think it's a coincidence?"

"Who knows?" said Hugo, a slight croak to his voice. "I'm going outside."

"Maybe, but probably not. Perhaps she knew these men through the Resistance." Clément took down the names in his notebook, and Evie thought this charming, especially as Hugo had already taken a photo. "I'll add it to my list of things to look up on the former Wehrmacht database."

Clément and Evie followed Hugo out of the chapel, and she was relieved to feel the sun once more on her face. She followed Hugo along a wide path that meandered from the chapel to a pretty clearing in the forest. Under different circumstances, it would have been magical walking through the golden dappled light amid elm, maple, and oak trees, but her throat felt dry and she found it hard to swallow.

So many brave people had walked this path, been lashed to a post, and shot.

In the clearing, Hugo was sitting on a log with his head in his hands. In front of him was a simple sandstone memorial slab and tricolor flag. Evie sat beside him and gave his back a rub. She'd expected him to pull away from her touch, but instead he relaxed. Not wanting to push her luck, she didn't offer any soothing words and just kept stroking his back.

Clément stepped to the other side of the clearing and walked farther into the forest, perhaps sensing they needed space. She was grateful for his thoughtfulness.

Together, she and her son sat in the clearing snuggled into the side of the mountain. She noticed some tufts of wild parsley at her feet and was moved by the way their fronds unfurled. She took out her sketchbook and started to draw the outline of the herb with an ink pen, shading one side and etching in the bark.

"Not bad," said Hugo, leaning against her. "You should do it more. I mean, you don't have many hobbies, and Papa always said you neglected your art by working all the time at the shop."

"Cheeky! *You're* my main hobby!" She nudged his shoulder while she continued to draw.

"Right! Better get a new one, then. I'm outta here next year."

Her chest tightened. Hugo was on the cusp of leaving to forge his adult life. Opportunity and freedom stretched out in front of him, because of the very people who had died here. They had given their lives fighting for what they loved.

Evie thought of the brave young men executed in this grove. Men whose freedom was torn from them. Still, they refused to be crushed, scrawling their own names and those of family and messages to loved ones all over the chapel walls. Prisoners whose heads and hearts were full of those they loved right until the end.

Chapter 14

JOSÉPHINE

FRESNES PRISON, FEBRUARY 1942

Weeks dragged into months, then a year. The Nazis seemed to want political prisoners to languish in jail for as long as possible. Fortunately, Joséphine had found she liked Margot and rarely tired of her company. They had become close friends and discussed Margot's case hundreds of times.

Finally, Joséphine's trial was due to begin. It was still dark at 6:00 A.M. when the kind warden twisted the key in the door and announced she was being moved to Paris. "I'm sorry, Joséphine, we need to leave now."

She had two minutes to wash, dress, and lace her boots. Margot, she noticed, was curled up on the opposite bed, watching her dress, before she stood up and stepped over to hug Joséphine. The girl said nothing, but Joséphine could feel her provincial cellmate had not lost all of her strength.

"Are you trying to kill me before I take the stand, my little bird?"

Margot started to cry. Joséphine looked up at the ceiling and fluttered her eyelashes to stave off the tears. She had no business with tears; she could count on the fingers of one hand the number of times she'd cried in her life, mostly in childhood. Prison forced tears from her.

"We have to go," said the warden, and he marched Joséphine out to the corridor, where she was instructed to stand two meters from the person in front. She spied Louis Martin, the lawyer. Just in front was Timothée, the young university student, who wore too-big clothes and whose hair touched his collar.

In all there were seven prisoners, and as they marched down the corridor and into the transport bus, she put a name to each face. No one made eye contact.

The truck drove past rows of elegant Haussmann apartments, neat lines of plane trees, parks and squares. Usually such places cheered Joséphine; she cherished the style and panache of her city. But today the skies were gray above the near-empty streets, and the shop fronts looked desolate.

The trial was conducted in a Paris town house overflowing with Boches and Vichy police. She and her fellow prisoners were marched up narrow stairs into a room with turbulent gold wallpaper. A swastika was pinned to the door. Lawyers spoke in low voices and directed people to tables.

Sieg Heil salutes started the proceedings, then charge sheets were read aloud. The political prisoners were accused of being "nationalists," which made Joséphine grimace—for weren't such dangerous sentiments the very kernel of what people like her were fighting against? The Boches shot Joséphine dark looks.

When Joséphine's charges were read, she was surprised they were for the production and circulation of *Liberté*. Also, espionage.

She swallowed. She'd expected three months for the misdemeanor of graffitied currency. Not this. *Seven years. Perhaps execution.*

Her lawyer's face looked grim.

❧

The trial went on for weeks, interrupted only by cell time and soup. She made no eye contact with Louis and Timothée and denied ever meeting them.

On the stand, she spoke in riddles and wove together the most fanciful threads of fiction, taking care to repeat the stories she'd told during that first Gestapo interrogation.

The night before sentencing, she heard screams from the man in the lockup beside her as the Boches tortured him. The screams eventually petered out, replaced by whimpers. Pleased with their efforts, the Boches laughed and slapped each other on the back as the thump of their boots faded down the corridor.

When Joséphine took the stand the next day, she was haunted by the sounds of screaming and laughter. She could barely focus on anything around her; only a hint of sympathy in the judge's eyes stood out. "You have conducted yourself with honor," he said before repeating the charges.

Finally, the verdict: *Coupable*. Guilty.

She held her breath as the sentences were delivered in pompous

German. "For Timothée Parsons, death by firing squad. For Louis Martin, death by firing squad."

She permitted herself to make eye contact with Louis, then Timothée. The older man nodded and closed his eyes for a beat, while the youth covered his face and sobbed. Joséphine's heart broke to see his pain. Louis lifted his chin and set his jaw, as if to say, *I regret nothing.*

"For Joséphine Murant, five years' imprisonment after deportation to Germany."

She gasped and tried to protest, but it was no use.

The Wehrmacht guards moved quickly, cuffing and dividing prisoners, then marching them from the makeshift courtroom.

Joséphine was numb. She ignored the prods in the back, sneers, and shoves as she was dragged into a transport bus and driven with the other female prisoners back to Fresnes Prison.

From the back of the bus she took in glimpses of Paris. Would she have the chance to return before the end of the war? She sighed, admiring the elegant iron balconies and the grand avenues of trees. She took heart that people still adorned their stoops with potted plants, and tufts of green shoots were pushing up in the spring air. Occasionally they passed a pop of yellow, an early-season jonquil. She was too heartsick, too broken, to be completely cheered by the flowers. How could she, when her friends were to be executed? Even so, it reassured her that Mother Nature paid no heed to the Boches.

When the warden escorted Joséphine back into her cell, Margot was red-eyed and huddled on her bed, hands about her knees. Damp straw tufted out the edge of the mattress. The trial had gone on for weeks, and poor Margot had been alone all this time.

At the sight of the Vichy guard, she jumped to attention. He shoved Joséphine in the back, and she stumbled toward Margot and fell facedown on the floor.

The door swung shut, and the key squeaked in the lock. Margot helped Joséphine up and ushered her over to the bed.

Joséphine studied her friend's pale face. A ribbon of freckles across the nose had faded, and her dark eyes were dull—dull, but not dead. "Still here, I see."

Margot wrapped her arms around Joséphine and started to cry. "Thank God! I thought you were going to be executed."

Joséphine felt something in her break and she leaned into Margot. She pictured her brave comrades, Louis and Timothée, being marched with the others to their deaths. Joséphine pledged to carry these men in her heart for the rest of her life.

As soon as the last door to the cellblock swung closed and was locked, all the inmates started to rattle their spoons against the bars. After a minute of boisterous clanging, one by one they joined in singing "La Marseillaise" at the top of their voices. Joséphine shouted so loudly, her lungs started to ache. Still, they kept singing, again and again, until their voices dropped away, and the cellblock was left in an eerie silence.

As darkness gathered, Joséphine broke down and sobbed, clinging to Margot, her chest tight. "I was only spared because I'm a woman." She spat into the slop bucket. "French law, apparently. The bloody Boches can occupy our country and steal us from our homes in the middle of the night . . . and *now* they pay heed to French law?" She felt delirious. "I should have been executed with the others."

Margot was stroking her back. "No, of course not! Don't say such things."

They sat in silence as Joséphine calmed slightly. Then she was struck by an idea. "Pass me that spoon." She held out a hand for it, and Margot obeyed.

"What are you doing?" she asked as Joséphine scratched on the wall.

She ignored her cellmate and kept scratching. When she was done, she sat back and showed Margot what she'd written.

"*Joséphine Murant, died March 1942*," Margot read aloud in a shaky voice. "You're not going to . . ."

"Take my life? No. Not today, anyway. Not after the special slice of bread with weevils I had in the bus back to this sanctuary. Too much to look forward to. But I wanted to make my own headstone." Joséphine's voice hardened. "When the war is over and Paris is free, I want to show the world what horror looks like. What fear *tastes* like. And I promise you I will *never, ever* give up any names to the Boches. You hear?"

Margot nodded solemnly and squeezed Joséphine's hands in hers.

"All right." Joséphine tried to smile. "I've been told we leave tomorrow at dawn for the German labor camp. You know, you really should start packing!"

Margot snorted, lifted up a leg, and waggled her holey boot. "Done!"

Joséphine laughed softly and tapped her own chest over her heart. "They can't separate us. I'll always carry you here, my little bird."

With a gentle smile, Margot nodded and squeezed her hands again.

Joséphine Murant Exhibition Catalog (Draft)

Chapter 4: Deportation: Nacht und Nebel
By Dr. Clément Tazi

Spared execution, Joséphine Murant was deported to Anrath Prison—an old fort near Düsseldorf, Germany—in March 1942. Here she was ordered into a Third Reich labor camp. She was to spend the next three years, until liberation in 1945, as a laborer in the nearby Phrix Rayon Factory at Krefeld.

Murant could not have known that Anrath Prison had been established as part of a Nazi program of intimidation and deportation code-named Nacht und Nebel ("Night and Fog"). Hitler had issued this code name for a decree he made on December 7, 1941—the same day as the Japanese attacks on Pearl Harbor—which allowed Nazi authorities to abduct people thought to be threatening German security, so that they vanished without a trace, often in the middle of the night, under cover of darkness and fog.

The code name was thought to be borrowed (ed: misappropriated?) from the great German poet Johann Wolfgang von Goethe (1749–1832). His poem "Erlkönig" ("Erl King" or "Elf King") tells the heartbreaking story of a father trying to soothe his child as they ride through a foggy night. The child knows they are being hunted by the Erl King, and the spine-tingling suspense builds until the fatal ending.

This sense of apprehension—of night and fog swallowing people up—was to play out in real life for Joséphine Murant over five years. She did not need to borrow her fear, her horror, from literature. She lived it.

The Third Reich applied Nacht und Nebel throughout the occupied territories of Western Europe: Belgium, France, Luxembourg, Norway, Denmark, and the Netherlands. It is estimated that under Nacht und Nebel, 7,000 individuals were arrested—almost 5,000 in France.

Closed courts (*Sondergerichte*) passed judgments for death and prison sentences. Prisoners would then be transferred to labor camps by Third Reich authorities. Swift deportation to Germany would unsettle local families and prevent future resistance action.

Joséphine Murant was one of hundreds of laborers forced to work with hazardous chemicals and machinery in the Phrix Rayon Factory. The rate of survival for political prisoners in labor camps was low. A chilling report by the de Gaulle government in 1946, *Collection Défense de l'Homme (ed: see cover image overleaf)*, suggests Anrath Prison was one of the deadliest.

Murant's novels have a pervasive sense of foreboding and share a universal truth: there is nothing a writer can invent that is more horrific, more terrifying, than what humans are capable of doing to one another in real life.

(Insert pics)

(Captions: L—R) Paris, June 1940, Adolf Hitler and senior members of the Nazi Party visit the Eiffel Tower; June 1940, Despondent, starving, and dehydrated Parisians flee the city in confusion, watched by filthy, defeated French soldiers; Checking papers at the demarcation line between Occupied and Unoccupied France; Prison hut of Anrath Prison; Commandant Gerhardt Jäger, Wehrmacht officer and chief guard at Phrix Rayon Factory, flanked by two lower-ranked soldiers; 1945, Captain James Blanch, 329th Medical Battalion, US Infantry Division, wraps the hands of an Anrath Prison evacuee: "We thought we had seen the worst. I saw more horror and hardship in two days' treatment of the women who served forced labor in Anrath than I will see for the rest of my life"; 1946, Cover of the Collection Défense de l'Homme *report.*

Chapter 15

EVIE

"*Nacht und Nebel*," Evie read out.

She and Clément had agreed to meet the following evening after catching the train back to Paris from Suresnes. The pair were savoring pinot noir at an outdoor café, and a platter of charcuterie, pickles, and fresh goat's cheese lay between them. Looking to the top of the alley, she could just make out the bold curves of Sacré-Coeur Basilica.

As soon as they'd arrived back in Paris from Mont-Valérien, Hugo had fled to Nina's house to hang out with Simon and do some "practice exams" for a couple of days. So now it was just Evie and Clément on what was verging on a date.

Evie studied the draft of the exhibition catalog that Clément had kindly printed out for her. "You write well," she said. "It's touching. I had no idea . . ." She tilted her head back into the sun as she finished reading, then wiped her hands on a napkin and pulled the photographs he planned to use from the folder. The bottom image in the stack was of a young blond doctor, wearing a helmet and with a red cross on his arm, kneeling in front of a prisoner who lay on the dirt, gently bandaging her hands. The second was of two American soldiers, again with the red cross on their arms, helping a woman step out of a building; under the woman's scarf, her eyes and cheeks were so dark and sunken she looked skeletal. Two of many nameless women.

Clément swallowed, perhaps a little nervous about her response. "It's an introductory piece. I think I've explained Anrath Prison. But how to explain what it *meant* for these women. For Joséphine Murant. She conjured trauma in her fiction, yet told no one of her reality. I'm explaining the history, or attempting to, yet revealing almost *nothing* of the author." He put his head in his hands and sighed.

Evie leaned back in her chair and held up the last photo. "You know how Joséphine always wore a headscarf . . . She must have looked like this when she was released from prison." Her voice broke as she finished the sentence, trying to imagine a young Joséphine, frail, filthy, hunched over, and almost unable to stand.

Clément lifted his head and stared at the photo. "Perhaps."

"Look, don't sell yourself short. Five thousand French were Nacht und Nebel prisoners. That's five thousand families—and many more now that we've passed down three generations. This is a shared trauma that needs to be documented."

Yesterday's visit to the memorial had shifted something in her. Forest ghosts had seeped into her bones. Last night, when she'd put her head on her pillow, she had imagined the texture of the wooden execution posts against her cheek.

She took a deep breath. "I've had my doubts about how much of Joséphine to share with the public. She was so secretive—"

"I understand." When she looked into Clément's brown eyes, she was relieved to see that he did.

"Okay, good to hear," she said, and their eye contact held for a moment. Feeling a bit flustered, she reached for some charcuterie. "I have good news. Gilles has managed to prize open several pages of Joséphine's Leroux, mostly toward the middle and the back. He's still working on the pages at the front and very back—they are pretty stubborn. We were right—it's a diary, and quite extensive. He's taken some pics on his document camera, and he sent a few to my phone to show you. The entries aren't in chronological order, sorry! Just the order Gilles opened them. I'll delete them when you've read them, just to be safe. This is a very valuable book."

"Of course," said Clément, beaming. "How exciting!" He patted the pockets of his blazer for his reading glasses, put them on, took Evie's phone, and started to read.

March 1942
Anrath Prison

Welcome to Germany! Though our greeting this time was without the usual treats of beer, Black Forest cake, and strudel. We were treated to a strip search and physical inspection on arrival (hooray, no lice!)

and issued a set of fetching threadbare coveralls and a mismatched pair of pumps.

Margot and I share a bunkroom with four others. The marks on the wall on my side of the bunk show the last occupant was here for thirty-one days. Either that or she got bored.

The director, Commandant Jäger, laughed when I informed him that I was a political prisoner (no petty thief) and that I would prefer to be on administrative duties, befitting my education, rather than manual work. He rewarded me for my impudence with two days in a solitary cell and a single meal of thin soup with a thumb of gristly pork sausage.

To be honest, if this is the food here in Germany, I'm content to have one meal a day! No bread!

"Joséphine loved her bread," Evie said with a laugh. "Insisted on it being delivered twice a day. Read out the last bit!"

On my way to my private suite, I asked the rather helpful guard what the factories we'll be working in are like. He replied that the cardboard factory is preferable. The Phrix Rayon Factory is hell, the director, Commandant Jäger, is a monster, and there are whispers of the acid eating away the limbs and internal organs of the women who work there.

Clément finished reading. Evie looked from Clément's draft to the photos of emaciated women. "We have to put a voice to this story. A name. There are so many brave, anonymous faces.

We can at least honor two names—and share the stories of the others."

"If you're certain," said Clément.

"I am. The foundation will agree to it. I've already spoken with them about this material. Keep reading . . ."

March 1942

It turns out the Spinnerei *is a giant factory for spinning the rayon. It's a huge shed—impossible to see each end once you are inside—with enormous machines the length of train carriages built in glass boxes. I presume this is to provide some semblance of protection for the workers, but even in these first minutes my throat itched with the rayon dust. Worse, my eyes stung, and I gagged at the bitter acid fumes. There are no windows, no fresh air. When I asked if I might go to the toilet to get some water, Commandant Jäger laughed and thumped me in the middle of the back with the butt of his rifle. I took that as a no.*

Margot is alongside me and it's a relief to speak in our own tongue . . .

Evie furrowed her brow. "I just realized . . . They traveled together from Fresnes Prison, but Margot wasn't a political prisoner."

"No, but she was a strong pair of hands."

"Not sure I follow?"

"Okay, so there's a theory that not just *any* convict was sent out from England to settle your homeland. They had higher literacy than others, were more able-bodied. Healthier and sturdier. The kind of convicts who could help set up a colony. Good workers, if you like."

"I see where you are going with this. But Australia wasn't *settled* by the English—it was invaded." She hoped she didn't sound too much like a lecturer.

"Touché. In fact, our museum is in the process of repatriating some artifacts to New Caledonia and Vietnam. About time," he muttered.

"That's very good to hear!" It took effort not to show just how much she was coming to admire him. "So, I get it. Margot was a strong pair of hands."

"Exactly," replied Clément. "The Third Reich did not care about the status of prisoners or justice. They just wanted good workers to power their war effort."

Evie picked up the phone and flicked to the next image. "Read this one."

March 1942

Today was as good as Christmas. When we entered the factory, we removed our thin, torn rags and put on the uniform of coveralls, headscarf, black apron, and a new set of comfortable clogs. (Unfortunately, we still have to wear our own drawers. Mine are so out of elastic they barely stay up, and I haven't been permitted to wash them properly for weeks.) The shirt has a fetching G on the back . . .

Evie said softly, "I've already Googled what it was for: *Gefangene*. It means 'convict.'"

She put her phone facedown as Clément said, "Since you guys are in Paris for a couple more nights, there's someone I want you to meet. I've been going through the list of possible contacts we drew up, and I tracked down an old friend of Joséphine's. The journalist Albert Remon—he was the first person who interviewed her, remember? I made an appointment at his house, ten tomorrow morning. I'll text you the address."

"Really? Thank you, that's incredible—he must be very old by now. So kind of him to meet us. I've not really spent time with many people who lived through the war, apart from Joséphine." Evie hesitated, sipping her wine. "I wonder how much he'll be able to tell us."

"Or how much we should ask," said Clément. "About the war, I mean."

She smiled, touched at his consideration. "That's your department."

The soft evening sun warmed her shoulders. While Clément ordered coffees, she deleted the photos and thought about his documentary series. She'd binged the whole thing over the weekend, and found herself enthralled by Clément speaking to the camera about different authors, or guiding his viewers through a war memorial with his signature white linen shirt, a scarf wrapped nonchalantly around his neck. He reminded her of Louis Theroux, only more reflective and earnest, more elegant. Certainly he kept his beard in better shape.

The sun was making her sleepy, though her thoughts zipped around her head like blowflies trapped in a bottle. She wondered what it would feel like to rub her cheek against Clément's beard.

Whether Hugo had eaten anything substantial at Nina's. And how well had this Albert Remon known Joséphine? How had he met her? Maybe he could tell them if she'd said anything about her early manuscript, off the record.

Threads of excitement began to gather in Evie's stomach. This was a chance to unravel more of Joséphine's story—and to spend a little more time with Clément.

Chapter 16

MARGOT

Rain pattered on tin. There had been dark, gray showers for days.

Margot was grateful for their German roof. No holes. That was something, at least. It felt like winter had set in early. Relentless wind juddered against the eaves. Sheets of water pounded the roof. On the rare occasion the rain paused, the silence was filled with the screech of an air-raid siren, then the boom and fire of artillery as planes roared overhead.

Rain pounded into concrete and mud. Rain, gunfire, bombs. Repeat.

She sighed and rolled over in her bunk, taking care not to tug too much of the blanket from Joséphine, who slept soundly beside her. Margot closed her eyes and remembered the sound of spring rain on her attic roof at Villa Sanary. On rainy days, she used to love waking up and throwing open her blue shutters to watch the wind create ripples across the lavender fields, then pick up and smash turquoise waves against the sandstone cliffs. The air would smell of the sea and pollen—roses, lavender, clematis. What Margot wouldn't do to smell that crisp, sweet air again.

Inevitably, her thoughts turned to her last day at the villa—as they always did. The day of Peggy Schramsburg's murder. Over the years, Margot had told and retold her story to Joséphine as she stepped the length of their tiny cells. Margot was convinced that she had been set up. But by whom?

Agitated, she rolled onto her other side and was dismayed that her hipbone dug into the thin straw, rubbing against the wood below. As she tried to find a comfortable position, she accidentally kicked Joséphine in the shin. "Go back to sleep," mumbled her friend. "Stop wriggling."

But Margot couldn't sleep. Instead, she took herself back to the morning of Bastille Day 1939.

꿐

Margot stepped onto the balcony to catch the last of the breeze. The rosy mist that crept down from the Provençal foothills was being blown out to the ocean and would soon be replaced with a hot, baking glare. It was her eighteenth summer, and the rhythms of the mist, the sun, and the sea were as much a part of her days as morning coffee and soup and bread for supper.

As she tilted her head to be bathed by the cool wind, she took the scent of wild herbs and seawater deep into her lungs. She looked down at the pool—so blue and alluring—and wished for the millionth time that she was not a maid, but one of the half a dozen elegant summer guests lolling about on deck chairs reading books, sipping cocktails, and summoning her to fetch iced water, champagne, or another cocktail.

The pale English guests, fresh out of first-class sleeper carriages on Le Train Bleu from Calais, stretched out like cats, purring in the sunlight. Poolside chatter was all about relief from the dreary rain, and what an unsightly mess they'd made in London parks, where air-raid trenches had been freshly dug and now lay filled with stagnant water.

"Trenches! So unnecessary!"

"Air raids . . . What on earth?"

"So dangerous for the *children*. Just imagine if they fell in. How ghastly!"

"Those bloody Bolsheviks have a lot to answer for," boomed Monsieur Munro as he glanced across the pool to his young American guest.

Mademoiselle Peggy Schramsburg lay on a striped towel in a low-cut swimsuit, back slightly arched and eyes closed, ignoring the chatter. Until last week, the American had been staying at Coco Chanel's nearby villa while the two women planned Mademoiselle's new-season wardrobe. Also there had been the man rumored to be Schramsburg's lover, Herr Bloch, a proud Nazi Party member, and things had allegedly become heated over Hitler's recent expansion into Eastern Europe. Mademoiselle had made a desperate late-night phone call to Tilly Munro, which Margot had overheard as she dusted outside the door.

"Of course, *darling*, you must come. Stay for La Fête Nationale. We'll wire your parents and put you on a ship from Marseille, soonest. Don't you worry, this silly business on the Continent will pass, and you'll be sailing back here for next summer in a blink."

The pallid guests and ebullient host, Monsieur Munro, glanced furtively over to admire Mademoiselle's golden tan and coltish long legs. She glistened like an exquisite jewel among this crowd.

Margot also studied the American. It was well after lunch: Madame Munro would already have informed her beautiful guest that she was to be murdered this evening.

As if on cue, Peggy shifted her weight a little so she faced the full sun. Her eyes were closed, shoulders loose. If she had thoughts about tonight's plans, it seemed she was relaxed about them.

⸎

Margot sat up in bed beside Joséphine. She ran the possibilities through her head for the thousandth time.

Madame Munro could have arranged for Peggy to be murdered; the fact that Madame had planned a game that was supposed to end with the woman's fake murder surely wasn't a coincidence. But whom else had Madame told about the game and its intended victim?

Madame *had* told Monsieur Munro, or at least she claimed to have told him. Could he have killed Peggy? Perhaps he was even the mastermind behind the game. Margot remembered the way he had admired his American guest beside the pool. Maybe they'd been having an affair, or just a dalliance, and he'd simply got sick of her. Or Madame had learned of his infidelity and taken revenge.

Margot's time in prison had shown her that people killed for much less.

Or perhaps it was over money, connected to the Munros' business affairs with Herr Bloch.

That filthy Nazi might somehow have been involved in the crime. Could he have threatened the Munros into helping him kill Peggy? He'd been her rumored lover, yet he hadn't hung around to be interviewed by the police, or returned for the trial. Presumably he'd disappeared back to his factory in Germany and was making uniforms for the Wehrmacht—or anyone who would pay him enough. Was Herr Bloch using interned labor arranged by the Nazis, just like at the rayon factory?

She sighed. Peggy's murder was proving an impossible puzzle to solve from jail. In the evenings, Joséphine sometimes helped her pick apart the possibilities and offered to help clear her name when they returned to France. She had access to contacts from her Resistance work—lists and lists of them, so many she'd never read them all. She was hopeful that there would be one with information that could prove Margot's innocence.

As a gust of cold air blew in the window, Margot snuggled against Joséphine's back as she imagined a younger sister might, and listened to the rain continue to fall on the tin roof, grateful for this moment's peace.

Chapter 17

Whispers about the German troops were circulating around the rayon factory. Nobody knew which rumors to believe.

The Germans had destroyed Stalingrad, while Allied forces had defeated Vichy troops in North Africa. Italy was a mess. The battles sounded bloody and merciless. Millions of troops on all sides were shunted between front lines and mountain ranges, a trail of broken countries and broken bodies.

Locked in the prison bunkroom, Margot ruminated on this as she lay curled up on her side of the mattress, licking the tips of her burned fingers like a kitten. It was a desolate existence, trying to survive work each day. Her single consolation was that she had company to survive with.

She shifted onto her back and stared up at the slats of the top bunk, trying to ignore the stench of the overflowing bucket they took turns to squat over in the far corner.

A sharp knock at the door.

"Time for work?" Joséphine groaned as she threw off her blanket from the other side of the bed. She scratched another line on the wall to mark the beginning of a new day—and a new month.

Their section of gray wall between bunks was almost filled with thirty-one blocks of fine lines. Had they really been in Germany for almost three years?

"You're annoying during the night," Joséphine told Margot in a good-humored tone, "what with all your wriggling and fussing."

Annika's dimpled face appeared over the edge of the opposite bunk, blond braid dangling down like a rope. "Sorry you two have to share. I'd offer to swap, but I need my beauty sleep." Her blue eyes glinted.

"You have enough to go around, Annika," said Joséphine. "Who did you seduce to get your own bed?"

"And shampoo for your hair?" muttered one of the other women.

"*Darlings*," the Russian said, mimicking the voice of a movie star, "I think the question is, who *didn't* I seduce? I look after the guards, they look after me." Her blend of flaxen hair, coquettish playfulness, and icy self-preservation reminded Margot of Madame Munro.

Above Margot, Syphilis Susie snored on the top bunk with the brutality of a chain saw. Susie's unfortunate bunkmate, Elsie, dangled her wasted legs over the edge. Margot saw her waver a little. She was the newest inmate from Belgium, but work in the factory had already made the poor girl's heart beat slower and occasionally thud in her chest at night—though the guards and wardress didn't believe her or anyone else who complained of similar ailments.

Joséphine was suffering too: Margot noticed her bunkmate was walking more gingerly and struggled to breathe, even when she was sleeping.

Prisoners who were slow or poorly were never given the day off to rest. Best they keep moving, without complaint. The previous resident of Susie's top bunk had been sent to the "first-aid room" only when she'd collapsed and rolled up the cuffs of her coveralls to show raw legs weeping. She hadn't returned.

The beefy warden rapped on their door again. "Twenty minutes to departure."

"Hate to be late! But first, a shower." Joséphine slid from the bunk and was first to the pail of icy water in the corner. Every day they all raced to be first, as the water was changed only once a day, and nobody wanted to wash *after* Syphilis Susie.

Margot sat up and removed her slip. She noticed in the morning light that the burns and welts from the viscose acid had wrapped their way around her arms like poison ivy. She thought of her mother, Vivienne, pressing calamine lotion into her hands when she'd had mere rose pricks on her skin—what would she make of these atrocious burns?

Margot rubbed her eyes and wondered if her mother was safe. She hadn't heard from Vivienne since her deportation to Germany. She had received the last letter just before they left Fresnes Prison. Although she'd never been one for praying—Vivienne had insisted on church every week, but Margot had attended only for the fancy lunch and crème brûlée afterward—she'd taken to saying a little something for her mother each night before she went to sleep. She didn't believe in God now. How could she? But each night she threw hope up into the fetid air with her dreams. It was just enough to get her through the day.

Her scarred arms were wiry ropes, her legs thin but still strong. Years of being in service had prepared her body well for hard labor. Not so for some of the others, who'd never endured tough physical work. Joséphine had grown skinny and weak. But it seemed that for Joséphine, as long as her body moved, her heart remained strong, and the pain did not become unbearable, she counted herself luckier than most of the prisoners who worked the twelve-hour shift at the Phrix Rayon Factory.

"Christ!" snorted Susie. "First, no breakfast. Now this freezing water." She swung her legs over her bunk, climbed down to the floor, then scooped her hands into the bucket of water and slapped it against her face, under her arms, and up her skirt, before reaching for another scoop.

Margot gulped and resolved to wash earlier tomorrow. It wasn't that she had anything against Susie; it was just she wasn't sure whether you could catch syphilis by sharing water.

She would have given anything for a decent bath. Clean warm water. Soap. She'd last had a bath up in her little attic room on the day of her arrest.

Margot spent a good half hour in the bath. For the first ten minutes or so, she finished the latest Agatha Christie she'd borrowed from Madame Munro's library. Usually she loved these exciting mysteries, but today she was put off because it was pretty clear where her employer had found her inspiration for this ridiculous murder game.

Annoyed and nervous, Margot tossed about in the tepid bath, soaping her arms and scrubbing the gold paint from the lily stems off her fingertips as best she could. A shaft of afternoon sunlight illuminated a square on the floor. Usually her baths were hurried affairs after supper. Every spare hand in the village was meant to be polishing glasses, placing silver candelabras in the entrance hall and on tables beside the pool, setting up fireworks, and pressing tuxedos. Still, she couldn't bring herself to climb out of the water.

Margot lolled her head sideways, her limbs heavy. The afternoon heat in her attic quarters was stifling, and all she wanted to do was take a nap. But that wouldn't do—what if she overslept? She cupped some water with her hands and let it drip over her breasts. As she lifted her arms, she studied the thorn pricks on her skin; some were deeper than she'd realized.

She needed to shake off her torpor and get ready for tonight. She sighed, hoisted herself out of the bath, wrapped herself in her thin towel, padded across the room—ignoring the puddles trailing on the floor—and dropped facedown onto her tiny bed. The heat was cloying as she dabbed at her clammy skin. She tossed about, restless and jittery, unsure how to quell this strange mix of dread and elation.

The truth was, she was finding it harder and harder to keep Gabriel Laurent from her thoughts. From their first meeting since their school days a month ago, when he'd walked up the gravel driveway toward her with a broad smile, an ill-fitting woolen jacket, and a reference in his hand, she had felt a frisson in his presence. He seemed to single her out whenever he could, flirting and trying to make her laugh and telling stories of his travels. And she could not deny her attraction to him.

Earlier in the day, she'd hurried out of the kitchen after dropping off the deliveries to Chef, then run through the side door so she could make her way to the garden uninterrupted by the guests who lounged around the pool, demanding champagne, olive tapenade, goat's cheese, and baguettes. Although she didn't approve of the murder game, it amused her to imagine the horror on these languid faces when they discovered that one of their own had been killed. How would they react when Madame Munro swanned in to declare the whole thing a hoax as she helped Mademoiselle Schramsburg to her feet? Would the guests lift their champagne coupes to whoop, clap, and celebrate as Madame hoped?

The gravel crunched under Margot's feet as she hurried across the terrace. Her pace eased a little when she made out the silhouette of a man balanced on a ladder, cutting back the huge bay hedge: Gabriel. Muscles strained across a tanned, sweaty back as he chopped and tugged at wayward branches. It took a mighty effort to tame the hedge protecting the villa from the harsh ocean breeze that whistled up the rocky cliffs.

Margot knew she should grab pruning shears from the garden

shed and get to picking the blush-pink roses as Madame had instructed, but she didn't want to—not yet. With all the party preparations, she'd hardly had a moment off her feet. She decided to duck into the orchard for a minute and sit with her back against one of the old apple trees. Dappled leaves protected her from the harsh midday sun and prying eyes. Six fat white hens clucked and pecked about her feet, hoping for a handful of grain. She shooed them away, kicked off her shoes and stockings, and allowed her legs to rest on the soft grass while she tried to imagine what her days would look like if she were free to choose how she spent her time.

Gabriel dropped a branch into the barrow at the base of his ladder, then pulled a handkerchief from his pocket and mopped up the sweat dripping from his face. His blond curls were tucked into a faded blue bandanna. He looked across at the orchard as he stuffed the handkerchief back in his pocket, but if he knew Margot was sitting under a tree watching him, he gave no sign.

Snip, snip, snip. He had turned again to his trimming, his back to Margot. A few times he held a rake across the top of the hedge, checking to make sure it was flat.

Margot had read about aha moments in the novels she pinched from the villa library. Heroines were blindsided by love, made sick with it, like in *Anna Karenina* and *Tess of the d'Urbervilles*. She'd devoured these books by candlelight up in her attic room while the rest of the villa slumbered. Within their pages, love seemed at once a blessing and a curse—powerful, cruel, and dangerous. She'd marveled at the noble sacrifices of the heroines, then raged against their hopeless circumstances. She found it curious that these fictional characters provoked such violent emotions in her, as she had never felt a man press against her, nor lifted her lips to be kissed.

She didn't really *believe* the novels. Not a word. She wasn't going to have her head turned by some giddy nonsense. But she wondered what it would be like to be kissed, and to have a different kind of life. She was jealous of Gabriel's freedom—his ability to escape from a quiet life of service on the Côte d'Azur to perform in cities that never slept. Now, as she lay on her bed, still damp from her bath, she imagined dancing with Gabriel in a sea of silk and sequins, spinning to the rhythm of Billie Holiday or Glenn Miller.

But what if his flirtations weren't serious? What if he saw her as a silly girl with a crush? And for her part, she wasn't sure exactly what she desired—just that she wanted something different.

Still, tonight offered her a chance to find out if there could be anything between them. And she realized she had to take it.

She threw off the towel, grabbed her notebook and a pen, and fell back onto her bed, resting the notebook against her knees.

Cher Gabriel,
Je vous adore . . .

She ripped out the page, tore it into tiny pieces, screwed them into a damp ball, and tossed it to the far corner of the room.

As she tapped her pen against the next page, she agonized over what to say. Should she explain that she was more—could offer more—than just domestic service? That she loved the way he described flying on a trapeze: how his heart thumped and time stilled in that long moment before he clasped the other acrobat's hands midair. His lunch break yarns of clams sizzled in Spanish sherry and silky shreds of the creamiest aged ham handed out on platters in the illegal jazz bars of Barcelona, where the air was thick with humidity, cigar smoke, and sex. That she both envied these adventures and yearned for them. But mostly, that she yearned for Gabriel.

Cringing and sweating, Margot scrawled out a short note that explained her feelings. She wondered how it could sound both too formal and too intimate, but she didn't have time for another attempt. In the next line, she asked Gabriel to meet her behind the hedge half an hour after the fireworks finished. Madame's foolish murder game would surely be wrapped up by then.

Margot hesitated, then signed off:

I will explain what I have done when we meet. Don't tell anyone.

She glanced at the clock on the stone wall: 6:00 P.M. Chef would be missing her in the kitchen, yelling about scampi and discipline. She finished drying herself, slicked her lank hair back into a braid, and tugged on her clean black skirt, matching shirt, and neatly pressed white apron. As she brushed her teeth, she studied herself in the mirror: mousy hair, medium build, eyes the color of whisky. Her skin was light brown, like the Côte d'Azur soil. Her stomach tightened and lip curled as she thought of the golden American, lying by the pool like some kind of queen, draped in turquoise silk that fluttered with the breeze.

Margot took one last look in the mirror, impatient for the murder game to be over. Then the second part of her night could begin.

She grabbed the letter, put it in an envelope, and wrote *Gabriel* in her neatest hand, before slipping it into her pocket. Finally, she smoothed back her hair, tightened her apron, knelt and wiped the dust off the toes of her shoes, hitched up her stockings, and slammed the door shut behind her. She stepped down the narrow staircase at the back of Villa Sanary that would take her from the attic into the chaos of a kitchen in full preparation for the party of the year.

❧

Margot dressed quickly in her threadbare factory coveralls and folded her slip under the pillow, hoping the two night-shift factory workers allocated to sleep in this bed for the day would not steal it. Next, she jammed her sore feet into wooden clogs and winced as they started to throb.

She'd decided not to wash from the bucket today, just in case. And she was still quite clean, relatively speaking, from last week's disinfectant indignity. All the women had been lined up in a tin shed, where they were instructed to remove their clothes and march into the shower block, one by one. As they walked, elderly women in white coats, face masks, and hairnets inspected all over their bodies for lice. They were then marched to a delousing room, then a steam room.

Wehrmacht factory policemen and SS guards stood in the steam room, staring at the women. Hitting some with rifles, pressing themselves against others. The men grabbed Elsie, who still had her long hair and curves, and shoved her up against the wall. Her arms were pinned above her head by a guard on either side, while her thick golden hair was hacked off with scissors by another at her rear. The belt buckle of the SS guard left a deep gouge in her buttocks.

When Elsie emerged from the steam room held up by Susie and Gertrude, Margot watched as Joséphine gently took her arm and said, "The shame is on those guards. On Germany." She brushed away Elsie's tears and held her gaze. "The violation is theirs. They have lost their humanity. Their decency." Then she opened her arms to embrace Elsie. "Come. Let me help you dress."

Back in the bunkroom, the women gathered to tenderly bind Elsie's feet and hands in rags, and brush her short, hacked-off hair.

Now, as they all prepared to leave for the walk to the factory, Margot eyed her warm bed with longing. At least the night-shift workers would be grateful for the heat.

When Joséphine had finished dressing, she reached under her pillow to the gap between the mattress and the wall, and pulled out the precious paperback and pen she had smuggled from Fresnes. She opened up the book and began to write in the margin.

"Hurry up!" Margot hissed at her. They were expected outside in ten minutes—if Joséphine was caught they would all be marched off to face punishment.

"Done," said Joséphine with a satisfied smile, exactly two minutes later. She shoved the book and pencil back into their hiding place.

A few minutes later, Margot and her fellow prisoners marched in two lines through the village. Nazi flags had been hoisted in the town square, and German women in thick coats, carrying bread under their arms, averted their eyes and hurried their curious children along.

A guard whacked a prisoner in the back of the leg with the butt of his rifle for failing to march in a neat line.

As the Nazi flags flapped, and the rain beat down and trickled under her collar, Margot saw the exhausted night-shift workers marching toward her group. In the middle row, an unconscious woman was carried by two sticklike others. At the back of the line, a prisoner shuffled and sidestepped with one hand pressed against her buttocks, her face screwed up in excruciating pain; crippled with a back injury, she was still forced to march.

As always, the groups of prisoners passed each other without speaking. Margot tried to give a reassuring nod and smile to the grimacing woman clutching at her back.

A tall German guard, new this week, made eye contact with Margot as he fell into step beside her. She braced herself for a blow.

Two steps. Nothing.

She relaxed her wince and glanced to one side: the guard's eyes were wide—sympathetic?

Joséphine, noticing this exchange, narrowed her eyes at Margot and gave a slight shake of her head.

Margot's foot clipped the heel of the woman in front of her, and she fell to the cobblestones.

"Margot!" Joséphine stepped from her row and bent to pull Margot up, but the tall guard ushered her away. "Stay in line," he said softly. "It is better if you keep in step."

After casting Margot a confused look, Joséphine marched to catch up.

Margot struggled to get to her feet. Her knee ached so much, she had to rub it.

As other prisoners marched away past the dreary, empty-looking shops flanked by soldiers, the new guard offered Margot his hand. Thinking this was some joke, or a preamble to a beating, she knelt forward and struggled to her feet without meeting his eyes.

He took a respectful step back, waiting for her to straighten her pinafore and tuck her foot back into her clog, before he indicated she should hurry forward to rejoin the two rows of prisoners.

Margot's breath caught in her throat. By declining to hit or insult her, this Boche had behaved with kindness—more than she had been shown by her captors since her arrival in Germany.

Chapter 18

Christmas passed the next week as though it were any other day. In the factory, worn-out women leaned on machines, emptied buckets, and stacked rolls of viscose as far as the eye could see. For twelve hours, Margot flung sticky filament, the texture of honey, into a glass funnel. Her hands were soaked with acid and stung, even though she had bound them in rags. Her eyes hurt. Her only consolation was that Joséphine worked directly across the aisle. Occasionally their eyes met, and each time a silent cheer rang in Margot's heart.

Late in her shift, the kind guard she'd met in the village last week approached her at the machine and introduced himself in shy schoolboy French. *"Je m'appelle Hauptmann Klaus Müller,"* he said, before stumbling through a description of a holiday he'd taken in Paris with his parents as a young boy. "A magical city," he said sadly as the machine clicked and whirred. His voice started to break when he said, "*Je suis navré.*"

Margot kept her eyes on the machine, loading and reloading as he talked. Anyone watching them would think he was giving instructions or perhaps reprimanding her.

Captain Müller said he was deeply sorry for the treatment of prisoners and factory workers, and for the conditions in the factory. He sighed, and his shoulders dropped. "I have a sister about your age—my mother sent her to stay with our grandparents. She thought it would be safer. They're Swiss. I haven't seen her for over a year. But I look around here, and I can't get the image of her out of my head. She's a strong girl, like you. The women here, none of you deserve to be treated like dogs. Worse, this war . . . it makes monsters of people . . . They force us into these jobs . . ." He dipped his head to hide his shame.

Margot glanced across the aisle at Joséphine, who mouthed, "Are you okay?" Her brow was furrowed.

Margot nodded and tried to concentrate on the machine.

Müller said, "The woman you saw being carried after the night shift last week—she died. I'm sorry. Her name was Karine."

Margot nodded again but said nothing, and the guard stepped away to oversee someone else's work.

As Margot stood there with the machine clanging beside her, she watched Müller pull a bandage from an inside pocket of his jacket and slip it to Annika as he strode past. The teary girl shot him a grateful nod and immediately used it to bind her bloody feet and stop them from rubbing against the rough wooden clogs.

She'd been reprimanded by Jäger yesterday for leaving a puddle of blood by the machine. It wasn't worth risking a second spray.

Later, as she passed Müller on the far side of a machine, she wondered how much she could trust him. She had only just met this man, a Nazi guard no less. But the agony and death that filled her days had shown her how precious life was. She had a feeling that despite his uniform, with its swastika that made her stomach curdle, Müller did not have the heart of a Nazi.

Müller *seemed* kind, but could he be trusted? There was one way to find out. It was a risk, trying to establish his sympathies so soon after meeting him, but nothing in prison was normal. Annika reached down to retuck the end of her bandage into her clog. At least the bleeding had stopped, for now. Margot turned and studied Joséphine: her hands were tender and she was wheezing. Time was not on their side. Not for any of them.

As Müller drew close to inspect her machine he blocked the view of the factory behind him. Margot held her left fist steady and took a deep breath.

Müller stood to attention and returned her clenched fist. Just as she'd suspected, he was a sympathizer. Perhaps even a communist. Their eyes met, and he extended a hand to shake hers. When she lifted her raw, infected hand and placed it in his, he didn't flinch.

He leaned in and murmured, "News from the Eastern Front is that Russia is making progress." Over the next few minutes, he gave her news on the latest developments. For the remainder of the shift, Margot was light-headed with hope . . .

As she lay in her bunk that night, her back pressed against

Joséphine's, she allowed herself just a moment to think of Captain Müller's kindness. She prayed she was right to trust in it.

Joséphine shifted position as she wrote in her paperback diary. Margot could feel her friend's rib cage through the thin blanket.

"That guard you were speaking to today . . ." Joséphine gave Margot a playful kick.

"Which guard? I was screamed at by many guards!"

Joséphine sighed and said softly, "Be careful."

Chapter 19

"Idiots! Back to your machines!" shouted Commandant Jäger, manager and chief guard of the rayon factory, a vein throbbing at his temple.

The factory was filled with the relentless roar of machines that rows of prisoners worked like automatons. The air was thick with dust particles; the scent of acid singed their throats and lungs with each breath. Margot's head clanged with wheels spinning and whirring, steam whistles and funnels pumping. She felt the noise ricochet off the factory walls and sear itself into her heart, her soul.

As she concentrated on stacking the cakes of viscose in a neat tower, she studied her dearest friend. Joséphine had been forced to operate a spinning machine solo for twelve hours each day. Though her eyes were not failing like those of her poor predecessor, who'd gone blind in a month, Joséphine's were bloodshot and constantly watered. Her hands and arms were chafed red-raw with acid burns, and at times she clung to the machine to remain upright.

Five-liter jars overflowing with human waste were stationed at the end of every row, ensuring each worker was only a few steps away from the putrid smell.

Margot recalled the lines of Leroux's *Le Fantôme de l'Opéra* Joséphine had read aloud to her the night before: "Take comfort in art, my little bird. We all have our own phantoms. Ghosts that haunt us. Lose yourself in the mystery and allow yourself to be carried to another place."

Dear Joséphine was only trying to lift her spirits, but Margot remained skeptical. What did Leroux truly know about humiliation and pain? Had he ever been forced to do his business in a bucket in front of dozens? To have a stomach that ached with hunger, a throat so dry it hurt to swallow? Hands red and raw, hair ridden with lice, and teeth so rotten that your breath smelled like a corpse?

Margot pressed the bib of her coveralls to her eyes to wipe away her tears. They came so frequently now that she was numb to them. Since she had received the formal news from the prison warden that her mother, Vivienne, had been killed last week, she couldn't tell if she was weeping for her loss or for her throbbing feet, jammed and bleeding in her wooden clogs. Each loss felt infinite as it bled and morphed into the next.

A whole day had passed before the magnitude of Vivienne's death had struck her. She would never see her beautiful, hardworking mother again. It was as if a piece of her had died also—she had no family left. No one to go home to.

It was an abyss of horror that those who moved through the world freely could never understand. Whoever would believe Margot if she told this story?

She'd come to understand why Joséphine spent hours recording her thoughts and snippets of the day in her beloved Leroux. Words were all they had left. Their only weapon.

Over the years, Margot had even grown more comfortable with Joséphine writing about Peggy Schramsburg's murder.

Then, last night, Joséphine had announced, "I've come up with a plan. As soon as I get the chance, I'll send your story to an old friend in Paris. He'll have no time, no resources, to look into the trial now. But I promise you, Margot, once this war is over, the case will be reopened. We can prove your innocence once and for all."

It was hard for Margot to share Joséphine's optimism, so she remained silent. Her fury about her wrongful conviction ebbed and flowed. Thoughts as to who might have killed Peggy still kept her awake at night, but she didn't want to let Joséphine see the extent of her bitterness. Her friend was a woman who didn't believe in revenge. When Margot had asked her why she didn't speak when their bunkmates took it in turns to say what they would do to the Germans on their release, her wise friend had simply said that her struggle was for France, for freedom, not against the people of Germany.

Margot had changed the topic. "What are you looking forward to?"

"Paris at twilight, walks in the Luxembourg Gardens, fresh croissants . . . friends." She grinned mischievously and sniffed under her arm. "Perfume and silk dresses, late nights in jazz bars, handsome lovers." Joséphine's cheeks grew red. "I wonder what's become of the Société Charles Perrault. Are any alive?" Her face fell. "I miss them. But, above all, I long to see my family. Even

Lulu, although she would be unlikely to come since she *hates* me. Sunday fish with Mama and Papa at a café beside the Seine, cherry pickles . . ." Her voice faded, and she turned once more to her Leroux. "I will go to Paris again and do all these things. Because to give up, to stop dreaming, would mean the Boches have won. Perhaps Leroux is right: the Nazis can contain my body, but not my mind. So"—she tapped her page with her pen—"I'll keep writing, keep resisting. One day, even if it's a long, long time from now, I want Lulu, Mama, and Papa to know." She stopped talking and continued to scribble in her book, with Margot reading over her shoulder:

The stories of this factory, this war, need to be shared.

As Margot now watched Joséphine on the machine and gazed around the factory, she realized something: the human spirit could not be crushed by concrete walls, iron bars, and brutality.

As if Joséphine could read Margot's thoughts, she winked and pressed the wet roll she was holding against the edge of the machine. This ensured that the viscose would be matted together. It would be completely unusable when it was transported and unpacked for weaving into Nazi uniforms and clothes for wealthy Germans.

Margot glanced over to where rolls of fabric were stockpiled in the corner. They could not be transported to Norway or Russia. Each pile of discarded rayon built hope in the prisoners' hearts.

Her heart full of love for Joséphine, Margot wanted to applaud her friend's sabotage—her determination—but instead she mouthed over the top of the machine, "Keep going."

Later that evening, Margot lay in her bunk, thinking about Captain Müller's story of his sister. He was kind and honest, Margot was sure of it. She wanted to do more than just escape, so perhaps she could convince him to sneak in some food for her bunkmates. Or medical supplies. Even a pair of shoes with proper soles.

She'd looked around for him during every shift for the past weeks when she had thought no one was watching. Sometimes she caught a glimpse. Occasionally they exchanged remarks about the weather; other times there was abridged news of the war. Margot preferred to stick to the weather. When she looked for Müller, it wasn't with the same tingling in her stomach that she'd had as she watched Gabriel. It was more a feeling of warm reassurance. She'd never had an older sibling, but she'd always longed for the comfort of someone looking out for her from afar.

But some of the women had noticed, judging from the comments flying about the bunkroom.

"I'll make a love potion for you," offered Annika.

"What, with piss?" teased Joséphine. "Do you have a secret stash of herbs and spices you would like to share with us?"

"Make sure he pays you first," said Susie as she lay prostrate on the mattress. "If you're not up to it, send him my way, love. I'll give him a little present to remember us all by!"

"Isn't that behavior why you're in prison?" asked Joséphine.

"Sure, I gave a German officer syphilis. But I gave him a *lot* more first." She laughed. "I don't care who wins, I'll be pounded and paid either way, thank you very much." She swung her head over the edge of the bunk and said, "Bastards won't beat me. I just need to survive this dump, then I'll save for a deposit on my own little place, and I'll be back in business."

The bunkroom filled with chatter and laughter, the women taking it in turns to tease each other. But when all the banter had settled down, and the knock had come at the door to instigate silence, Joséphine snuggled against Margot and whispered again, "Be careful."

Chapter 20

The next morning at the factory, Commandant Jäger allocated Margot to the spinning machine. As she worked, her pinafore clung to her back with sweat, a vein throbbing in her forehead.

Jäger marched a few rows along to scream at Elsie for being too slow with her stacking. He was in a mood, and they needed to be careful. Elsie started to sob and missed turning a cog on her machine. Jäger exploded, picked a metal pot up from the floor, and smashed it into the back of her skull. As she fell to the floor, he followed through with a second blow to the back of the neck. She screamed and gurgled as she spat blood.

Her eyes closed.

Margot knew she would never forget the crack as Elsie's head hit the concrete.

Susie, Annika, and all the other women gasped and bit their lips, averting their eyes as they struggled through their tears to keep the spools spinning and the machines turning. For what could they do? To help Elsie was surely to accept the same fate.

Jäger swiped her identity card from her pocket, and yelled at two guards in the far corner to remove the body and toss it in the incinerator. Margot blanched. Elsie Bergmont would be added to a death list in Wehrmacht headquarters, thousands of miles from here. A statistic in human horror.

After a quick glance at each other, Margot and Joséphine ran across to where Elsie lay in a pool of blood on the concrete floor. "Useless cows, get back to work or it will be both of you next!" Jäger screamed.

The guards stepped toward them, and Margot could just make out with her weepy eyes that one was Captain Müller. He and Margot exchanged a cautious look, and he whispered, "Be careful. Don't test him today—the Allies are getting closer." He indicated for another guard to help remove the body. Clearly he wanted to stay nearby and see no harm came to Margot.

Joséphine touched Margot's arm. This was what their life had become: devastation, cruelty, and hope in the same fleeting moment. Margot studied Elsie, being hoisted away by guards as if she were rags, and her throat constricted so tight she thought she might choke.

"Idiot women!" shouted Jäger. "Back to your machines. If I have to tell you one more time today, you will both be sent to solitary!"

Müller started to guide them back to the machines with a gun and a solemn face, being careful not to make eye contact.

Margot shuddered, but Joséphine was inscrutable.

Just as she got back to the machine, Margot turned and spat on the floor. "Monster!" She no longer cared who heard her.

Behind her, Müller gasped.

"Take that woman to solitary!" shouted Jäger. "All of you, consider this a warning. The next one to make a noise will meet the same fate as that imbecile."

Müller marched Margot from the factory floor, gun pointing into the small of her back. She imagined he was holding it to look fierce, but she could barely feel it. Elsie's death had numbed her. The ghoulish image of the woman's crushed skull played through her brain. Blond hair matted with blood.

As she marched past the rows of machines, she glanced at the newest Russian prisoners, whose embroidered scarves she had so admired when they arrived. There were so many beautiful young Russians streaming into the prison now, ripped from their country homes and farmlets, round faces as sweet as peaches. After six months, these sweet women now cussed in German, curled their hair with leftover rags they used for cleaning the machines, and had sex with predatory guards under the machines at the end of each shift. For bread. For touch.

Some of the women had diseases. Susie had warned the girls against it, but what could they do? Others were pregnant, and as their bellies swelled they struggled to lift the viscose cakes, their foreheads dripping with sweat, their breath wheezy from inhaling acid fumes all day. Margot feared for these women and their unborn children, for how could a baby survive this place?

Müller tapped her on the back with his gun. He ushered her outside and across to the solitary cells. "I'm sorry," he said. "If you like, when we get close to the building, you can make a run for it. I can give you an address of someone who can hide you."

"Don't say it," implored Margot. She wouldn't leave Joséphine and the others. How could she seek safety for herself and leave her friends here in this sulfurous hell?

"I trust you," said Müller.

"That doesn't matter."

They trudged across the gravel from the factory, and her breath was visible in the chilly air. Lamps lit up the barbed-wire security fence, and their shadows loomed large like dancers against the pale concrete buildings in the dim light. Then Margot heard the thud of distant bombs and gunfire. The evening sky burned like a giant sun, blazing red and orange with death and destruction. Different pockets of the horizon were lit up by air raids over nearby villages. It was both macabre and magical.

As she watched the light in the sky explode into millions of shiny pieces, she was transported back to Villa Sanary. The fireworks, the perfume, the incense, the champagne and silk. Peggy Schramsburg, Madame Munro. Vivienne's tears.

Madame's words jerked Margot back to reality: *You, my darling are the only one I trust around here to do things properly.* Margot had trusted Madame too, and she had turned her back when Margot had needed her most.

Margot stepped to one side. She was all alone with a Nazi guard; now more than ever, she needed to be careful.

The sky burned again, and they stared at the light thrown up by the blaze. Müller pointed, his voice soft. "Those flames, all that gunfire, means the Allies are gaining ground."

This was no comfort to Margot. She could only imagine the horrifying inferno, incinerating all in its path. Nazi soldiers, to be sure, but also women, innocent children, tiny babies. How could she take any relief in the demise of others?

"There are no winners in war," he whispered. "Even if we have peace . . ."

The solitary confinement cell looked like a concrete toilet block set into surrounding concrete. It was a few hundred meters from the factory.

Margot shivered. She was all alone here, and if she was hurt—or screamed—no one would hear her.

He shook his head. "Come inside, quickly. I have something to dress your hands." After unlocking the cell, he showed Margot in. It had a single bed neatly made, a slop pail, and an enamel jug of water. He gestured for her to sit on the bed. She held out her infected hands, palms facing up. As he studied them, he sucked in his breath and muttered, "Christ, the suffering. This factory . . ." His eyes started to fill with tears. "What you women endure . . . It's my fault." He looked broken. "I'm sorry. It's *you* who is suffering, yet here I am crying like a baby!"

"You can't shut down the factory any more than you can shut down this war. We are the same, you and I. Just cogs. Just surviving."

Müller winced at Margot's candor. He glanced at her hands. "Let's try to fix these. I was going to slip this to you tonight, but as you'll be in solitary for a week, perhaps we can heal your hands." Pulling out some ointment in a glass jar, he said, "I went to the pharmacy. Told them my mother burned her hands on a pot—"

"You live with your mother?"

"Since the war, yes." He blushed. "My father was killed in the last war, at the Somme. My older brother is a senior SS officer, and it was he who convinced my mother that I should join up. He promised her he'd keep me safe. Wouldn't let what happened to Papa happen to me." Margot winced as Müller smoothed the ointment onto each finger and gently rubbed it in. "Sorry, I know it's painful. But I promise it will ease."

"Thank you—for the ointment, for telling me about your family." She held his gaze. "I don't think you are a coward. You promised your mother you would survive this war. Keep your sister alive. And you have."

"So far." He grimaced as anti-aircraft fire cracked across the sky just a few villages away.

"So far," Margot agreed. "And you are kind to us at the factory."

"Your friend doesn't trust me."

Margot snorted as he pulled a brand-new bandage from his pocket and unwrapped it from the packaging. "She doesn't trust anyone much. She's a journalist, it's in her nature to be skeptical. But once you have her trust, you'll find none more loyal."

Margot sucked in her breath as Müller started to uncoil the bandage and bind her fingers, one by one. His strapping was firm and methodical, but gentle.

"I'm assuming you aced your first-aid class?"

"Sorry, is this too tight?" he asked as he tucked the end of the bandage into the thick strapping across her palm, his brow sweaty and furrowed with concentration.

"I'm kidding. You make an excellent first-aid officer."

"If only!" he said wistfully. "I inflict more pain than I heal."

"That's not true."

He started to bandage her other hand, neatly wrapping each finger before finishing with the palm. Her words hung in the air, filling the cold room. She looked at their enlarged shadows, leaning into each other on the far wall.

With a meticulous fold of the white bandage, Müller finished wrapping her hand.

Margot swallowed and repeated, "That's not true. You don't inflict pain."

"I don't stop it."

"You try."

"It's not enough," he whispered. "I thought if I joined my brother, I could find a way . . . I *detest* him, but not as much as I detest myself."

Their breath synced and grew heavy. Neither spoke, overwhelmed with their own sadness and horror.

Rat-a-tat-tat. It was the butt of a rifle against the wooden door.

Müller jumped up, smoothed his hair, and replaced his hat. Another rifle banged against the door. He paced across the room and threw it open.

"Captain Müller. Reporting for duty," said the junior-ranked factory guard, looking surprised and holding his rifle in midair.

"*Heil Hitler.*" Müller saluted, and Margot turned her head so he wouldn't see her flinch.

"*Heil Hitler,*" said the other guard, who returned the Nazi salute.

"When I've gone, lock the door. Don't let anyone in, and don't let the prisoner out. Understood?"

"Yes, sir."

"Good." Müller spat on the ground. "Filthy *Pissflitsche*. Don't contaminate yourself by stepping inside the cell. I give you strict orders to stay outside. Understood?"

Margot's stomach fell; she crawled up on the bed and started to cry. She knew Müller insulted her to protect her, but that was also just how the Boches spoke. It was impossible for her to be truly friends with a Nazi.

A key turned in the lock.

In Fresnes Prison, Joséphine had joked about getting a set of keys as a keepsake to jangle around and use as rosary beads. But Margot knew that if she survived this, she would never again take comfort in the click of a lock.

She cried herself to sleep, hungry and tired, as the little window flickered with light from distant fires and shadows danced across the wall. As she drifted off, her mind wandered—as it often did—to Villa Sanary. Tonight she sought comfort in a memory of her last visit to the market.

⁕

Usually Margot loved the walk from the villa along the sandstone cliff tops. But that day she felt overwhelmed—there was so much to do. While Madame Munro was full of compliments, her trilling and swooning only extended so far. Everyone would be in trouble if a course was overcooked or under-catered, or the blush-pink roses were not in the centerpieces.

Out the stairwell window, Margot spotted little Maxime pottering about behind his father, head gardener Pierre Laurent. The boy was puffing as he pushed a tiny barrow full of compost, wobbling it sideways so it threatened to tip over at any moment.

She finished lacing her boots, ran down the stairs, and snuck out across the terrace to where Maxime and Pierre worked in the vegetable patch.

"Ma-Ma-Margot," stuttered Maxime as he jumped up and down.

"What a good little helper you are! Would you come to the village with me to help carry some bags? If your papa can spare you, of course." She winked at Pierre over the top of Maxime's head.

"Can I, Papa, *please*?" Maxime said, jumping again for emphasis.

"Put the barrow over there, boy, and be off with you," said Pierre, in a voice gruffer than he meant. He returned Margot's look with gratitude.

She held out her hand to take Maxime's and passed him a straw market basket to sling over his other arm. Together they walked out of the vegetable patch, swung past the iron gate, and meandered along the sandstone cliffs. Maxime skipped and kicked stones, while Margot bent to pick a twig of wild rosemary, crushing the tiny leaves between her fingers and breathing in the woody oil. She loved to gather the herbs along these cliffs. She and her mother had been harvesting them since Margot was

Maxime's age: rosemary, thyme, oregano, catmint, marjoram, and lovage.

Vivienne would still sneak down to the kitchen most evenings—when Chef had gone home—to bake bread rolls, prepare soup and pistou, and sprinkle them with whatever herbs she and her daughter had collected. Sometimes Vivienne would chop the herbs and mix them with salted butter, spreading it thickly across a fresh-baked roll and letting it melt.

Margot's stomach groaned for the second time that day as she and Maxime entered the village. Scents from the vine-covered boulangerie lingered in the main street. She pushed open the door, smiled at the jangly bell, and tugged Maxime inside. "Are you hungry?"

The child nodded shyly and pressed his face up against the glass counter filled with baguettes, rolls, croissants, tarts, and cakes.

"Bonjour, Monsieur Moreau," said Margot to the portly baker across the counter. "Two fougasses, please. And may I please arrange for two dozen more baguettes to be delivered by four? The Munros have some extra guests Chef hadn't catered for."

The baker handed over a brown bag filled with warm bread. "Of course, I'll drive them up myself. Good day, Mademoiselle Bisset. Wait!" He plucked four tiny lemon tarts topped with strawberries from his cabinet and wrapped them in wax paper before handing the parcel to Maxime. "A little something for your afternoon tea. To share with Mademoiselle Bisset and your family."

"*Merci*," said Maxime as he tucked the tarts into his basket.

Margot fished in hers for her purse, trying to hide her blush as she was sure she did not have enough coins for the two fougasses and the tarts.

"*Non*," said Monsieur Moreau, "it's my pleasure. Villa Sanary has ordered so much bread this week, it's the least I can do. And how is that American guest of yours? Mademoiselle Schramsburg. I haven't seen her this week. Usually she visits, for my pain au chocolat . . ." His ears reddened.

"She's quite well, thank you, but the villa has been frantic with Fête Nationale preparations—she's been busy," quipped Margot. Was every man in the village under Peggy Schramsburg's spell?

"Please send my regards."

"You may be able to deliver them yourself when you deliver the bread," said Margot, trying to feel kindly toward him. He was a besotted old fool.

She didn't have time to take afternoon tea—and doubted the Laurents did either—but perhaps, if she remembered, she would give a tart to her mother. Vivienne would not have had a break, and her only indulgences were a cassoulet and glass of pinot noir after church with Margot.

The baker nodded, still looking a little embarrassed. "Perhaps . . ." Then he cleared his throat and said softly, "Mademoiselle Bisset, I know your mother is worried about her outstanding account. But please, there have been such large orders for the villa, I consider it settled."

Margot's chest tightened, her eyes growing wet at the baker's kindness. It was this kindness that had kept her and Vivienne going since her papa died. Few men had returned unscathed from the Somme, but Marc Bisset had been particularly affected in the years before his death, and ever since the end of the war many villagers had been moved to assist his family. Piles of coal had been left by the back porch of their little cottage in winter, fresh fish delivered by the men from the wharves, thick coats dropped off in brown paper tied with string.

Eventually, the Munros offered Vivienne the housekeeper position for the full year instead of the summer, with the condition that young Margot also be employed full-time. When Vivienne had taken the offer, she and Margot had given up their cottage and moved into adjacent attic rooms.

So Margot, a studious child who could already read English, had left school at fourteen, just like her mother. She gave her books to a girl at the desk beside hers and fed her notes into the flames on the final day before summer break. It had been silly of her to imagine she could finish school. Selfish, really, when she'd been offered a job with firm prospects. Her mother worked her fingers to the bone to provide a roof over their heads—working hard was the very least Margot could do to earn her keep. As a child, she'd been ashamed that her mother labored away at the villa; by young adulthood, she'd begun to realize what an achievement that was.

Now, as she swung open the boulangerie door to leave, she studied the calluses on her hands and the muscles in her arms. Four years had hardened her body; any dreams of finishing school were buried. But she still dreamed of a life beyond the village—a life like Gabriel's.

Outside, Maxime snuggled into Margot's side as they sat on

a bench, his legs swinging as he ripped his bread from the bag and tore it open, stuffing big pieces into his mouth. She longed to pull out the Agatha Christie book she had smuggled into her basket and read for a while in the sun, but it was unfair to expect the boy to sit quietly.

"Slowly, Maxime!" she admonished as she watched the old men in the town square take turns to play pétanque and drink pastis. She could have set her watch by the rhythms of this village. Growing up, this had given her comfort, but after hearing Gabriel's stories, reading Madame's novels, and listening to the tales of guests at Villa Sanary, she yearned to pack her suitcase and the little savings she had, and catch the next train to Paris.

Chapter 21

EVIE

Before her appointment with Clément and Albert Remon at ten, Evie met Gilles for an early breakfast at a café overlooking the Luxembourg Gardens. They needed to discuss an assortment of nineteenth-century illustrations by William Hooker that a collector in Hong Kong had contacted them about.

"The collector's kids are going to college in the States next year," Gilles told her. "Twin girls, to Johns Hopkins and Brown."

"Sounds expensive," she said as she ate a spoonful of Bircher muesli and wondered if Hugo had given any thought to university applications. All his talk lately was of his gap year. So far activities mooted had been hot-bathing in Reykjavík, heli-skiing in New Zealand, and going to some music festivals just outside Rio. Last week he'd mentioned getting a job at one of the infamous weed cafés in Amsterdam. She'd chosen to ignore this last suggestion, but felt pleased he was making plans with his friends. He seemed less and less bogged down with grief.

Gilles handed his laptop to Evie so she could look at the illustrations. She flicked through images of cherries, pineapples, and nectarines, all etched in colorful detail. After pausing to study the disappearing edges of some oranges, she gazed at a trio of red-streaked Bramley apples, complete with brown scabs. "I love this one. They are so imperfect. So real."

Gilles smiled. "I knew you would. Hooker was big on capturing things exactly how they were. Didn't matter if a stem was mangled or an apple scarred, he wasn't afraid to show the struggle that comes with growth. To thrive, a plant might sometimes have to push out at an awkward angle to get the sun, or an apple might be constantly pecked by birds. But that little apple will cling to its seeds and ripen anyway, letting the flesh be torn away."

"Hmm. They really are something."

"Like your Joséphine Murant. It's a challenge to survive, to thrive. An achievement worth commemorating, isn't it?" He grinned. "I'm close to having more pages of the diary ready for you. Her handwriting becomes increasingly difficult to read—you'll see how the ink has bled into the page, and the letters are very scrawled and ill formed in some sections. Of course, it's understandable because of the injuries she endured in Anrath."

"Yes, her factory work damaged her hands severely. I hate to think of the pain she must have experienced—and yet she kept writing!"

"Indeed. Unfortunately, the notes in the margins of her manuscript you texted me weren't very helpful because her handwriting changed so much."

"I can get Clément to email you more samples, just in case?"

"Thank you. Might just help me compare and clarify some of the letters, the turn of her hand."

Evie ordered a second coffee, sat back in the sunshine, and chatted with Gilles about Margot Bisset. Joséphine had recorded their conversations in her diary, mulling over possible suspects in Peggy's murder.

"The thing is," said Evie, "Joséphine was an acerbic observer of the people around her. She used words to paint them in all their complexity, just as Hooker layered his oils and watercolors to paint plants. And she believed Margot. See this entry." Evie tapped on a photo that Gilles had sent her earlier, one of those she'd deleted after her meeting with Clément.

Margot has said she didn't commit murder. Said it was a misunderstanding. That she is innocent. Somebody else fired the bullet that killed Peggy Schramsburg.

When I first met her, I didn't quite believe her. After all, she was imprisoned for life. Everyone at Fresnes pleaded their innocence, even me. And I definitely did all the things on my charge sheet—and more.

We've all done things in this war, in prison, we thought we'd never do. Lie, cheat, and steal. Dignity lies not in being righteous, but what you can do to make life a little easier, a little more bearable, for those around you. To find a way for the spirit to prevail.

But now I'd swear on my life that Margot Bisset is no killer.
The little bird simply doesn't have it in her.

After finishing her breakfast chat with Gilles and agreeing on a price for the Hooker collection, Evie walked the few blocks to the house of Joséphine's old friend, the former journalist Albert Remon. It was one in an avenue of Haussmanns, its gray stone façade covered with ivy, window boxes spilling over with bright red geraniums. It looked a little wild compared with the other impeccable houses adorned with prim topiary.

Clément was waiting outside, and he beamed and greeted her with a kiss to both cheeks. Evie savored his smell for a moment. He looked very smart in his crisp white shirt and navy blazer. "Ready?" he asked, sounding excited, as they rang the doorbell.

A young woman in jeans and a T-shirt answered with a broad smile. "Monsieur Tazi, Madame Black, please come inside. I'm Izzy. Monsieur Remon is in the salon, this way." She ushered them into the grand hallway. "I'm his great-granddaughter and carer. He looks tired but, trust me, he's still very much firing up top." She tapped her head and opened an oversized oak door. "Albert, your guests are here," she said cheerily.

She led Evie and Clément into a large library with floor-to-ceiling windows, its walls papered in faded gold silk and lined with bookshelves, its floor covered by overlapping Persian carpets. Monsieur Remon sat in a wheelchair under a sash window, bathed in sunlight, with a checked blanket over his knees. Introductions were made and Izzy left, closing the door behind her.

"You wish to ask me about Joséphine Murant?" said Monsieur Remon as he gestured to his bookshelves. "You can see I have all her novels. First editions."

Clément nodded. "I have the article here you wrote along with a review in *Réalités* journal in 1950. I think you were the first person who got to interview her for a feature." He produced it from a folder in his leather satchel.

"I see. That was a lifetime ago." Monsieur Remon closed his eyes.

"What was Joséphine like as a young woman?" asked Evie as she sank into the sofa opposite the old man. Clément sat next to her.

"Well." Monsieur Remon's eyes opened. "That depends."

Evie and Clément looked at each other, puzzled.

"Depends on?" asked Clément, still pushing. Evie reflected that he could have been a journalist—he was so thirsty to uncover hidden voices and find the truth.

"I knew Joséphine before she became an author. We were colleagues at *Le Monde*. Then, when the Occupation started, we met with a group of friends and founded the Société Charles Perrault."

"A literary club?" said Clément, who had pulled out his notebook and was taking down everything Monsieur Remon said.

"Of sorts. We met as like-minded people each month at a café on the Left Bank. But soon we started doing other . . . work."

Clément leaned toward the old man. "Resistance?"

"Resistance." Monsieur Remon gave a firm nod. "I haven't spoken of this in over seventy years. But, young man, when I got your letter . . ."

Evie smiled: Clément and his charming letters.

"Well, I knew I had to help with this exhibition. You see, before the war, Joséphine had so much verve, she could light up Paris. She'd arrange meetings, take minutes, draft stories, edit—she even did the drop of the first few issues of *Liberté*, our newsletter, at Métro stations. Stuffed five-franc notes in her garters that she'd stamped with *Vive de Gaulle* in red ink. She was fearless. In the evenings, before the Occupation, she'd tear apart jazz clubs, drinking whisky, dancing, and smoking till dawn. A different silk dress every night, fur stoles around her pale shoulders. Even after the Boches took Paris, she still managed to keep her verve."

"I have a couple of early photos," said Clément. "She was something."

"She sure was!" Monsieur Remon chuckled, before going still. "But that was before her arrest. The Gestapo—they took her in the middle of the night. At the time, none of us had any idea where she was." His face fell as he picked up an envelope and passed it to Clément with shaky hands.

"From Joséphine, in Germany," Clément said as he examined the postmark. "How did she send this from Anrath?"

"Must have bribed a guard. But go on, read it."

Clément pulled the thin paper from the envelope. "Swastika letterhead. A thoughtful touch." He grimaced as he held it so Evie could read as well.

Our days are twelve hours, the women here suffer shortness of breath, our heart rates are dropping. Our hands are burned with acid, as are our legs and feet. Each month there are fewer of us, and I fear by the end of this war there will be none at all.

But enough of this. My days are full of this.

I write because I want to reopen an investigation. My cellmate Margot Bisset was wrongfully convicted of the murder of Peggy Schramsburg. Marseille Courthouse, 1940.

She is innocent. Please help undo this wrong. I know there are many innocent victims of this war, but she deserves a life.

"You see," said Monsieur Remon, "I did investigate. It was difficult, of course, with the war. But I had friends—ex–court reporters and police—who could get me information. That's what I dealt in then, cigarettes and information. I tried my best, but I found nothing to suggest that Margot Bisset was innocent. I felt that I had let Joséphine down, but what could I do?" He sighed. "Years later, when I finally saw her again for the interview, she was almost shy. We exchanged hellos and swapped pleasantries. She kept her face, and that fine mane of hers, under her scarf. Understandable. The scarring across her nose and cheeks made her unrecognizable. Her eyes . . . they were full of pain. She could hardly look at me," he said sadly. "I decided not to bring up her request. What would have been the point?"

Evie was gutted. She'd come to believe Margot had been innocent. Obviously Joséphine had too—why would she advocate for her friend otherwise?

Clément sensed Evie's mood and shrugged at her as if to say,

I'm sorry. They'd both wanted to believe the young maid was not a murderer.

She was.

The three of them sat in silence as light spilled through the tall windows.

"Joséphine must have thought highly of Margot, to vouch for her under those circumstances," said Monsieur Remon. "To risk sending that letter to me."

"Yes," said Evie, with a pang of sorrow, "they must have been very close."

"Perhaps too close for Joséphine to see the truth," said Clément. He glanced down at the *Réalités* interview, and Evie watched with fondness as he switched back into investigative mode. "I wonder, monsieur, if you might help me with one more matter. You quoted Joséphine in this article as saying she'd had a manuscript rejected. Did she tell you about it?"

"No, I'm sorry. She was—"

"Brusque?" Evie asked.

"No! I was going to say withdrawn." He fixed Evie with his bright blue eyes. "The last time we had met in Paris, during the war, she had arranged with a friend of ours, a printer, to make contact with a town planner, who gave us access to important maps. The Resistance and the Allied soldiers used them to detonate some sites. Secret airfields outside Paris. Munitions factories, warehouses full of weapons." His voice was full of pride, but then he leaned back in his wheelchair, his gaze dimming. "Joséphine was arrested that night, along with Timothée and Louis."

Evie and Clément exchanged a glance. "Timothée Martin," she

mouthed. "Mont-Valérien Chapel." Joséphine *had* known those men, and honored them with her endearing, courageous detective character.

Monsieur Remon spoke again, his voice hoarse. "I owe them my life—all of this . . ." He gestured around the room. "My beautiful wife and her brothers—all passed, bless their souls. My lovely Izzy. My career as a journalist." He coughed, pressing a hand to his eyes. "I owe them everything, for they gave me my *liberté*."

Evie glanced across at Clément and saw he too had tears in his eyes.

"I'm going to tell you something I've never told a soul." Monsieur Remon leaned forward again and dropped his voice. "I was at Mont-Valérien the morning when Timothée and Louis were . . ." His voice wavered, and he reached into the pocket of his tweed jacket for a handkerchief to dab his eyes. "Our network had just heard from our contacts at Fresnes Prison that the men from the last round of trials were being transported and executed. So many political prisoners were being killed at Mont-Valérien, sometimes dozens a week. There was nothing we could do against the regiment of Nazis that guarded the fort."

Evie recalled the clearing in the thicket. Birch and oak trees huddled around the edges, branches overlapping. The rough texture of the telegraph poles used as execution posts. The charred bullet holes.

"But," Monsieur Remon continued, "I wanted to honor these good men, so I got up before dawn and, as the sun started to break up the fog, I hiked through the forest in a filmy golden light—well, I ran like a mountain goat, weaving between those elms and oaks. It was magical, with the dappled canopy overhead, mud and leaves underfoot. Morning birdsong. The most perfect spring morning. When I got closer, I heard the engines of German trucks—the soldiers." Monsieur Remon wiped his nose.

Clément nodded.

"I reached the clearing and there they were: Timothée, Louis, and eight other brave men, tied to posts like dogs. Louis cried out, 'Liberté, égalité, fraternité,' as twenty Nazis lifted their guns. Our men sang 'La Marseillaise' one more time. I sang it too, from behind my tree. And then . . ."

Evie held her breath.

"And then they shot them. My comrades. Bravest men I ever met . . ." His voice faded, and he dabbed at his eyes and closed them. Seconds later, he started to snore.

"We should go," Evie whispered to Clément, brushing away her tears.

"Of course." He squeezed her hand.

The pair moved quietly across the room, but at the creak of the door Monsieur Remon stirred. His eyes opened a fraction, then he mumbled, "That architect, he told me . . . he told me where to find . . ."

"Where to find?" asked Clément as he quickly stepped back to Monsieur Remon and knelt beside him.

"Where to find?" repeated Monsieur Remon, sounding surprised, before he yawned, closed his heavy lids, and went back to sleep.

Keen not to wake the old man a second time, Evie gestured to Clément that they should slip away.

Chapter 22

Izzy met them in the hall and went with them to the front door, where they said polite goodbyes and shook hands. Clément told Izzy that he would be in touch about obtaining official permission to use Joséphine's letter in the exhibition. As the door closed behind them, Evie and Clément shared a grimace. Evie was gutted that they had no leads on the missing manuscript. Perhaps it was time to gather the material they did have and prepare the final list of artifacts for the exhibition.

"A drink?" suggested Clément with a raised eyebrow. "I need to debrief." He lifted his satchel. "Unless you have plans?"

"No plans for lunch. Just some invoicing and emails, but they can wait."

He hailed a cab. "Le Comptoir Général, Canal Saint-Martin," he instructed the driver as he ushered Evie in before him.

"Oh, I don't know this place, is it new?" she asked, trying to sound casual.

"Not sure," he said, "I just like the ambience."

She really wanted to go for a drink with him—and more. But uncertainty and fear skipped about in her stomach. There was Hugo to consider; she didn't want something *casual* dipping in and out of their lives. Besides, Clément lived in Marseille.

She sighed and looked out the window, watching Paris slide past in the bright noon light. Tourists and students lolled about in parks and on nature strips, and the road was filled with cyclists.

"What do you think Monsieur Remon was trying to tell us at the end?" Clément asked.

"Oh, it was probably nothing," said Evie, although now that he'd brought it up, she wasn't so sure. She'd meant to ask Izzy about it, just in case, but it had slipped her mind, so she made a mental note to follow up.

A few minutes later, the taxi stopped in a nondescript street. Clément led her past a traffic island until they reached what looked like an old wooden barn, overgrown with vines. They stepped inside to a vast warehouse filled with mismatched velvet couches, fringed lightshades, art deco posters, African sculptures and artifacts, and a long bar shaped like a ship's prow.

Evie gave him a playful smile. "No wonder you like this place—it's part thrift shop, part museum."

"Indeed. It's also very *Midsummer Night's Dream*."

They sat in a blue velvet corner booth, and each ordered a glass of wine. Soft electronic music thrummed. Although it was just after midday, the place was full of office workers, students, and musical boho types.

As their wine arrived, Evie said, "That letter from Joséphine was hard to read. And having read some of the diary entries, and your catalog draft . . . I keep thinking of those poor women. What brutal conditions."

"Yes. The *Collection Défense de l'Homme* paper was written in 1946 to investigate the labor used for factories. And all the camps, actually. Anrath was considered one of the most extreme. In the factory, the carbon disulfide destroyed airway passages, weakened hearts, damaged eyes, and ate away at flesh."

"All for rayon." She shivered. "I'll never wear it again."

"That's understandable! But during the war people had no choice—cotton and wool supplies were blocked or eradicated. Germany needed that Phrix Rayon Factory to clothe their soldiers *and* civilians."

"Well, I hope the prisoners found a way to stuff it up for those bastards!"

Clément laughed heartily, and she felt a warm glow as she met his eyes.

"You are very . . . Aussie, do you know that?" he said, still chuckling.

"I hadn't noticed."

They sampled their wine, then Clément's expression grew serious. "Your husband, Raphaël . . . What was he like?"

Her chest tightened. It was a reasonable question—but what to say?

"I'm sorry." Clément looked sheepish. "You don't have to talk about him. I shouldn't have asked."

"No, it's fine. He was . . . We were a close family, the three of us. A unit. We loved each other very much. Raph enjoyed food, wine, skiing. He worked as a commodities trader, but out of the office he was sporty and fun, very carefree. Unlike his aunt Joséphine." She laughed and shrugged. "She *adored* him, of course."

"Sounds like a great guy."

"He was. I'm not really doing him justice—he was an *amazing* husband. I miss him. I wish he were here to see what we've un-covered, to hear these stories." It was awkward: she felt like she was comparing the men, and that wasn't her intention. Where Clément was rangy, bookish, and considered, Raph had been athletic and outdoorsy. They were so different, yet Evie found Clément more and more appealing each time they met—his hunt for forgotten war stories, his admiration of strong women like Joséphine, his self-deprecating humor, and the way he squinted when he laughed.

"You're honoring them both," he said, "Raphaël and Joséphine, with this project."

Her face grew warm. "Yes, thank you." She sipped her wine and tapped the menu. "We should order."

After they ordered some bao, meze, and samosas to share, Evie shyly asked Clément if he had a partner.

She had assumed he didn't, but as Camille had said on the phone last night, *It's best to just double-check the girlfriend situation before you jump in with both feet. Long-term single men, sometimes they're not entirely up front.*

Thanks for the vote of confidence.

I'm not saying your Clément is like that, but it's always good to do a basic clearance check. You've been out of the game for a while. Everyone's got some baggage!

Evie held her breath as she waited for his response. She didn't think he was the type to connect with another woman when he had a partner, but as Camille said, best to check.

"I had a partner," he said. "She's also a museum curator." He pulled a face as if to say, *I know.* "Ana. We broke up last year because she wanted to move home to Stockholm to be nearer to her aging parents."

Evie imagined a six-foot Nordic supermodel striding through a museum dressed in a white duster and cat-eye glasses, with a bevy of Scandinavian Nobel Prize winners at her beck and call.

"We keep in touch, actually. I'd hoped to see her at a conference in Bilbao later this year. She emailed me last week about it, sent me some papers," he said absentmindedly. "She's very insightful and warm. You'd like her."

Evie nodded, surprised at how disappointed she felt. She tried to keep her voice light and casual as she asked, "Do you miss her?"

"Sometimes. She's smart. Loves hiking, like me. Also books, that's important."

"Very!"

"I mean . . . I *did* miss Ana. Very much."

"*Did?*"

He smiled. "We're friends. But her life needs to be in Sweden. Mine is here." A waiter brought the snacks and Clément pushed some meze toward Evie. "Eat." He picked up a bao and bit into it. "This is good. Getting back to Ana . . . I guess if we were going to keep being a thing, I would have moved to Sweden."

"You'd have given up your *curating* job?" Evie asked, incredulous and impressed. He looked young for a head curator, and she imagined that leaving the role would have been a huge sacrifice. Raph, in contrast, had never considered moving to Australia—it was Paris or nothing. She realized she still felt some resentment about that, now tinged with guilt.

"There'd be another job," Clément said simply.

Evie nodded, touched. She dipped her samosa into some minty yogurt and took a bite. Keen to change the subject, she said, "He was so brave, Albert Remon, walking up through the forest of Mont-Valérien all alone like that. Imagine if he'd been caught!"

"So brave. Like your Joséphine. We just keep peeling away layer upon layer of these war stories. I took notes—I think it will be good to have a quote by Monsieur Remon in the exhibition. We can display his interview with Joséphine, then reveal the link they had during the war with the smuggled letter."

They called for more wine and discussed the possible staging of the exhibition and the likely dates it would run. Clément made checklists and notes in his diary before recommending exhibitions for Evie to check out at the Pompidou Center while she was back in Paris.

They whiled away an hour, then two, and when they walked outside Evie blinked at the sunlight. She fished in her purse for her sunglasses.

"I have to go if I'm going to make the train," said Clément, then stepped forward to kiss her goodbye.

But something had shifted between them, and a simple peck on the cheek wasn't enough. Evie reached up and put her hands on his cheeks, as if to ask a question.

He blinked, then held her gaze when she slowly moved her hands into his hair, tangling his curls in her fingers as she pulled his head to hers.

How long they stood on the footpath kissing, Evie couldn't say. But when they finally peeled themselves away from each other and said goodbye, she was left wanting more.

Chapter 23

MARGOT

Margot awoke in her solitary cell and watched her breath plume for a few beats before she threw off her blanket and crouched by her pail of water.

She cracked the thin layer of ice with her elbow, cupped the water, and tried not to flinch. Freezing liquid slapped against her skin as she began her bathing ritual. When she was clean all over, she brushed her teeth using the toothpaste and toothbrush Müller had smuggled her the night before. Her hair was braided, and the threadbare blanket was folded neatly into quarters and draped at the end of her bed. She pulled on her thin pinafore and mismatched socks and slipped on her clogs.

Margot had been in solitary confinement now for ten days—or was it eleven? Her hands were healing well, as Müller dressed them again every evening when he did his final round. She'd tried to tell him last night that it was a lost cause—her hands would be every bit as raw and infected again as soon as she went back to work in the factory—but he persisted with the re-dressing.

She understood his reasons. To survive, they needed to cling to tiny gestures. To quit the rituals that made up a life—even the worst kind of prison life—would be to give up.

She thought of Joséphine, Susie, Gertrude, and Annika, who would be fighting over the slop bucket and performing their own ablutions before heading off to their shift.

Gertrude had swallowed a few gulps of acid last week. A handful of women committed suicide every month the same way. But Commandant Jäger had been nearby and forced the antidote down Gertrude's burning throat by holding her mouth open with his fingers as if she were a dog. She had been taken to the "first-aid" room by Müller, who insisted she have at least a day to recover. Jäger gave Gertrude twelve hours before he dragged her back onto the floor by her hair. "Let her be an example to all of you human waste."

Margot's body remained thin but hard. Her will to survive was strong. She traced one of her braids and felt something like pride. Or at least felt *something*. The trick to survival lay in the details, seemingly inconsequential moments. A clean face. A folded blanket. A neat braid.

She'd taken the everyday moments for granted when she was growing up, and again when she went to work. Seen them as necessary, but unremarkable. Now these rituals were all she had.

Margot thought of her mother. To think she'd railed against Vivienne's insistence on routine and strict grooming. Margot had been embarrassed about her mother's persnickety ways—her job in service—along with her aprons and gloves. Now she understood the gift her mother had given her.

She counted out the seven steps of her cell.

The factory guards would be stationed outside her door. They didn't even bother to check in now; it made no difference to them if she was alive or dead, she supposed.

Her small square was gray. Thudding could be heard from a distance. The walls murmured but didn't shake. Her chest tightened—were the Allies getting closer? The thudding and rumbling seemed to be unchanging. Just like her days.

With a sigh, and a check at the door, she felt under the mattress for her last gift from Müller: a paperback novel—German, of course. "My mother is partial to them," he'd said, the tips of his ears turning red, as she'd imagined this tall grown man smuggling a crime fiction paperback from his mother's front parlor.

Hard to believe that when Margot had arrived three years ago, she could barely count to ten in German. Now she hungrily devoured their paperbacks, and could cuss and count respectably in Flemish and Russian too.

With one ear to the door and the other to the window, she curled up on her bed and started to read.

❧

On the fourteenth night, a key turned in the door. Margot sat up, blanket over her knees. Her slop bucket had already been tossed in the latrine; the younger of the two guards marched her there at the end of every shift.

Müller had not visited for days, and she'd been surprised at her disappointment when she thought that he might not come again. She missed the news. The reminders that there was a world waiting for her outside these walls.

And now, this scratching at the lock. Usually the metal scraping made her cringe—like when classmates used to run their fingernails down the blackboard at school—but tonight the turn of a key in the lock was as merry as village church bells.

She heard his voice dismiss the guards. *Heil Hitler.*

She stood, as had been demanded in the presence of all Germans since the day she'd entered Fresnes.

"Sit," Müller commanded when he entered the cell.

Shocked at his abrupt tone, she dropped onto the bed. He slammed the door and took some agitated steps to the window.

"What's happened?" she asked.

"Dresden has been bombed, *destroyed*, by the Allies. *A whole city is burning.* Nazis killed. Innocents dead."

Müller's brother was in Dresden.

"Have you . . . ?" She let the words hang in the air.

He shook his head. "Nothing. I need to go home and tell my mother. I'm not sure what is worse. I'm relieved my brother is dead. His cohort of monsters are dead. *But the civilians . . . the children.*" His eyes were full of shame. He swallowed. "Lukas was my mother's favorite son. The scholar. The eldest. The captain."

"You're a guard—"

Müller gave her a withering look. "I neither earned nor wanted it. At least my brother had conviction. He stood for something—for Germany, the Third Reich. I'm a coward."

"You are not. Look!" She held out her bare palms. "My hands are healing. I removed the bandages to let them dry—but I still use the ointment. I owe my hands to you. Gertrude owes her life to you. You've helped Joséphine smuggle her letters, and you bring us news of France. The Eastern Front. Belgium, now Poland."

Müller hung his head with shame.

She'd been surprised when Müller had told her last week that Joséphine had asked him to post a letter for her. Her skeptical friend must have begun to trust him after all.

A flicker of light at the window—was it fire or anti-aircraft shells? She no longer cared if she got hit. It might be a quicker, less painful death than the ones she saw every day at the factory. She caught his eye. "Herr Müller." She shivered but held his gaze.

"Klaus. Please, just Klaus." He stepped to the far side of the room, as if wanting to put as much distance as possible between Margot and himself, to show he wasn't a threat.

But she couldn't bring herself to call him by his first name. After all, they could not properly be friends.

He slid down the far wall and sat on the floor, cradling his head in his hands.

Margot crouched in the corner of her bed. She wanted to reach out to him, to offer him some comfort. To hug him and brush away his tears like she used to do for Maxime. But he was still a guard—and a Nazi. The gulf between them was too great.

At another thud of a faraway bomb, she imagined herself checking into a seaside hotel with fresh daisies on the bedside tables, lace curtains flicking about in the breeze. With each breath, she started to fantasize about what her life would be outside this cell.

She would move to Paris with Joséphine—there was nothing at Sanary for her now. They would pick their way through the markets, buy bushels of white asparagus, cockles, and fresh bread.

She breathed in as if she could smell the bread. Germans knew nothing about bread. Or salted butter, croissants, and pains aux raisins.

Chapter 24

A cube of light from the window. A scratch on the cell door.

Müller had spent the night curled in the corner opposite Margot's bed.

"Hauptmann Müller, you dirty dog," said a young guard, laughing, as he yanked open the door. He spat on the ground. "Time for breakfast," he said as he grabbed the buckle of his belt. He tossed down Margot's metal bowl of porridge, and it clanged and spattered all over the concrete.

Mortified, she swallowed as she hurried to give Müller back the coat he had thrown her from his corner to protect her from the cold. He buttoned the coat and straightened his uniform.

Margot remained in her bed, pressing deeper into the corner as the young guard stepped right in front of her, blocking her view of Müller. He had pulled his flaccid penis out of his trousers and was tugging at it between his thumb and forefinger.

She looked away. Her slow heart started to pound.

"You can eat this," he said to Margot as he tugged again at his penis and winked over his shoulder at Müller. "You can go, sir. My turn." He leered at Margot.

Müller had finished tying up his boots, and he jumped to his feet. "How dare you, soldier. Nothing untoward has happened in this cell. You'll be punished for your insolence."

Cheeks burning, Margot pulled the blanket up under her chin.

"Oh, no need to pretend, sir. She's ready to go again!" The guard chuckled as he reached for the corner of her blanket.

"*Stop!*" Müller shoved the guard to the floor.

The shocked young man shouted, then pulled out his gun.

"Put the gun down," ordered Müller.

"We'll see. What's the problem with sharing the slut? Everyone does it in the factory. Haven't had a Frenchie. Last week I dined on Russian and Flemish." He studied Margot. "Though this one looks a bit bony. I prefer the fresher meat."

"Leave!" ordered Müller, his face blank, eyes cold.

The guard looked confused. He held the gun steady.

"Give me the gun, Fischer."

"Why should I? You either let me have a piece, or I tell Jäger. You choose."

"The gun."

"Either way, she's dead." Fischer's voice grew bolder, while his face reddened.

"Calm down. Give me the gun."

Fischer shook his head. His pants sat below quivering buttocks that looked like a plucked chicken. His penis was hard now, protruding from an angry scribble of hair.

Margot flinched, and the temperature—already icy—seemed to drop.

Yanking at his pants, Fischer flew toward Müller with the butt of the weapon raised, ready to strike him on the head. He was a little taller than Müller and just as broad. When Müller shoved the young guard, he grew visibly angrier and more confused as he tried to throw a punch. Müller stopped the fist with his hand and wrestled Fischer to the ground. The gun dropped beside them as they tussled, then Fischer flipped Müller onto his back, holding a knee to his throat. "Now who's in charge?" he said with a chilling smile. He raised an eyebrow at Margot as he continued to mock Müller. "I won't break your neck, weakling. I'll let you up on the count of three. Then, if you promise to play nice, I'll let you stay and watch me fuck your whore."

Margot pounced on the gun and held it to Fischer's head.

From the corner of her eye, she saw Müller's kind face—his shock.

The crack of a gunshot. The smell of singed flesh. The sweet metallic scent of fresh warm blood as it seeped into the dirt.

Chapter 25

EVIE

VILLA SANARY, PRESENT DAY

Evie sat at the kitchen table working while Madame Laurent chopped apricots for stewing.

"Here, try one of these." The housekeeper handed one to Evie. "Had to stop the young lad from eating them all. Headed for a bellyache, he was."

"I hear you. That kid could eat for his country." She bit into the apricot and juice dribbled onto her chin; she wiped it off with her sleeve.

"How are you getting on with the exhibition, then?" asked Madame Laurent, still chopping. "How was Paris?"

"Good." She tried to hold her voice steadier than she felt. Avoided looking at Madame Laurent. Instead, she recalled her fingers in Clément's hair, her hands touching his cheeks, his arms about her as he hugged her goodbye and jumped in the taxi.

It was just a kiss. She'd definitely wanted more, and so had

Clément, judging by the way he'd held her tight. But it was complicated. There was Hugo, the exhibition, different cities . . . Plus, they'd both been a bit tipsy. Clearly, she should *not* day-drink. It wouldn't happen again. Would it? Part of her would kiss him again in a flash—most of her, in fact.

"We had some good meetings," she said lightly.

She also hadn't told Madame Laurent about Maxime's older brother, Gabriel, handing over the letter that had helped convict Margot Bisset. Evie was conscious of what the housekeeper had said about her husband: *He still shakes his head and goes quiet when it comes up on the rare occasion. You'd think it was his fault the murdering maid went to jail.* Hopefully she and Clément would find something to shed more light on the matter before the note went on display at the exhibition.

At least there was something she *could* tell Madame Laurent. "The publishers are sending through some of their notes and correspondence with Joséphine. She was always published with the one company, Mallory."

"Loyal to the end, that one," said Madame Laurent. "Doesn't surprise me."

"Actually, I got an email from the publisher this morning with a scanned letter that they had on file, squished up under her first few contracts. It's the rejection letter for her first manuscript, 'The French Gift.' Nobody there can remember what it was about." Evie scratched her head. "We've looked everywhere. She must have destroyed it."

"Sounds like Joséphine. If she thought it wasn't good enough . . . I'm sorry, love." Madame Laurent frowned as she tipped the apricots into a large copper pot. "I know how hard you and Dr. Tazi searched for it. What it would mean for your foundation."

Evie's face grew hot at the mention of Clément, and she hoped Madame Laurent wouldn't notice. "One good thing has come from this search. We met with the journalist who wrote that first feature piece on Joséphine. He was in the Resistance too. An old acquaintance of hers, though they only met just the once after the war."

"That's our recluse!" Madame Laurent chuckled as she poured sugar over the fruit and dabbed it about with a wooden spoon. She tapped the spoon on the lip of the pot and let it rest there before walking over to where Evie sat and pulling up a chair. "So, go on then, show me this rejection letter. Joséphine didn't much like being disagreed with, so I can imagine she kept this to herself. Just another of her funny little secrets, or quirks, if you like."

Evie took a gulp of water and opened her email as the sunny scent of sticky apricots filled the kitchen.

September 16, 1948
Mallory Press
Paris

Dear Mlle. Murant,
I wish to thank you for sending us your manuscript "The French Gift" for consideration.

 Please understand that we are not so large a publishing house that we can take a risk on an incomplete work, and I must admit to finding some of the plot implausible. Should you see fit to include the pieces of missing evidence and provide a satisfactory revelation for the ending, we may be persuaded to look at this manuscript again.

If you will permit me to make a personal observation, this fiction is quite a departure from the style for which you established your byline as a journalist. The topic you have chosen is perhaps too complex for a first-time novelist, and too severe for writers and readers of the fairer sex. However, your fiction has a charming turn of phrase and a jolie voice, and I would encourage you to develop your hand.

I would be happy to consider any subsequent (finished) manuscripts.

Yours sincerely,
Jean Mallory III
(Manuscript enclosed)

Madame Laurent tutted. "*Manuscript enclosed.* Well! You're right, she must've got rid of it at some point. Good thing she kept so much of her other work."

"Clément Tazi is certainly grateful for your excellent organization."

"He's a good egg, that one." Madame Laurent touched Evie's hand. "Forgive me if I'm overstepping, love, but he does seem to fancy you. I know you miss Raph—we all do. He was a good egg too."

Evie couldn't help laughing, even as her eyes filled.

"Sorry! My dear, I know you have Hugo, and it's a business getting them into the world—believe me, I understand that much." The older woman rolled her eyes. "But you've done a good job. Monsieur Laurent doesn't stop talking about the lad, who apparently spouts philosophy and talks biology as he helps in the garden. Hugo has a big heart, like his dad. Like you."

Evie nodded, swallowing back tears, and Madame Laurent patted her hand.

"Anyway, I'm talking too much." She pushed the chair back and returned to the stove, where she picked up her wooden spoon and started to stir. "You know, Joséphine was all about second chances, Evie. Look at her—such a tough life, in Fresnes Prison, Anrath. She even had time for that murderer, Margot Bisset. Though for the life of me I can't think why."

Chapter 26

MARGOT

Margot quietly stepped back into the fetid bunkroom.

Captain Müller had reported a rogue guard attempting to rape prisoners, caught in the act. The young man had gone wild, threatened to shoot. The incident was reported, documented, stamped, and sent to Wehrmacht headquarters. Case closed.

"Margot!" The women all jumped off their bunks and huddled around her. Susie, Annika, Gertrude, and Joséphine smothered her bony body with hugs.

Questions were fired between the roars of the Allied aircraft blasting overhead: "Where've you been?" "Where did they take you?" "Did they torture you?"

Margot swallowed, gathered herself, and produced a slim silver hip flask from her coverall pocket, which Müller had slipped her to help with the shock. "I brought a gift," she said, proffering it in the air.

Gertrude grabbed it, unscrewed the lid, and took a swig. "Schnapps." She winced. Then, "Kraut-piss," as she took a second, longer glug and wiped her mouth with the back of her hand.

"Better than the glass of acid you skoaled last month," said Joséphine. "Gave us quite the scare."

"You should have let me die," said Gertrude, softer now.

"I wish it too, sometimes." Susie sighed, reaching for the flask.

Joséphine squeezed Gertrude and ruffled her matted hair, while Susie tucked herself into Joséphine's shoulder and snorted.

"Sorry, they didn't have vodka." Margot grinned, almost feeling cheeky as she took the flask and passed it to Joséphine.

Margot studied this motley group who pressed their cheeks together, laughed, and teased. They passed the flask around as though they were clinking martini glasses in the most sophisticated of nightclubs. Instead they were riddled with lice, with infected eyes and abscesses on their legs. Her mother, Vivienne, would have wanted Margot to hold her head high—even when she felt she couldn't take it any longer. Margot was grateful for her friends. She thought, *These women keep me going.*

The flask was passed to Margot, and she took a swig. As the alcohol burned a sweet, heady trail down her throat and into her belly, she kissed Joséphine's sallow cheek and raised a toast to friendship.

Chapter 27

The rising howl of bombers echoed through the prison at dusk. It had been like this on and off throughout the weeks since Margot returned to the bunkroom. All the prison wardens and factory guards had fled for the underground shelter on the far side of the prison, leaving prisoners abandoned in their unlocked cells or hunched on their knees in flimsy outhouses.

As soon as the first siren sounded, Joséphine grabbed Margot by the hand, and they hobbled down the stairs to an old cellar they had discovered last week. Margot produced the big iron key slipped to them by Müller, slid it into the lock, and pushed open the heavy door, as they'd done several times this past week. In the cool cellar, they lit a candle and stood huddled together examining their blistered hands.

Joséphine produced a safety pin from her apron, waving it in the air and swaying her hips as though it were as tantalizing as a block of chocolate.

She passed the pin to Margot and ordered, "You first."

Margot grabbed the pin, pierced her blisters, and squeezed the pus so it spurted like fountains against the wall. After only a week of being back in the factory, her hands had already become raw and infected.

Joséphine took the pin and did the same. They would often play this silly game with the others in the afternoon as they trudged back to the prison in two lines through the village, each prisoner seeing whose blisters squirted highest. The game usually gave Margot and Joséphine something to laugh about and helped them ignore the repulsed faces of the locals as they stared at the lines of limping, festering, stinking women who carried each other as they marched.

Margot glanced down at her threadbare pinafore, purple ankles, and flaking red feet thrust into wooden clogs. Her eyes stung from the viscose dust and carbon disulfide fumes. Though she would never admit it, her blistered hands, her eyes, her chest all throbbed with pain. She tried to swallow, but her throat was dry. She patted her tongue against her arm, hoping it would be a salve, and thought of water. Clean running water.

To distract herself, Margot talked about the stream above her village on the Côte d'Azur. The sparkling sapphire pool at Villa Sanary. The clink of ice against crystal on silver trays as she served guests every summer.

As she babbled with faux cheer, Margot looked to the stone

wall and remembered the bloodstains in the corridors at Fresnes, where inmates had had their foreheads rammed into the bricks. She thought about bashing her own head against the wall, warm blood streaming from the gash in her skin.

Would it bring relief? An end to this horror?

Margot then studied her friend from the far corner and stepped closer, trying to conceal her black thoughts. "Sorry, I was babbling. I don't know why I keep going on about Villa Sanary. About my village."

"It's your home, Margot. You've told me a thousand times that the soil is in your blood—it's where you go in your dreams." Joséphine hesitated. "Though for the life of me, I hope you do a better job of that murder game in your dreams. You need comfort. Happy dreams. You're still shaken. What happened in solitary . . . you mustn't blame yourself." She reached out and squeezed Margot's hand.

Margot had told her friend what had truly happened in the solitary cell. As the story unfolded, she'd expected to feel guilt. Or shame. But instead she felt fury and disgust. How dare that man try to demean her. Hurt her. Joséphine said she would have done the same thing. Captain Müller said the guard deserved it. He had repeatedly reported him to Jäger for similar incidents, and nothing had been done to remove him from the vicinity of women. *He deserved to be locked up. Not you.*

Still, she could see how a Boche guard would regard her as meat for the taking. Her life was worth nothing. A woman whose only role was to do as others bid. A pair of strong hands in a garden or kitchen, a lever on a viscose spinning machine, a pawn in a rich woman's silly games. Margot was reduced to shadows and gristle. It was enough just to get to the end of each day. *If* there was a moral line, she no longer knew for certain where it lay, or if she had the energy to care.

Joséphine, however, still fizzed with energy and intent. She refused to let Margot feel anything but pride. "Remember, when we get out of here you'll come to Paris. Don't give me that doubtful stare! You *are* coming to live in my apartment. I insist. We've discussed this many times. You'll study. And then at night we'll dine on steak, salmon, or oysters, then hit a nightclub and drink champagne by the coupe as we foxtrot with handsome and heroic soldiers till dawn." She took Margot by the forearm and gave her a twirl. "We are the same size—you can wear some of the dresses I haven't had a chance to yet. I think green is your color."

Margot's cheeks warmed. "I—do you think?"

Joséphine reached for Margot's hands. "Show me yours, and I'll show you mine." She laughed. They opened their palms and stood shoulder to shoulder, raw skin visible in the candlelight.

"But I have a life sentence. Suspended execution, for now!"

"You didn't do it."

"I need to find out who did. Only then do I have a chance of being released. Otherwise, I'll be back in Fresnes for the rest of my life."

"I'll help you. I have contacts—"

They held their breath as the air raid began again.

"We've nothing to dress our hands with," said Margot. "We need to moisten then bandage them to give them an opportunity to heal." She remembered Müller's careful dressing.

Then she thought of her mother.

⁂

Margot carried an apron full of blush-pink roses and presented them to her mother in the dark scullery tucked at the back of the villa. "Put them down," said Vivienne gruffly, pointing to where the white lilies were spread out on a sheet. She dipped a brush into a pot of gold paint and proceeded to run it over the stems and stamens.

Margot dropped the roses into a bucket of water. "Mama, let me do this! You've been going all morning in the kitchen with Chef, now this. Let me help." She grabbed the brush from her mother and started to paint the lilies.

"Nonsense, girl, you've enough on your plate." Vivienne snatched it back. "Don't think I didn't notice Madame call you into her chamber. She hasn't hoodwinked you into one of her schemes, has she?"

Though Vivienne and Madame were the same age, Margot lamented that Vivienne could be Madame's mother. Her legs were knotted with purple veins, hands callused and red, and shadows darkened her eyes.

"I don't know what you mea—"

"Look! You've got gold all over your hands."

They both stared at Margot's hands, then at the drops of blood on the white sheet by her feet.

"You're bleeding!" said Vivienne, voice softening.

Margot looked to where the rose thorns had caught on her skin. Blood seeped through her sleeves and dripped down her wrists.

"Quickly now." Vivienne threw her a towel. "Go up to your room, draw a bath, and take this and put it on your arms." She thrust a bottle of calamine lotion into Margot's hands. "Dab it on your wounds so they don't get the rot. I'll tell Madame I sent you on an errand for an hour. Take your time. Lord knows you won't sit down for a wink tonight, and you'll need all your strength for running up and down those stairs."

Margot coughed, relieved her mother didn't know the half of it.

"Go! Scat." She was shooed out of the scullery like a stray cat, equal parts annoyed and grateful to her mother. Vivienne would not stop working until the last course had been served, yet never once did she complain.

As Margot moved to go up the stairs, she looked at her mother hunched over the lilies, wiping her brow and harrumphing before she turned to wave her daughter away, her face full of concern and pride.

⚜

"Here. Try this," wheezed Joséphine as she pulled off her coveralls, whipped off her knickers, and squatted down. "I saw one of the Belgians doing this on the machine opposite me yesterday. She said it helped. Worth a try . . . It's all we've got at the moment."

"What are you doing?" asked Margot, mortified.

"What does it look like?" Joséphine grinned as she started to piss on her hands. "Try it. I read once that urine is sterile."

Margot gave her a skeptical look as if to say, *Have you finally lost your mind?*

"Look. It's either do this, or wash your hands in that filthy slop bucket upstairs with our syphilitic sisters. You choose."

"It's hardly a choice." Margot squatted and felt warmth trickle over her hands, stinging her blisters before it soaked into the dirt of the cellar floor.

Joséphine stood, then ripped some strips from the hem of her pants and bandaged Margot's hands, before doing the same to her own.

The pair stood with their hands wrapped in gray linen as the roar of planes grew louder, peppered with the cackle of anti-aircraft fire. The bombers were definitely getting closer.

Margot glanced around the candlelit room and then closed her eyes.

Joséphine whispered, "Let me guess, you're trying to remember the sun on your face, the scents of rosemary and thyme along the cliffs, the smell of bouillabaisse filling a kitchen." She touched Margot gently on the shoulder. "Let's stay here awhile with our dreams. No point going upstairs just yet. No one will miss us—the wardens and Commandant Jäger will be in the bomb shelter."

"And Captain Müller," whispered Margot.

"And Captain Müller. I'm sorry—" And she stopped, for what else was there to say? He was kind, and he was a Nazi.

A tear ran down Margot's cheek.

Chapter 28

JOSÉPHINE

ANRATH PRISON, MARCH 1945

As Joséphine sat on the dirt floor beneath the low ceiling, she studied the resigned face of her friend and marveled at Margot's steadfastness. Pressing her cheek to the cold wall, Joséphine felt the vibrations of planes thundering overhead. Outside these walls, the world was imploding with hate, greed, and violence. But here in this cellar, just for this moment, their life was calm and still.

Margot put her head on Joséphine's shoulder.

Joséphine had just been told by the prison warden that a telegram had been received from a Mademoiselle Louise Murant. Apparently it read: *Mama and Papa killed by gunfire. Apartment building evacuated.*

Such simple words. Yet each was more painful than a knife wound.

Joséphine was not allowed to read the correspondence; the

warden had tossed it into the fire as though it were rubbish, leaving Joséphine bereft.

Now that their parents were dead, Lulu would have no further reason to contact her. She could feel her sister's scorn, the blame, through the telegram. Joséphine would never see her family again.

The pain in her heart melded with the pain in her feet, her hands, her eyes. Would there be no end to it?

She tugged her dog-eared copy of Leroux from her pocket, pulled the candle a little closer, and started to write an entry with the new pen Captain Müller had smuggled her.

March 1945
Today I pissed on my hands and the Allies breached the Rhine . . .

When she was done recording her thoughts, she started to flip through Leroux, looking for the parts she had underlined and annotated over the years. *Except our own thoughts, there is nothing absolutely in our power.* The beautiful French words filled the tiny cold space like a warm bath.

Margot sighed, moving her head to find a more comfortable position on Joséphine's bony shoulder.

Joséphine studied her moist bandaged hands, still incredulous she'd pissed on them but relieved because the stinging had subsided. Perhaps there was something to it. Tomorrow would tell.

As Joséphine started to read more Leroux, Margot opened her eyes and asked, "What did this Leroux know? He knows nothing of a thirst so painful we're forced to sneak water from a toilet cistern. I can't *think* my way out of these walls."

"Ah, but you *do*—don't you, my little bird?" She stroked Margot's hair, full of pride.

In truth, she agreed with Margot. Humiliation, hunger, torture— if she'd had the strength tonight, she would have pissed on her Leroux too. How ridiculous to suggest that mental pain was worse than physical degradations! She could see why Margot clung to the paperbacks Müller had given her.

"Where are your crime ~~books~~?" she asked Margot.

"I lent them out. One to Gertrude, the other to Susie. They plan to swap when they're done."

"I didn't know Susie could read German."

"She learned it from her . . . patrons—sharp mind, that one," said Margot, with typical generosity.

"I have a theory about why you love your mysteries."

"Please tell."

Joséphine turned to look her friend in the eye. "Because in an Agatha Christie—or any other crime novel—the *real* murderer gets caught. There's betrayal. Horror, certainly. *Then*, right at the very end, there is justice—truth. The villain *always* gets caught."

"Or killed," retorted Margot as a rain of bullets fell overhead.

Surely the Allied bombers knew this prison was full of Allied inmates. They wouldn't kill their own, would they?

"Either way," Margot said, "I agree, there's satisfaction in the neat endings. But also, the thrill of the hunt." Her voice had a bite.

"Well, well! My little sparrow has become an eagle. A noble

predator, and every bit as mighty and beautiful." Joséphine squeezed her friend's wiry leg. "When we get to Paris—"

Margot gave a weary snort and shook her head.

Joséphine's blood ran cold. Her friend couldn't give up, not after all this time.

Margot muttered, "You're assuming we'll make it out of here alive."

"Where? Do you mean prison—our lovely factory—or Germany?"

"Both!"

"We've escaped execution once. I'm counting on avoiding it again."

Margot shook her head. "I'd never fit in, not in Paris. Isn't it funny? All I dreamed about was leaving my tiny pocket of the Côte d'Azur. Roaming the world. Now all I dream about is the red soil, the cliffs, the herbs. The way the mistral tugs the winter down from the mountains."

"As I was saying, when we get to Paris you can stay with me. Then you can decide what you want to do. Where you want to live."

Margot laughed. "I didn't even finish school! I went into service at fourteen. What on earth could I possibly *decide*?"

"I'll help you find work." The gunfire halted, and she looked up at a sliver of moonlight falling between the bars. "I promise, I'll help you."

"Who is going to employ a convicted murderer?"

"You didn't do it!"

"Who'll believe me? No one has in the past."

"I'm sorry about that, Margot." Joséphine wriggled her legs to stop them from going numb and kept her stinging hands still. "I'm sorry no one in power helped you. Believed you. I've been meaning to tell you, I wrote a letter to that friend I mentioned, a journalist colleague, Albert Remon. I asked him to find the coroner's report, look at court findings, witness statements. He does the court beat, you see—and now that France is free, he can start looking into the old files."

"So that was the letter you asked Captain Müller to send."

"Yes, via his network."

"Great! Now they will add espionage to my charge sheet."

"Touché! Don't be so dramatic." Joséphine elbowed her bony friend, whose smile was wry. "We'll see if anything comes of it. You've always said some of the guests were Nazis, or sympathizers at least."

"And my employers had business links with Germans."

"Well, who knows, perhaps something in my files could point us in the right direction. A contact. That's a start, isn't it?"

A spray of artillery fire shook the wall. Dust fell onto their hair. Their faces.

"Looks like we're here for a while," said Joséphine. "So why don't you tell me *again* what happened that night at Villa Sanary?"

At this, Margot's face broke into a sad smile. "You really are incorrigible, you know that?"

Joséphine lifted a bandaged hand. "Start at the beginning. Tell me every little detail." Her eyes lit up. "I know"—she jiggled on the spot—"to make it fun, tell it to me like it's one of your precious murder mysteries."

Margot sucked in her breath and held it for a beat. "Ridiculous. But . . . okay. I'm only doing this because, well, I don't have anything else on at the minute. I'll start with the party, set the scene."

"Go on, then. I'm listening. This time make it a snappy opening."

Margot settled back against the wall. "The housemaid tucked herself behind the potted palm on the villa's balcony so she had a clear view to watch the murder."

Chapter 29

EVIE

Evie sat at Joséphine's desk overlooking the pool and sipped a cup of green tea. Outside, Hugo lay sprawled in his favorite lounge chair, a biology textbook opened across his lap. Judging by his dark glasses and the way his head was tilted back, she assumed he'd dozed off in the sun.

And why not? When they returned to Paris for good after this summer, his head would be full of assessments, college entrance essays, and exams. Soccer training and games would be squeezed into every moment in between. Her role would be less counselor, more shuttle driver and caterer, she suspected. This summer had shown her—shown them both—that Hugo was ready to fly.

She smiled as he shifted his weight, and his head lolled to one side. Definitely *not* studying.

Her chest tightened. She would miss doing Hugo's life admin. Affirmation that yes, he was seventeen, male, and . . . still required her signature. She wished Raph could see the man Hugo was becoming.

Beyond the pool, the dark leaves of the bay hedge rippled like feathers in the wind. She leaned toward the window and opened it a fraction, so the sunlight and a warm breeze stroked her face. Just as the mistral was starting to gather for the change of season, something was shifting in Evie.

Working with Clément to put together the exhibition had shown her how much Raph's great-aunt had endured. She'd been brought to her knees by depravity and horror time and time again, but refused to stay there.

Evie had been up all night reading the latest diary entries, emailing back and forth with Clément and Gilles. They were still deciphering some of the writing, and Gilles had sought help from an expert at the Louvre.

Evie tried to imagine Joséphine hunched over the book, pouring her thoughts into the margins. The photos didn't show the patina, the knocks in the spine, the curved corners that had been thumbed night after night, words smudged with sweat and oil. The Leroux had survived alongside Joséphine. And she'd kept her mother's words tucked inside the front cover, like one last hug.

Evie shivered and opened her laptop. Once more she was drawn to the very last entry. She had read this over and over last night, marveling at Joséphine's acerbic wit.

March 1945
Today I pissed on my hands and the Allies breached the Rhine . . .

Prison and labor camp hadn't knocked the spirit from Joséphine. She had shown Evie just what was important.

Evie would always miss Raph. Their stories would always be bound. It was crucial to fold her grief and loss into a corner of her heart and carry it always. She didn't need to let it go or close anything; Raph wasn't something to be packed away or to move on from. He would always be with her—and that was okay.

But just like a hellebore under a giant chestnut tree, Evie had learned to lean toward sunshine. She'd learned to maneuver her heart and find pockets of happiness with Hugo, in her sketchbooks, and studying the line of a perfect geranium or camellia with Gilles.

Also, a generous pour of rosé always helped. Joséphine had taught her that too.

Evie swallowed as she realized how much she would miss this project—and Clément—when she and Hugo returned to Paris. She remembered her hands in Clément's hair, his lips on hers.

They'd spoken over the phone only once since that kiss, as she preferred to email. The conversation had grown stilted when she'd said, "Listen, about that moment on the footpath . . ."

"I remember," said Clément with an awkward chuckle. "How could I not?"

"I'm just not sure . . ." She paused and tried again. "It's just that things are complicated. Hugo, work . . . Are you there?"

"I'm here," Clément said softly, "and I understand, Evie. Honestly."

"Maybe in different circumstances."

"There's no need to explain. Let's focus on the exhibition."

That brief moment was buried. It was better, more meaningful, to focus on Joséphine's story. Margot's story.

Also, getting Hugo to launch into *his* story. For everything up until now had just been the introduction; it was up to him where it went from here.

Chapter 30

JOSÉPHINE

PHRIX RAYON FACTORY, APRIL 1945

Joséphine and Margot had been working at adjacent machines for twelve hours. Each time Margot picked up a cake of viscose, she made sure to smudge it against the nearest metal pole. Joséphine's heart quickened. Who would have thought this timid little sparrow who'd perched on the end of Joséphine's bed in Fresnes Prison would end up doing her part for a country that had tossed her away?

Joséphine did a few steps of the tango between spins. Margot laughed and whistled.

Commandant Jäger growled at this show of affection. How dare anyone show amusement in this dusty hellhole! "No more talking today. Idiots, do you understand?"

Joséphine nodded, her head bowed to hide the slightest smile twitching at the edges of her lips.

"Yes, Commandant," Margot replied with her head also

bowed deferentially. Once again Joséphine caught a glimpse of the resigned young maid who'd stepped into Fresnes Prison all those years ago.

This time, though, Joséphine knew it was an act.

Whether at Villa Sanary or Phrix Rayon Factory, Margot had been considered nothing more than a sturdy set of arms and legs, ready to attend to the next task as instructed. Invisible. Dispensable. It had become her greatest strength. Joséphine wondered if she knew how remarkable she was.

Jäger marched across to where a viscose pipe was shuddering beside Margot's spinning machine. A plume of steam spurted from the top.

The commandant cursed: an airlock.

Joséphine held her breath and tried to look busy. She *did not* want to be near this machine when it was drained. The commandant would need to run all the acid from the machine into a bucket to unblock the airlock. Someone would need to hold the bucket steady as the acid spurted from the bottom of the machine, otherwise the force would tip the bucket over and acid would spill across the floor, spreading fumes, burning anything it touched. The spinning would need to be stopped while they cleaned it up.

Joséphine did not want to be the one to hold the bucket. What if the acid spewed out too quickly and overflowed?

"Are you listening to me, lazy cow?" Jäger only ever addressed the women with insults. Never by name.

"Yes, Commandant," replied Joséphine.

"Hold the bucket under the pipe."

With quivering arms, she moved one of the waste buckets under the pipe to collect the viscose and acid as it spurted out.

The bucket filled quickly. Too quickly. It was almost full, and still more acid poured from the machine. She needed to empty it, but one accidental spill and the acid would burn her hands and her feet. It was too risky; she wasn't strong enough to lift it. "Commandant, I need help to lift—"

"How dare you address me," he bellowed, face reddening. "Empty the bucket. Now!"

"No," she said softly. "I can't." It was true: her back, her legs, and her arms were so weak she couldn't lift the pail.

Margot dropped another cake on the stack and approached Joséphine. "Commandant, may I assist?" Margot slunk closer like a cat, nimble and ready to jump to one side at the slightest sign of a fist.

Jäger glanced from one woman to the other with narrow eyes and spat a glob of phlegm onto Joséphine's clog. "What a pair of *hässlich* twins you are. Get out of my face."

Joséphine opened her mouth to snap that the commandant was no oil painting either, but thought better of it when she saw Margot's thin arms straining to replace the bucket. Any wisecrack would only see her friend punished too.

A shaft of light from a high window fell across Margot's forehead. There was nothing ugly about her.

Margot put her bucket under the pipe and helped her friend carry the acid to where they could pour it into a holding tank. Five minutes later, bucket emptied, both women were back at their adjacent stations.

But the airlock on Joséphine's machine was not fixed, even though it had just been drained. The faulty pipe started to clank and shudder and let out a high-pitched whistle. She pressed her palms over her stinging eyes to protect them from the acrid yellow steam filling the factory. She leaned against the spinning machine and wheezed, and her hand went to her chest, as if pressing her breastbone could steady the weakened heart within.

"Straighten up," Margot warned as the commandant spun on his heel and started to march toward them.

The thud of steel-capped boots on concrete blended with the menacing whirr of the machines. The marching drew closer, accompanied by a volley of angry words. "Idiot! Bucket!"

Jäger kept screaming instructions at Joséphine, but she couldn't hear him. The factory walls had started to judder, and the air was filled with the crackle and scream of anti-aircraft fire. She strained to hear the magical buzz of an aircraft over the factory noises and gunfire. Was it possible? Could the Allies really win this war? End it? One of Susie's civilian patrons had eagerly fed her news as he unzipped his fly under the spinning machine. "Jabbered like a schoolboy," Susie spat.

This factory could be liberated soon. They all just needed to hold on a little longer.

Then Joséphine thought of Elsie and felt wretched. She resolved to track down Elsie's family when she was released and tell them the truth.

She looked at Margot through the sulfurous haze and grimaced. Margot's brown eyes were twinkling, even though she winced at the cacophony of artillery. Joséphine tried to be reassured by Margot's smile.

"Concentrate!" screeched Jäger.

Joséphine was rewarded with a smack to her cheek from the base of his gun. She fell to her knees, clutching at her face.

"Joséphine!" Margot dropped her cake and took a step toward her.

"*Halte!* Bucket!" yelled Jäger as the light fixtures trembled above him.

Looking up from where she was curled on the floor, Joséphine shook her head slightly, warning Margot to stay where she was.

"Back to your machine, you troll. Now!"

"Not until I help Joséphine to her feet."

"Now! Do you want to go back to solitary?" He stepped toward Margot and raised his rifle.

Joséphine pleaded silently with her friend to stay away. To protect herself.

Margot ignored the pleas and instead tried to help her friend, bending down to replace the bucket with her back to the machine. The pipe on Joséphine's machine gurgled and started to spurt. Acid and viscose shot out the end and flooded the bucket.

Jäger lunged for the lever, and Joséphine pulled herself up off the floor and leaped across to protect Margot from the torrent of acid spilling out the end of the pipe.

What felt like warm honey smattered across her cheek and nose. She lifted her hand to wipe it off but realized too late her mistake. Her face and hands started to sting as if attacked by ten thousand bees.

Beside her, Margot rocked on the floor with her knees curled up under her chin. She was taking short, shallow breaths, and her uniform had been burned away. Her beautiful face was already starting to blister.

"Christ. This is not my morning. I need coffee." Jäger indicated for the guards to deal with the two howling women crumpled on the floor. "Clean up this mess." He ordered everyone back to their stations, and his heavy boots stomped away.

A soft hand squeezed her shoulder. Captain Müller.

"Margot—" croaked Joséphine. "Please help, Klaus."

"Of course." He gently slipped his arms under Margot, and Joséphine watched as he lifted her onto a steel trolley. When had that arrived?

He knelt to help Joséphine. Her back arched with pain, she clawed at her burning face, her legs stiffened as if cramped. Her breath was louder now, gasping. "Margot," she pleaded as she flung out a limp hand.

Müller soothed Joséphine. "Margot's here. I'm just going to lift you up on this trolley, and we'll get you both to the hospital."

Joséphine's head lolled to one side, and her eyes rolled back. Rasping even louder, she grabbed Müller by the lapel with a strength that surprised her and pulled him closer. She licked her burning lips and struggled to speak, her words sticking in her throat like shards of glass. But she persisted, because what she needed from the guard was crucial. "I'm dying. This is what I need you to do." She gave her instructions.

Müller nodded, his kind face strained, veins standing out

from his neck. He was still for what seemed like minutes, face expressionless.

But as Joséphine's trolley was pushed away, he gently touched her wrist before he quickly removed something from her coverall pocket.

The last words Joséphine heard in the Phrix Rayon Factory were "*Je promets.*"

I promise.

Chapter 31

EVIE

PARIS, PRESENT DAY

Soon after the meeting with Albert Remon, Evie had called his landline to follow up. His great-granddaughter, Izzy, had answered the phone and said that she would ask him what he might have been talking about as he drifted off to sleep. Evie hadn't heard anything since—until this morning.

Izzy had called to say that her great-grandfather had remembered what he'd wanted to tell them and would Evie like to come to morning tea. Glad not to have any pressing work commitments, Evie had hopped straight in a cab.

Afterward, she'd immediately called Clément with the news. "Can you come to Paris tomorrow?"

"Sounds urgent!"

She was so excited she wanted to jump down the phone. "We have some new information about the Resistance. I've just this minute finished having tea with Monsieur Remon." She'd also had two pistachio macarons and contemplated the raspberry, but Clément didn't need to know that. "He knows where Joséphine hid secret Resistance documents. The architect showed her how to conceal them under the parquetry in her apartment, so she became the repository for their part of the network. But after her arrest, they felt it was too risky to break into the apartment, partly because her concierge was suspected of reporting her. Monsieur Remon said that half the time she didn't know what she was hiding, just that it was important. She made a point of not reading anything, only the handwritten notes she took. Apparently, that was their golden rule—the less they knew, the better."

"Incredible," said Clément, sounding stunned and impressed. "This is a huge find for the exhibition and the museum, and for all historians. Text me the address, and I'll meet you there at 10:30 A.M. tomorrow."

❧

As planned, Evie met Clément outside the art deco–style building in Montmartre. Red geraniums spilled from the window boxes, and plane trees brushed against the balconies on the upper levels. Evie loved the way the trees cast a pretty tracery over the whole street, and she longed to press her cheek against their smooth gray trunks, as she had with the smooth bark of eucalyptus trees when she was young.

Greeting each other with broad smiles, she and Clément kissed on both cheeks, and she took in the scent of his clean shirt and aftershave.

She stepped back quickly, leading him into the apartment building, and strode across the black and white marble tiles in the foyer, waving at him to keep up. He whistled and raised an eyebrow. "Nice place."

"Joséphine's father bought it for her on her graduation from the Sorbonne, apparently. She lived here until—"

"The eighties, when she bought Villa Sanary. I've done a little research, remember! Even made a documentary."

Evie grinned and tapped the bell on the oak concierge counter.

"Oh, Evie, back again!" The silver-haired concierge shuffled out from her rooms, a Chihuahua in a pink turtleneck sweater under her arm.

"Madame Arnaut. Coco." Evie rubbed the tiny dog between the ears, and the old lady beamed. "So good to see you. Are you feeling better?"

"Well, my back is still sore and I cannot get my new knee until October, so . . . same, same." Her eyes narrowed. "Provence suits you—you have a tan." She leaned sideways to look behind Evie. "And a *friend*, I see." She raised her eyebrows, pursed her lips, and said nothing, but her twinkling eyes told Evie the old concierge was busting to say more. "Are you here for the night? Remember, I told you last night that the next Airbnb guests are not arriving until tomorrow."

"No worries, we'll just be here today. I'll also grab the latest landlords' notes while I'm here, please." The concierge had made a habit of taking notes on all the maintenance jobs that needed doing in the building and making it into a newsletter for all the landlords. The woman ran a very tight ship.

"Bah, of course," said Madame Arnaut as she handed Evie a list folded neatly into pigeonhole 16.

⁕

Evie and Clément ran upstairs and entered the apartment using the old-fashioned metal key. Light fell in pretty squares across the oak parquetry from tall sash windows.

Evie stood staring at the floorboards and around at the apartment: home to Joséphine, then, decades later, to Raph and Evie as newlyweds. He'd carried her over the threshold, and they'd danced to Eurythmics and U2. After some champagne, they'd pulled each other's clothes off as fast as they could.

They'd been so happy here.

She looked out the window across the rippling canopy of green leaves and thought about reinvention and renewal.

Then she focused back on Clément, who was counting his steps from the far wall.

"What are you doing?" she asked, confused.

"Searching for Joséphine's hiding spot!" He looked endearingly excited. "You said the architect told Albert Remon it was five feet from the far wall."

"Stop. I already know where it is." She walked across and stood at a spot where the parquetry creaked. "This has always made a noise—we always meant to get it fixed . . . In her will, Joséphine asked us to replace this floor, among other jobs."

They bent to look at the boards. There were no indentations or clues that they had ever been lifted, and the oak had aged to the color of honey. Evie pulled her pocketknife from her handbag and knelt to angle herself into position.

Clément laughed. "Of course, you brought your own equipment."

With force, Evie rammed the knife into the gap between the boards and repeated the movement until a couple of pieces loosened enough to be lifted up. She tossed them to one side and brushed the dust away at the edges with the hem of her skirt.

Underneath was a package wrapped in what looked like a silk scarf. *Very Joséphine.* She bent down to grab it.

"Wait," said Clément as he pulled two packets of cotton gloves and some archive folders from his bag. Next, he took out a sheet of plastic, a roll of velvet, and an archival camera, and arranged them in a semicircle.

"Thanks," said Evie, admiring his competence—actually, if she was honest with herself, it was kind of a turn-on. She cleared her throat. "Okay, I'll unwrap it slowly. We'll document it as we go."

Clément nodded and shone his iPhone into the void. Her hand shaking, Evie plucked out the parcel.

She smiled at Clément, shifted from her knees to sit cross-legged on the floor, then placed the parcel onto the strip of plastic overlaid with velvet, unwrapped it, and started to sift through the pages. Carefully transcribed on lined notepaper was a list of more than two hundred names with columns beside them allocating tasks, contact details, code names. Evie recognized the same confident hand that had written the prison entries in the Leroux paperback.

She and Clément sat side by side, finding the names they had expected:

Timothée Parsons
Louis Martin
Albert Remon

Air caught in Evie's throat. She would never forget the image of a young Albert Remon running up Mont-Valérien through the forest, his footfalls masked by soft soil and moss.

Clément and Evie sat for a while passing pages between them, humbled by what they were reading. Joséphine's neat hand had recorded minutes for each meeting and a list of topics for articles in the *Liberté* newsletter.

"I suspect some of these annotations were not for committee eyes," said Evie as she nudged Clément.

Jean Paul not to write on Métro network—too sappy
Roland Bertrand to meet with pilot—dishy

Underneath was a substantial list of Allied pilots rescued and escorted from Paris, plus addresses and contacts of safe houses. In addition, there were maps of arrondissements, certain country areas, and rivers, all with a series of color-coded dots and lines. Hundreds of people who'd never met one another were grouped together on this pile of paper for their resilience. Their resistance.

Evie shivered. Joséphine had been interrogated in Paris by the Gestapo and then in Fresnes Prison. Not once had she given up a name.

When Evie and Clément were done photographing and recording each item, she gathered up all the papers and handed them to Clément. He sorted them into annotated archive envelopes, before tucking them into his satchel for safekeeping. "I think perhaps after the exhibition," he said, "these should go to Fort Mont-Valérien."

"Perfect. It's full circle." His generosity made her feel like opening up to him. "Why do you think she left all this here? All these years without telling a soul."

Clément frowned in thought. "Monsieur Remon said something about Joséphine Murant that reminded me of my *jadde*. Maybe, like him, she had *severe nerves*—PTSD, they'd call it now."

"Of course," said Evie. "Her days in the rayon factory were barbaric. Even so, how could she not do anything with this material, or the diary?"

Clément said softly, "When she returned to Paris, she must have been traumatized, sick, and weak. And there was a lot of paranoia: suspected collaborators were being lynched, and she was fluent in German. But even if she'd wanted to hand over the material—to whom? The Vichy government tortured her then threw her out of her own country. The new de Gaulle government had good intentions, but perhaps she thought no authority would believe her, not straightaway." He paused, his brow furrowed. "And think of the hundreds of families affected by what lay under these floorboards. In her mind, perhaps, why dredge up confusion, loss, and pain? Why not let these families have their peace? They earned it."

"But," said Evie, confused, "she didn't destroy these documents. She *intended* for them to be found, one day. Hence the note in her will."

Evie peered into the darkness below the floorboards once

more and cast her arm about, in case they'd missed anything. Her fingertips brushed against something soft. She grabbed the ends of what felt like a knot and lifted it gently to where she could get a better grip on the item.

As she pulled it into the light, her gloved hands rushed to unpick the knot. "Look!" Her skin tingled as she ripped away the green silk to reveal a manuscript title page.

Clément was clearly trying to contain his excitement. "It's the same typeface as all the other manuscripts we cataloged that first day in Joséphine's library. I'm sure of it."

```
THE FRENCH GIFT
A novel by Joséphine Murant
(Final Draft)


The housemaid tucked herself behind the potted palm
on the villa's balcony so she had a clear view to
watch the murder. She had been directed to give the
signal, and so she snapped a particularly stubborn
leaf at the mid-stem to improve her view.
```

"This manuscript," said Evie, as adrenaline rushed through her, "it's about Margot Bisset! I need to know what happened."

"This is *fiction*," Clément said softly, as though he were trying to coax her from a cliff edge.

"I know." Evie tried not to sound too irritated. "But weren't you the one who said first manuscripts are often the most auto-biographical?"

"Yes. And I had nothing whatsoever to base that on."

"Okay, keep reading." She hushed him with her hand.

He shot her an amused look but obeyed, reading each page before passing it to her. They were equally transfixed, and they were both fast readers. For one hour, then two, the only sounds in the little apartment were their breathing, the clock ticking, and the flicking of pages.

Well into the third hour, Clément gasped.

"What is it?"

With a grave face, he passed her the page he'd just read.

To think a single moment—an accident—thrust the young maid into a life that wasn't hers. One minute she was a country girl on a stretcher, screaming as her dearest friend's breath drew ragged, then stopped. The next, she was wheeled from the factory with a new identity—revered journalist and Resistance fighter—and a Parisian address.

The scars on her face protected her, in a way. She was so disfigured, nobody dared stare at her for too long lest they seem rude. From time to time, people she suspected were on the journalist's list hidden under the parquetry would come calling at her apartment. She'd open the door just a fraction and see their faces fall—or an involuntary hand fly to their necks—as they surveyed her face. The celebratory hand waving a bottle of red wine or champagne would drop to their sides.

The French Gift

One by one, the jubilant visitors stopped turning up at her door. She never accepted an invitation to catch up with "old friends" and instead spent her days walking the streets of Paris, or at her desk writing. Perhaps they'd heard that the war had damaged her, the burns seared into her soul.

At any rate, the invitations dried up. Requests for the journalist to write for her old newspaper, *Le Monde*, fell away.

To break up the monotony and earn a little money, the woman took a job cleaning other apartments in the building two days a week—her concierge recommended her. Her needs were modest: fresh bread, croissants, and a little left over for a Sunday visit to the cinema. She lived frugally off the money the German guard had given her, augmented by her cleaning.

She had worried about being contacted by the journalist's family, but everyone except her sister had died in the war. They never corresponded, but the woman was able to connect with the journalist's niece.

The woman sent only one postcard, to the address in Germany the guard had made her memorize when he'd offered to shelter her. The postcard was of a picture of the Champs-Élysées with rows of plane trees in bloom. She wrote, *Spring in Paris. All well here.* The maid walked to the far end of the

Luxembourg Gardens to post it—past the lake where
children poked at colored wooden sailboats with
sticks and anxious mothers yelled at them not to
fall in. She thought of the little boy she used to
babysit at the Côte d'Azur villa. Would the child
have finished elementary school by now?

The older brother's face was in shadow. The high
cheekbones and dancing eyes she'd had a girlish
crush on had become hazy. The dreamy, hopeful
girl whiling away her spare time in the orchard
no longer existed.

Life started to thrum and take new directions.

The woman decided to try her hand at a little
fiction.

And there, the manuscript ended, abruptly.

Evie frowned and scratched her head. *Could Joséphine Murant
have been Margot Bisset?* She swallowed, trying to get her head
around what she'd just read. "Could it be true?" She tapped the
manuscript.

"It's possible," Clément said evenly. "But this isn't proof, of
course."

Evie's head swam as she reread the first chapter. The driving
force of the narrative was not the identity switch—it was that
Margot Bisset was innocent. Written from the maid's perspective,
it trawled over every minute detail of the murder party. Coupes
of Krug, trays of smoked-salmon canapés, blooms of blush-pink

roses and gold-painted lilies. Mountains of fresh oysters set out on silver trays beside the floodlit pool. The dizzy and selfish English mistress and her boorish husband; his German business associate, the Nazi Party member who arrived with Coco Chanel; the Duke and Duchess of Windsor; the beautiful, athletic acrobat who swung from the ceiling.

"Joséphine—Margot?—is meticulous with every detail," Evie mused. "The maid was clearly set up in some way by her employer or her husband or both of them, or someone else who knew about the murder game."

There was just so much to take in. Overwhelmed, Evie pressed her face into her hands. Clément gently patted her back, as one might soothe an upset toddler. He was right, she told herself. It was fiction. How much should they believe? Evie looked up at Clément. "She never again tried to publish it, even when she became famous. Maybe because she never finished the manuscript. It doesn't say here who the murderer was. Just that Margot Bisset was innocent . . . Maybe she didn't know?"

"Or she did, and she was protecting someone. Remember in the documentary interview, she corrected me when I assumed crime novels were about finding out who the killer was. *You assume a crime book is about the crime.*"

"I remember," said Evie, as her cheeks grew hot; she must have watched it three or four times now.

"Joséphine said mysteries were about justice. Less about the who, and more about the why."

"So, let's say we believe Margot was innocent—and I think

I already do. If she did live and take on Joséphine's identity, she must still have wanted to work out why she was framed. She would have wanted justice. A resolution."

"She must have spent so many years lying in her tiny cell thinking about that night," said Clément, "talking it over with . . . with Joséphine."

They sat in silence for a few moments, lost in bewildered thought.

Eventually, Evie took a deep breath and said, "I deal with precious manuscripts every day. Texts that were crafted with painstaking care—the drying of the vellum, the precise placement of the lapis lazuli, the annotation of a specimen, and occasional gold leaf. We see them as artifacts, something profound that brings medieval days into the present on the page. But they are not static objects—they encapsulate emotion. Care. And reflect that back onto the reader. With a botanical manuscript it's up to the conservator or the reader to put together all the parts. To look into the margins, as Gilles always says."

"And that can also be done with a crime novel," said Clément, nodding. "There are so many unknowns, mysteries we are unable to resolve in life." He glanced at his satchel, full of the neatly sorted pages of names, notes, and maps, then back to the manuscript. "But we're trying, just as Joséphine tried. And, it seems, Margot too."

Was that enough? Evie wasn't sure. But for now, it had to be.

Shadows had started to dance across the walls, the sunlight fading. The plane tree leaves were shaking with the evening breeze. Evie took Clément's hand, turning it over so she could spread her palm against his. They linked fingers and squeezed. She tugged him closer, and he shuffled across to sit beside her, took her other hand in his and kissed it. They sat together in the shadows, holding hands and kissing softly as ghosts filled the room.

Evie pulled away slightly. "I've changed my mind." She waved her hand at the manuscript. "*That* is complicated. *This*"—she waved her hand between their chests—"is not. I want this."

"Very good to hear." He kissed her again. "Because I definitely want this. Us." He ran a finger up her calf, then her thigh, before resting his hand on her hip and kissing the crook of her neck.

She turned to smile up at him.

"This exhibition . . . it's huge for me, professionally," he said. "But the best part has been spending time with you."

"Really?" Her voice caught in her throat.

"Beautiful, generous . . . a little bit wild." He tucked a curl behind her ear and placed a hand over her heart. "And strong."

Evie said gently, "I want this, I just don't know how. I haven't . . ." She hadn't been with anyone except Raph for over twenty years.

When Clément held her gaze, she could see that he understood. He didn't need her to voice her fears.

Her cheeks warm, she dropped her head so her curls covered her face. He bent toward her, cradling her head, then ran his hand up her leg, this time under her skirt, before he leaned over for a long, lingering kiss.

She moaned and lay back on the floor, pulling his body with her. They moved slowly in the evening light, caressing each other as they removed their clothes piece by piece. Evie savored each kiss, each touch, and let herself have what she wanted.

Chapter 32

MARGOT

PARIS, OCTOBER 1945

When Margot finally reached Paris, she walked the last part of the journey to Montmartre.

The train from Germany had been packed with weary soldiers and hollow-cheeked refugees. Sweaty bodies swayed and pressed together as the train crawled through the countryside. Bombed bridges and hastily repaired tracks made the journey painfully slow. Days. At the border, the carriage burst into a throaty rendition of "La Marseillaise" as they passed an avenue of French flags some thoughtful citizens had set up along the tracks to welcome their comrades back onto home soil.

Margot thought of all the times she'd sung the anthem, first at school in village fetes and Bastille Day celebrations, then among the prisoners lifting the roof off at Fresnes and Anrath. Voices she'd come to know so well had bellowed so hard she could imagine their red faces on the other side of the concrete walls.

Allons enfants de la Patrie,
Le jour de gloire est arrivé!
Arise, children of the Fatherland,
The day of glory has arrived!

Margot looked around her carriage at the singing faces of men, in uniforms that hung limply off skinny shoulders, and mothers, who clutched confused children under their arms like hens sheltering their chicks, and wondered, *Is this what glory feels like?*

As Margot joined the chorus, a little girl on the seat opposite peeked out from under her mother's arm and stared at Margot's face. Margot shifted to one side and tugged at her headscarf, so it covered more of her forehead. Still, the girl kept staring as the adults around her started to belt out the final verse of "La Marseillaise." Emboldened, Margot stuck out her tongue at the child and wiggled her nose. The child giggled and pointed. The mother, mistaking her daughter's attentions toward Margot as unkind, hushed the child and forced her across the aisle to sit with her father.

"*Très désolée*," the woman apologized, without looking at Margot's face.

Margot tried to give her biggest smile to reassure the woman there was no harm done—but her face was unused to such spontaneous smiling, and her cheeks ached. If she wasn't careful, she'd be committed to an asylum as soon as they hit Paris.

The singing ended, leaving the carriage with an electric charge. Nobody spoke. Margot imagined herself back in the tiny cellar in Anrath, her head on Joséphine's bony shoulder while her friend hummed these same lines as she made notes in the margins of her beloved Leroux.

When the conductor announced they were three hours from Paris, Margot finally succumbed to sleep. As she drifted off, she told herself she was doing the right thing: the plan had always been that they would return to France—to Paris—together.

Only someone who has been locked up for six years can know how strange it feels to walk down an avenue freely. Margot walked along the pavement at her own pace, feeling lost without rows of women in rags beside her marching in time to soldiers' orders. Newly planted flowers peeked out from window boxes. Shop fronts were being repainted, some in colors so bright they dared the gray sky to grow darker just to prove they would not be dimmed. Couples walked furtively arm in arm, rejoicing at neat rows of late roses and asters in garden beds lined with green hedges. Restaurants were throwing checkered cloths over outdoor tables and placing blackboard placards that boasted about their *menu du jour* in curling script—though there still wasn't much to offer. Soup and bread. A measly salad.

As Margot climbed the hill to Joséphine's favorite patisserie in Montmartre, she was relieved to see it was open. Joséphine had described the tiny window as always filled with immaculate rows of croissants, pains aux raisins, and baguettes. Now it just had a few bread rolls, but that was enough. Margot startled herself with her confident tone as she leaned against the counter, speaking to the cherub-faced waiter. She hadn't spoken a word since leaving Germany two days ago, afraid the very act of speaking aloud would define who she was going to be from this point.

She was not the timid country maid—the *provincial girl*—who'd been ripped from the Côte d'Azur six years ago. The brash voice ordering bread told her she carried more of Joséphine with her than just her Leroux.

Margot sat at the tiny round table out front in the sunshine, drinking water and letting fresh bread crumbs sit on her tongue. She had never been to Paris before, and she found herself besotted with the cobbled streets, ornate shop fronts, and curved avenues of elegant apartments.

A swarthy man dressed in a shabby coat and red silk cravat knelt at the corner painting canvases that replicated the boulevards and dancing spires that unfurled down the hill from Sacré-Coeur.

A woman carrying a baguette longer than she was tall brushed past Margot, her other hand gripping a wire rack stacked with six bottles of red wine. Margot's mouth watered as she imagined the cheese board and charcuterie bound to accompany this extravagance—though the woman's apron, brown plaid dress, pinned-back hair, and worn shoes made Margot suspect she was merely delivering these treats for someone else.

Margot was soon afraid that if she spent any more time wandering the streets and lingering outside shop fronts, she would be arrested on suspicion of being a collaborator. She shivered and tugged at her headscarf. The last thing she needed was to be interrogated by a jumped-up officer at the local police station. If they asked to see her papers and then traced her to Anrath, well—she'd heard on the train that French soldiers and vigilantes were rounding up suspected collaborators and hanging them in the streets.

Margot arrived at Boulevard de Clichy. She started counting down the numbers in her head, noting the elegant wrought-iron gates, heavy wooden doors, and wide stone façades. It was even more impressive than Joséphine had described.

Margot stood looking up at Joséphine's apartment building.

Third floor, at the end of the corridor. 16.

If she craned her neck, she could just make out the last window. Joséphine's gift.

Margot squared her shoulders and pushed on the blue wooden door. A bell rang in a far room as it swung open, and she stepped into the dim foyer. Black and white tiles covered the floor, and a curved wooden desk for the concierge sat empty in the far corner.

A squat woman with stockinged legs appeared from a doorway carrying a miniature gray French bulldog. This had to be Madame Thomas.

She's a witch. But her dog, Bonaparte, adores me.

The concierge peered at Margot and waddled closer. "Yes?" she barked.

Margot tugged off her scarf and turned her head. The concierge flinched as she took in the seams of scars that ran from Margot's cheek across her nose.

Before Margot knew what she was doing, she had reached out to rub the dog behind the ear. The dog licked her hand, and Madame Thomas stepped back, clearly not wanting this monstrosity standing in her foyer to have any further contact with her precious pet.

With a voice far steadier than she felt, Margot said, "Madame Thomas, I wondered if—"

The woman raised an eyebrow as if to say, *How do you know my name?*

"I wondered if I might have the keys to my old apartment," Margot said boldly as she put her hand, sticky with dog saliva, into her pocket and pulled out her identity card.

JOSÉPHINE ELOISE MURANT

"Mademoiselle Joséphine!" Madame Thomas's hand flew to her neck. "Your face! I'm sorry, I did not recognize you. And you are thinner, but aren't we all?"

The concierge looked pretty stocky to Margot, and she wondered if Joséphine's suspicions had been well founded.

It was Madame Thomas who reported me, I'm sure of it. Sold me out for a leg of ham and some vegetables . . . She'd give up her own child for a leg of ham, that one! Joséphine's hands had balled into fists and her jaw clenched.

Bonaparte cocked his head at Margot and yelped a little.

"He always liked you . . ." The older woman let the sentence hang in the dim foyer. Her silence left no doubt that the remainder of the sentence was: *I have no idea why.*

She unlocked the safe behind her desk and pulled out a large black key. "Here. No one has been inside since . . ." She pressed the key into Margot's palm. It was cold, heavy. "The Gestapo commandeered all the other apartments. Perhaps yours was too small. Who knows?" She pursed her lips and shrugged, but when Margot looked up into her eyes, she saw shadows. Sadness. Hadn't they all seen things—done things—they regretted?

Margot had been sure that she would rage against Madame Thomas. But now that she was faced with an old woman who clung to her dog as if he were her soul, the urge to take revenge on her for Joséphine was gone.

Margot realized she didn't have the energy to be bitter. She still ached to know who had been involved in Peggy Schramsburg's murder, but that mattered less to her right now than making a fresh start. France was climbing to its feet, and Margot needed to steady herself and find a way to exist in this new world. Otherwise, what was the point? She might as well have bashed her head against the prison wall, swallowed the acid, or peeled away the lifesaving drips and cords while she recovered in the overflowing German hospital.

So, Margot smiled at Joséphine's cursed concierge and said sweetly, "*Merci*, madame." Then she turned her back on the concierge and made her way to the stairwell, crying tears of relief. She'd spoken as Joséphine to Madame Thomas, and . . . nothing! With a wave of her identity papers, a sassy voice, and a firm step, she'd become someone else.

Joséphine had written on the wall in Fresnes: *Joséphine Murant, died March 1942.* But Margot Bisset, the village maid, had also died in prison. She wasn't sure what to do with this freedom.

As she climbed the grand old staircase, she ran her fingers up the mottled walnut balustrade. She needed to touch it all—take it all in. *This* was her life now. Her home. She swallowed down her guilt and loss and squared her shoulders as she passed a window, glimpsing blue sky above golden autumn leaves that stretched hopefully toward the sun. The stairs, newly waxed and polished, smelled of honey. Paris was rebuilding, and she must find a way to rebuild as well.

⁓❧⁓

Margot hadn't understood what was happening as she'd watched Joséphine tug Captain Müller down by his lapel. They'd murmured to each other between Joséphine's pained grimaces, then Müller had fished her identity card from her coverall pocket. Quickly, he had done the same for Margot.

A guard and a medic were approaching them.

"Joséphine, lie still," Müller said to Margot.

"I'm not—"

"Shush, you've been badly burned. Your friend is dead, and we have to get you to the hospital." He turned to bark at the other prisoners, "Fräuleins, stay back from the acid!" Then he faced the guard and the medic, who stood beside him now. "Take this prisoner to the hospital. Here."

He handed the identity card to the medic, who squinted slightly to read. "Joséphine Eloise Murant."

"No," groaned Margot as she was rolled away on the trolley. "Margot—"

"Margot Bisset is dead," Müller said firmly, sounding every bit the stone-hearted guard. "Joséphine Murant, you will be taken to the hospital now."

Margot was wheeled away, her head spinning and heart more broken than she'd thought possible. Then she fell unconscious.

Days and nights blurred. She awoke at the hospital dazed and painfully alive, with overworked German staff hovering over her at intervals. Captain Müller had demanded a corner bed with a tiny window. She could see the days pass—from sun to ink and back again.

Outside her area, the corridor hummed with the rattle of trolleys, the chatter of staff, the patter of feet on clean floors.

She ached for Joséphine—her laugh, her spirit. How strange it was to lie with her head on the pillow and hear the kind nurses say that name. *Joséphine.* How could she do her friend, this name, justice? Her face stung with the burns: no ointment could take away the sting. Her face was also no longer her own. Instead it was a red, mottled, weeping cobweb of scars. Scars that would never heal.

One morning, she turned her head to find Müller standing nearby. He walked over to the hospital bed, heavy boots squeaking against the white tiles.

"Hello, Joséphine. They tell me you are making a good recovery."

"I can't! I'm not . . ." Margot struggled to lift her head off the pillow.

He dropped his voice. "You are. Joséphine wanted this. You must go to Paris. I promised her that you would have another chance, another life."

"But how do I become Joséphine? She's educated. A writer. Parisian."

"You'll find a way. You're strong." He spoke more urgently. "We don't have much time. You already have the identity card." He gestured to where it was clipped on the hospital chart at the end of her bed. He pulled a small brown parcel from his pocket.

"These are travel papers, and Joséphine's Leroux. Your bunkroom friends gave it to me."

"But—"

"Listen very carefully. Joséphine has an apartment in Paris. I'm assuming you know where it is?"

Margot nodded.

"Well, when this war ends, you'll have your liberty. And it will end soon. In fact, the Allied soldiers will be here within days."

Margot sighed. The tube in her arm hurt, and she could hardly speak. When the Allies arrived, she would be free. But Müller would be arrested; he would almost certainly face trial and imprisonment, perhaps execution.

He studied her tube and gave her a sad smile.

"What will you do?" she asked.

His face fell. "Nothing. I will do nothing. This is the end of the war, finally, and there will be consequences."

"I'll testify! You were so kind to me—to all the prisoners."

"That won't be necessary. I'm prepared, come what may." He reached out, lifted Margot's hand, and shook it. "Goodbye, Joséphine."

Chapter 33

Margot stood outside apartment 16, placed the key in the lock, and turned it.

Nothing.

Agitated, she jiggled it from side to side, pushing a little harder until she was rewarded with a click. The door swung open to reveal a small room with large windows. Sunlight fell diagonally onto the parquetry, giving the room a pretty golden hue. An antique cupboard sat against the wall with bits of cloth peeking from under the doors, as if the clothes were jammed in too tight and the doors slammed shut. *How very Joséphine.* She grinned. Nestled under the window were a desk, a chair, and a pretty typewriter. In the far corner was a cast-iron bed; beside it, a tiny table with a blue china jug. A glass lay on its side, perhaps knocked over as Joséphine was hauled out of bed in the wee hours of the morning.

Margot's stomach roiled as she imagined just how petrified her friend would have been.

There were two. The younger one pulled me off the pillow by my hair and covered my mouth with his oafish hands so I couldn't scream. The other cuffed my hands and feet. They carried me from the building in my nightdress. I was not even allowed to put on shoes.

A second wave of nausea hit as Margot realized the same fate could befall her now, if she was accused of being a collaborator. She needed to keep her head down.

She righted the glass, then opened the wardrobe and gasped at the colorful sequinned sleeves and waterfalls of silk that spilled out. She reached for a long green gown nipped in at the waist and set with a glittering brooch at the shoulder, and was reminded of poor Mademoiselle Schramsburg.

After slipping the dress back into the wardrobe, she pulled out gown after gown in hues of sapphire, emerald, and gold. She turned to the mirror to hold up a particularly pretty dress in peacock blue—but gasped when she saw her face.

She lifted a finger to trace the lines of scars. The German doctors in the Krefeld hospital had held a mirror up to her every week and assured her that the seeping wounds were healing, that the infection had passed. But the welts remained. The doctors said she would always carry the scars on her face and hands. Though she'd never been vain, it upset her to see her ruined face. It was as if the hurt, fury, and shame she carried with her were on display.

Swallowing her tears, she lifted the peacock-blue dress to chest height. The bias-cut silk must have looked superb hugging Joséphine's curves. She pictured her friend clutching a glass of champagne in one hand and a cigarette in the other, head thrown back in laughter as handsome men took it in turns to charm her at nightclubs all over Paris.

This was how she would remember Joséphine: flamboyant, elegant, and colorful. Not the shriveled, lifeless woman on a cold concrete factory floor.

Margot pressed the dress against her boyish hips before returning it to the wardrobe and closing the door. She had no idea what she would do with those dresses, let alone where she would wear them. But if she was going to be Joséphine, she would need to camouflage herself with some of her friend's sassiness and color.

She picked up a stole thrown nonchalantly over a chair and wrapped it around her shoulders, rubbing the soft fur and giving herself a small hug. It was a comforting gesture that made Joséphine seem close.

Finally, Margot stepped over to the little desk positioned under the biggest window overlooking Montmartre and marveled again at the spires of Sacré-Coeur. Perhaps it was the trees reaching into the sky, the rooftops glinting in the sunlight, but she thought she saw a glimmer of magic.

She dropped the lace curtains.

After we get out, my little bird, we'll go to Paris together. You can live in my apartment—Papa bought it for me as a graduation present. I know I'm lucky, dear Margot—don't give me that look!

Joséphine had tapped her friend on her nose.

You'll come and live with me—I'll show you Paris. The first thing we'll do when we hit Paris is drink hot chocolate and eat croissants at Boulangerie Bleue.

Joséphine's eyes had narrowed.

I'm certain someone will want to know what happened to us in Paris, at Fresnes, then here at the factory. That not everyone was a turncoat. We fought for our grandchildren and their grandchildren. The time will come when I tell my story. And you, Margot, must tell yours.

Margot stepped to the middle of the room, just as Joséphine had instructed: five feet from the northern wall toward the front door. Once Margot was certain of the spot, she reached for the black mink coat at the back of the wardrobe and felt along the hem until she found something hard. Then she pulled away the lining to extract a small screwdriver. She slid the tool into the gap between the boards, and did it over and over until a couple of pieces came loose. After tossing them to one side, she wiped off the dust with her sleeve.

Hand shaking, she plucked out a parcel wrapped in baking paper and tied with string. *Probably the only time Joséphine ever used the stuff!* Margot smiled, shifted from her knees to sit cross-legged on the floor, and placed the parcel on her lap.

Half an hour later, Margot recrossed her legs to get comfortable as she tried to make sense of the documents spread out in front of her. She started looking through the alphabetized lists of names for any she recognized, partly out of curiosity, as many politicians, celebrities, writers, and other well-known public figures had stayed in and around Villa Sanary in the lead-up to the war. But also with the faint hope she might find someone who had attended that final Bastille Day party; Joséphine had come up with various theories, some outlandish, that the murderer had had a political motive.

Some names were crossed out, some were annotated by region—Dijon, Tulle, Paris. There was also a list of friendly foreign contacts in France, labeled by country: *Allemagne, Angleterre, Amérique*.

Then Margot found a name that made her shiver. A name scratched out with a neat line of ink: *Margaret E. Schramsburg (Amérique)*.

Margot lifted the paper up to the light and gaped at the name.

Were all these crossed-out names people who had died?

Her throat was tight and dry. She could hardly breathe.

The list had no title. It must have been put together by an anti-Nazi French group in the late 1930s and then passed into Resistance circles.

In July 1939, two months before war broke out, had Peggy Schramsburg been an American contact working against Germany? This list left no doubt.

Herr Bloch had owned several cloth factories across France and Germany, and the Munros were key suppliers. Was the American gathering information about their sources, their supply chain? Peggy's parents were big industrialists in America. She'd have grown up with talk of manufacturing at the dinner table. The American woman was no fool: a war had been brewing and the Germans—and the Munros—were on the wrong side. Margot thought about the piercing blue eyes of the American: honest eyes. The girl was no doe-eyed socialite; she was trying to make a difference. Perhaps for her family's gain, but mostly for America's gain. Also, for France . . .

Margot recalled Peggy's look of fear when Herr Bloch stepped into the foyer, with Coco Chanel swathed in layers of dusty-pink sheer silk at his side. As the sequinned acrobat had twirled around the trapeze, the heiress's face had grown pale. Resigned. She'd waved away the plates of brioche rolls stuffed with lobster and salmon canapés and the coupes of Krug being served, opting for water.

Margot had assumed this was the face of a rejected lover. But as the list fluttered in her hand, she saw that Peggy Schramsburg had been trapped that night. And she'd known it.

Herr Bloch had made no secret of the fact that he was a Nazi Party member. He'd boasted that Hitler had toured his German cloth factories in 1936 and actively encouraged him to expand them into France and Belgium. Factories with which the Munros had business links. Factories like the one Margot had been forced to work in. She studied the mottled scars that smothered her hands and shivered as she imagined them burning once more. Acid eating her flesh. Peggy Schramsburg had an inkling of the evil that was unfolding across the continent, and Josephine's documents concealed under the parquetry proved she was working to stop it.

The smell of orange and clove incense mixed with summer sweat came flooding back. A jazz quintet. Laughter and the clink of crystal. The sapphire blue of the pool. The salty breeze on her cheeks as she crouched behind the palm; the rustle of the pencil pines as they bent and swayed with the mistral. The scent of rosemary and lavender thickening the hot evening air. Fireworks.

The man in a white tux on the balcony bickering with Peggy Schramsburg. She couldn't tell if it was Herr Bloch or Monsieur Munro. She'd assumed it was a lovers' tiff. But now she saw it was something more sinister.

The acrid smell of a bullet.

The sound of the back of Peggy Schramsburg's skull being pierced by a bullet.

The warm spatter of blood across Margot's face.

Furious, confused, and hurt, she lay on the floor of Joséphine's apartment for half an hour watching a tiny brown spider weave a web in the dusty corner. Then she sifted through the rest of the papers, wondering what had become of all those people. Were they still alive? Did they have families? Had they been sent to labor-camp hell?

Her own story was not so bad. She was alive, and during her time in prison she'd made friends. Found a community.

She had shot a man through the skull. She had watched friends die.

She had learned what was precious, and if she ever found it again, she would clasp on to it and hold it tight.

When Margot had finished going through Joséphine's papers, she wrapped them back up and placed the parcel in its hiding spot, tucking it in and patting the parcel as tenderly as a newborn. She had decided to wrap the papers in some of Joséphine's collection of silk scarves; the rest she would use to cover her scars, so she always held Joséphine's exuberance close.

Perhaps it would rub off on her.

Exhausted and missing her friend, she reached for the coat a German nurse had insisted she leave the hospital with and pulled out Joséphine's beloved Leroux paperback.

But it was not the writer's words Margot was seeking. She had her own ghosts. Instead, she sought comfort in the neat, steady hand of her friend.

She flipped through the pages, noting that Joséphine had marked their first meeting with a sketch of a sunflower in the margin.

They can't separate us. I'll always carry you here, my little bird.

Tears welled in her eyes and fell onto the page, causing Joséphine's crisp letters to bleed, obscuring the words. Margot dried her face with her sleeve, blotted the page to preserve the words, then flipped through the book until the final page.

March 1945

It was the night they'd sat together in the cellar as the Allied aircraft bombers raged overhead.

My Margot is innocent, of that I have no doubt. Over the years, we have picked apart everything she was accused of, like one of the crime paperbacks she loves to read.

She insists I write her story, but my Margot has her own way with words—and her own story to tell. When the war is over, I'll take her to Paris, dress her in the finest silks, and dine with her on lobster at Georges before we dance the night away and walk home carrying our heels. In the morning, we'll bid our lovers farewell, drink coffee, and walk through Montmartre, before sitting to write at our apartment.

I'll enroll her in a course at the Sorbonne and set another desk where she can polish her craft.

What will we write? Well, I shall find a way to tell the fragile stories of my compatriots.

And as for my Margot . . . well, that is up to her.

But first, let me share the opening lines of her story.

> *The housemaid tucked herself behind the potted palm on the villa's balcony so she had a clear view to watch the murder. She had been directed to give the signal, and so she snapped a particularly stubborn leaf at the mid-stem to improve her view.*

Touched, Margot closed *Le Fantôme de l'Opéra* and put it in the top drawer of the little cherrywood desk. She intended to keep it close, like a talisman, for the rest of her life. She knew what it was to have people recoil from your face.

She turned her attention to Joséphine's metal typewriter, a present from her papa on her enrollment at the Sorbonne. A box of paper sat underneath the desk, slightly curled and browning at the edges, the top sheet covered in dust. Margot picked it up, shook off the dust, stuck it into the typewriter, and made a start.

AAAAAEEEEEHHTHEJOSÉPHINEMURANTWWWWWPT

For hours, Margot pressed the keys with her index fingers as she taught herself how it worked. It was slow, and she was surprised at how hard she had to press and how easy it was to strike the wrong key. But there was comfort in the rhythm of the letters pressing onto the page.

Margot sat at Joséphine's little desk until dusk. Then, without bothering to go out for food—her stomach was still bloated and gurgling from that morning's bread roll and coffee—she walked the few steps to the bed and fell asleep curled up with Joséphine's stole snuggled against her cheek.

The next morning, after inhaling the coffee and precious croissant someone had left on a tray at her door with an abrasive knock—a peace offering from Madame Thomas, perhaps?—Margot bathed, dressed, and once again sat at Joséphine's desk.

She took out the Leroux and set it at her elbow, then started to type.

```
THE FRENCH GIFT
A novel by Joséphine Murant
(First Draft)


The housemaid tucked herself behind the potted palm
on the villa's balcony so she had a clear view to
watch the murder . . .
```

Chapter 34

Margot sat at her cherrywood desk with a clear view past the pool to the rose garden. She leaned back for a stretch in the fancy new office chair Madame Laurent had insisted on buying. Dear Monsieur Laurent—Maxime—had proudly unloaded it from the back of his truck last week. *"J-J-Joyeux anniversaire,"* he'd declared shyly as he slipped it under her desk and carried her old one away above his head with wiry arms. The decades had done little to curb his energy, or his stutter.

Of course, she'd wondered over the years if he'd recognized her and kept silent about it. But every time that thought snuck into her head, she snuffed it out. The truth was that Margot Bisset had died half a century ago.

She put a hand out to steady herself and allowed it to linger on the blue silk wall. It reminded her of the cupboards upstairs stuffed full of the silk and sequinned dresses Joséphine had worn as she strutted around Paris.

Images of her dear friend flashed through her mind, making her dizzy: sparkling eyes, a throaty Hollywood laugh as she teased Susie, the way she used Margot's back as a book rest. The *scratch, scratch, scratch* as she poured her words—and her life—into the margins. Except in old photos, Margot had never seen Joséphine in anything other than a factory uniform or ragged clothes, but sometimes when she closed her eyes at night, all she could see was an intoxicating woman full of joie de vivre, her elegant hand clasping a cigarette set into a mother-of-pearl holder.

Margot took a sip of her tepid water and wished she had some ice to press against her neck. It was a hot, dry Saturday afternoon, and the incessant Sanary sun beat down on the sandstone walls and paving around the pool, giving the day a dull pink haze.

Joséphine's great-nephew, Raphaël, bobbed and splashed about with little Hugo, the delighted baby staying afloat thanks to yellow tubes on each arm.

Over in the orchard, Evie had set up her easel and watercolors. She was painting a vignette of chickens pecking about under the apple trees. Her paintings were better than she gave herself credit for. She'd turned red when Margot insisted on buying a trio—plums, apples, and olives—for her library wall.

Margot used to love sitting in the orchard when she was young. On any given break she'd be under an apple tree, reading a book or just lying on warm fresh-cut grass watching the clouds dip and swirl. It was to the orchard she'd retreated in a lull between chores the day of the murder party. She had watched Gabriel trim the bay hedge.

In the pool, Raph dunked Hugo under the water, then lifted his squidgy little body high above his head, dark eyes brimming with happiness and love. Hugo squealed and cackled with laughter, and Margot thought she might burst with joy. With pride. She had no right to this love—this family—but now they were as much a part of her as any limb.

The years had passed and still Margot kept living. Sixty, seventy, eighty . . . the decades were marked only by box sets of mysteries, special hardcover editions, and now, perhaps, a documentary.

She could barely recall the quiet, fresh-faced young maid who'd roamed the cliff tops and dreamed of a bigger world than her sluggish pocket of the Côte d'Azur. Since then, she'd seen how ugly the world could be—blackened with torture, prison, starvation, humiliation, and war. The innocent country girl was lost. It still shocked her, the ease with which she could lie and deceive. Margot studied her mangled hands and thought of what a hollow wreck of a woman she'd been.

But inspired by the joy that family and the villa had brought her, Margot had rewritten a happier tale, one that would live on long after she'd gone. She looked at Hugo and hoped that Villa Sanary would continue to be filled with laughter and happiness. Celebrations and new beginnings, instead of shadows and ghosts.

A new day. Fresh starts. Newborn children. All these things were gifts. She intended to give one more to this family. She'd left a parcel—a partial manuscript—hidden under the floorboards in the Montmartre apartment and instructions that would ensure it would be found after she was gone. Tied up with string. It was the only thing she could tie up, because she had never finished the damn thing. How could she finish the story when she didn't know the ending? Margot had learned over the years, with her thirty-nine subsequent, completed novels, that the key to planning a good murder mystery was to start with the ending: you had to know who the killer was. The purpose of the plot was to work out *why* they did it. And then: justice.

This was one of the reasons she'd bought Villa Sanary—she had hoped it might somehow help her finish the novel. She thought of the pages wrapped up under the floor in Paris. Her unfinished manuscript. Now that she was an experienced writer, she understood why it had been rejected—who wants an unresolved mystery?

Fortunately, she had not been crushed. That was the upside of a war that no one could imagine: her spirit and body were already so dehumanized, so desensitized, that something as trivial as a rejected manuscript was a walk in the park.

Her next manuscript was published, then the next and the next, never another rejection. Her novels sold well. She developed a reputation as a recluse, and the more her star rose, the less she did interviews.

One morning over coffee and *Le Monde*, her breath caught. A half-page advertisement for a Côte d'Azur villa featured on the back page. Her villa.

À VENDRE
FOR SALE
Villa Sanary

A perfectly located villa in a quiet residential area of Sanary,
500m from the sea, offers spectacular views across the bay
of Villefranche. The residence is situated on a large plot
of five acres with a spacious main villa and a guest house
with independent access from a separate street. No major
renovations required.

Margot read the advertisement over and over, holding her breath
to see if the villa's dark history—her history—would be mentioned.

This is a charming property with incredible sea views and
direct sea access only 20 minutes from Monaco and 30 minutes
from the International Nice Airport.

Nothing.

Margot booked a flight to the Côte d'Azur the next day.

She'd had a lovely surprise when she found Maxime working
here. And it warmed her heart that he would clam up whenever
journalists pestered him for the history of Villa Sanary and
the story of Margot Bisset. He would shake his head and walk
away, muttering, "*Occupez-vous de vos oignons.*" Mind your own
business.

About a decade ago, Margot had taken him an iced tea in
the garden. It was a hot July day, and the sun beat down on

the pink soil. He was picking tomatoes and plucking sunburned leaves from the vines. As she approached, he passed her a warm cherry tomato, and she popped it onto her tongue—the sweet, tart taste of summer exploded in her mouth. Rows of curly chard and lettuce unfurled in neat beds, and adjacent to the vegetable patch was the rose garden—Maxime's pride and joy, as it was his father's before him.

They perched on the edge of the planter with the sun scorching their bare necks and looked out across the sparkling pool to the villa.

He pointed to the balcony where Peggy Schramsburg was murdered and spoke softly. "I gave a letter from Margot to my older brother, and he passed it to the police. No one believed Margot. She never stood a chance. And my brother, he disappeared the next day back to his circus troupe. But the thing is, I never saw him tumble or do any training. And you'd think if he was a clown, he'd have performed for his baby brother."

Margot wasn't sure what to think. Everything was hazy in the heat. She popped another cherry tomato into her mouth.

"Last year I replaced some of the bay hedge with saplings. And when I dug up the roots, do you know what I found? A buried rifle. The roots had wrapped around it and tugged it deep into the earth. I remembered seeing Herr Bloch—the German friend of the Munros—give Gabriel a copy of *Mein Kampf*. Of course, I had no idea what it was as a lad. Just that I was curious—I was quite the reader." He finished his iced tea and rolled his glass between his hands. "I promise you, Margot did not shoot that American. But it's too late." He shook his head sadly. "Margot is long dead. And when Gabriel never returned, Papa said he was dead to us. Why drag up that muck?"

"The gun, what did—?"

"Ah, the crime writer!" He grimaced, pointing along the line of cypress down to the cliffs. "I tossed it into the ocean. Margot deserves peace, bless her soul." He crossed himself, stood, and hitched up his trousers before heading over to pick some dark, curly kale.

The tomato she was sucking burst and juice dribbled from her lips. She wiped it away as she remembered Gabriel on the ladder, resting his rake on the bay hedge as he checked to see if the surface was level. The handle had pointed toward the balcony.

Not long afterward, he'd approached her as she'd snipped away with the pruning shears in the rose garden, picking blush-pink flowers for Madame Munro. "Here, let me do that for you," he said as Margot focused on cutting far down the stems.

"I'm fine," she said, without looking up. Where had he appeared from? He'd still been taming the hedge when she'd left the orchard. His presence beside her made her heart thump so loudly, she worried he could hear it.

"Mademoiselle, why don't you let me finish cutting these, while you hold the roses?"

How ridiculous she must look, clumps of roses gathered into her apron, chopping madly with her free hand. He must think her so primitive.

"Oh, roses!" An American drawl filled the garden. "Look at all these pretty colors—the pink is my *fav-or-ite*." Peggy Schramsburg appeared in a turquoise caftan with one bare shoulder proudly on display. She unfurled a gold-bangled arm and plucked a rose from Margot's apron haul. "May I?" she asked, even though she'd already taken it.

"Of course." Margot's ears reddened. The roses were surprisingly heavy in her apron, and she needed to get back to help her mother. But she didn't want to leave Gabriel alone with this . . . this . . . goddess. It was as if a snake had crept into Margot's belly and taken hold. Gabriel had also been doing some work for the Munros' neighbor, Coco Chanel, these past few months on his free days. He must have seen the American there when she was a guest.

He stood motionless, seeming to watch the American apparition waft around the garden, smell her flower, and disappear out the far gate. Or was he just casting a gardener's eye over the bushes? Margot couldn't see his face. Perhaps she was being unfair.

From the corner of her eye, she caught sight of Monsieur Munro and Herr Bloch striding across the lawn in their tennis whites, then looping behind the hedge to the garden shed—no doubt looking for Gabriel, to set him another impossible task for the afternoon. The pair seemed to be giving him plenty of orders, though what matters of Villa Sanary and the garden had to do with Herr Bloch, she had no idea. Perhaps he was just a plant lover. He obviously liked giving orders—for he certainly seemed to be doing much of the talking—though Margot was always too far away and too busy to catch a word.

As Gabriel examined a few bushes nearby, Margot resumed her rose collection, swiping at the stems with her rusty pruning shears. Soon her apron grew too heavy to hold with just one arm, so she put down the tool and gathered the second apron corner to carry her scented haul to the villa.

"Margot, please!" said Gabriel, moving closer. "Let me help you."

He tried to fish the roses out of her apron, but she lifted it and pressed it against her chest. Thorns pricked through the fabric and gouged the tender skin of her forearms, but she didn't flinch. She could not be caught by Monsieur Munro alone here with Gabriel, his hands in her apron. And he was so handsome and being so kind to her—it was all too much.

"I have to go!" she said, her cheeks burning as she rushed away.

&c&

Margot jolted herself out of her reverie and focused back on Hugo, Raph, and Evie. One day, she hoped they would find the hidden parcels. The unfinished manuscript. Joséphine's notes. She hoped they would understand she'd preserved these documents for Joséphine. For the others who had not made it. Also, for her family.

She'd found the ending for her manuscript, but it would serve no one to publish it. "Margot Bisset" was dead. She had long ago destroyed the page with Peggy Schramsburg's name—for hadn't that girl suffered enough? Her terrified eyes, her pale thin arms, and the smell of fear shrouded in a slinky green ball gown would haunt her forever. The American was working for the right side—her angry words with Herr Bloch certainly suggested she was no Nazi sympathizer. Madame and Monsieur Laurent led a rich, gentle life nurturing their beautiful family, Villa Sanary, the garden, and all who moved within their world. Why shatter their peace?

There were more important stories, more important names, under the parquetry that she hoped, in time, people would find.

She closed her eyes and nodded in the sun. This was one manuscript she didn't need to finish. It was better for everyone that she didn't.

Margot drank more water and tugged the T-shirt where it clung to her sweaty skin. She placed the glass back beside her typewriter. At her elbow sat the well-thumbed Leroux. Behind it sat her favorite slim blue vase with a sprig of rosemary. She plucked at a leaf and rubbed it between her thumb and forefinger, and the heady, woody scent filled the library.

She'd once read somewhere that rosemary enhanced memory. At her age, though, her recollections clanged and clashed about in her head like cymbals, and there was nothing she could do to dull the noise—no matter how hard she tried.

Chapter 35

EVIE

PARIS, PRESENT DAY

They gathered at Olivier's restaurant on the Left Bank where Gilles had arranged for the best corner table to celebrate Hugo's graduation. Nina and her son Simon, and Camille and her son, Victor, had joined them, and Monsieur and Madame Laurent had made the trip up from Villa Sanary. "We'd be honored!" the older woman had said over the phone, sounding quite moved. "Our Hugo, all grown up. Tell him if he needs a bed in California, our Bess and her family would be happy to have him."

Gilles was already pouring champagne for the Laurents when Evie and Hugo arrived. Camille was on to her second Negroni, and Nina was making introductions. Coats were peeled off, hugs exchanged, and the Laurents clucked and plucked at Hugo's new navy jacket, teamed tonight with his shabbiest T-shirt. He had bought the jacket from the music-blasting boys next door under duress for the official school graduation night, spending precisely double the budget Evie had given him. She'd gone over to give the boys a lambasting about why an eighteen-year-old needed a Comme des Garçons sports jacket but lost her nerve as soon as she stepped into the store. All thoughts were drowned out by a ripping bass. Then they'd offered her a cocktail as a salve, and all was forgiven.

Platters of grilled white asparagus, terrine, and charcuterie were shepherded to the table by Olivier. "To the guest of honor." The portly chef poured himself a glass and proposed a toast. "*Bon voyage.*" He and Gilles looked like a pair of proud uncles.

"Congratulations!" everyone said as they clinked glasses.

Gilles laughed. "May the fun begin!"

"But not *too* much fun," Evie said as she joined the toast, voice breaking. Madame Laurent shot her a look, and it was all Evie could do to stop herself from crying.

Victor and Simon sniggered and were given matching dark looks by their mothers.

Hugo would die if she cried. She'd already gotten teary before they left the apartment, and he'd rolled his eyes.

"Thanks, guys," he said now. "Don't worry, Mum, I won't do anything you haven't done. Like switch countries and marry someone you'd only known a few months for a visa."

Everybody roared with laughter as Evie's face heated. "I *didn't* marry Raph for a vis—"

"Oh, love, he's only teasing," said Madame Laurent as she squeezed Evie's leg.

"Anyway," Hugo said, "you lot won't have time to miss me, with the exhibition coming up and all." He put his hand out for a champagne top-up.

"Another worthy celebration," said Gilles as he filled Hugo's glass. "Joséphine Murant was an icon. I'm so looking forward to the launch."

"As are we," said Monsieur Laurent. "Madame Laurent has already planned to make you her famous bouillabaisse."

"You'll have to try the fougasse too. Dad's favorite." Hugo gave Evie a meaningful glance.

"We'll come," said Camille. "I've already booked a hotel."

"Hotel?" Evie asked. "No, there's plenty of room, you can stay with us."

"Oh, really? Seems to me it could be crowded by then . . ."

Evie gulped down a mouthful of her bubbles, hoping her face was not as red as it felt. She and Clément had spoken about next steps, like perhaps taking a holiday together when the exhibition was all over. He had sent his apologies tonight; he had a shipment of dinosaur skeletons coming from the Smithsonian, and he needed to receive them into the holding room. She couldn't help but admire his dedication—she would have done the same for a rare botanical illustration.

She hadn't been able to get back to the Côte d'Azur during Hugo's last term of exams and graduation. So the pair were taking it slowly and courting via old-school phone calls and FaceTime like giddy teenagers. It was early days, and they were both hoping there could be more.

Last month, Gilles had sent her and Clément the findings of

the Louvre handwriting expert, who had compared the material from under the floorboards and the Leroux diary to the manuscript annotations. According to him, they were in different hands.

Evie wasn't sure what to do with this information. Should she try to have Margot Bisset publicly exonerated? Could that be done without revealing that Margot had become the world-famous author Joséphine Murant? Evie wanted justice, but not at the expense of Joséphine's reputation. And what would happen to the charitable work of the foundation? Evie also wanted to avoid the media chaos that could ensue, for her and Hugo's sakes. She wasn't even sure if she should tell her son all the details.

A fork clacked against a plate, startling her. She realized she was getting caught up in her thoughts and focused back on the moment. She reached for a piece of baguette.

When Gilles tapped a fork on his glass, the table hushed. "To endings and beginnings," he said as he shuffled back his chair and got to his feet. "None of us know where we are headed. Look at your mother's life, Hugo. And Joséphine's. Such different roads from what they expected. Victor and Simon, you boys are included in this. I hope and pray for your safety, for your good health. That you never have to live through a war. I also know that whatever lies ahead—good and bad—you'll confront every situation with grace. *Bonne chance pour ta nouvelle vie.*"

Empty plates were cleared, and Olivier delivered entrées to the table: sautéed scallops, baked goat's cheese with honey, and a salade Lyonnaise. Monsieur Laurent and Gilles talked about plans to extend the southern garden at Villa Sanary. Camille pressed a red lipstick into Nina's hand and complimented Madame Laurent on her pink sweater. "So chic." Madame Laurent blushed. The three teenage boys were having an in-depth discussion about a computer game.

Watching them, Evie remembered the night a year ago when Hugo had helped convince her to throw her full support behind the exhibition. His words had stayed with her: *I'm not sure that covering things up . . . It's not always for the best.*

He was right. She shouldn't hide this from him.

She leaned over, put her hand on his forearm, and said softly, so the others wouldn't hear, "When we get home tonight, there's something I need to talk to you about."

He pulled a face. "Seriously, Mum, I'm going to be *fine*. I don't need the 'talk.' *Please!* I have condoms. Won't take drugs. Will text when I arrive in a new city. Check. Check. Check."

"No, it's not *that*!" said Evie with a laugh. "It's about Joséphine. There's something I need to tell you before you go."

Review: The Joséphine Murant Retrospective

ESTELLE AUBERT PEEKS BEHIND THE POLICE TAPE AT AN EXHIBITION CELEBRATING FRANCE'S MOST FAMOUS CRIME WRITER.

There's a chilling circularity to this exhibition at Villa Sanary, Côte d'Azur. The villa itself was the site of a notorious society murder in 1939.

It's a twist that could be lifted straight from one of Joséphine Murant's bestsellers.

The first stop in the exhibition is Murant's library, complete with a cherrywood desk and antique typewriter (the only one she ever used, as she refused to write on a computer). There are annotated versions of all her manuscripts, assorted papers and Post-its stuck along the walls.

While adults absorb Murant's working space and perhaps seek out her muse for themselves, children are encouraged to explore the villa's elegant grounds. They can even have a go at solving a cute mystery set up in the rose garden.

For serious sleuths, the balcony overlooking the pool has a replica of the taped-off crime scene—taken from police-file notes on the notorious 1939 Bisset murder case—where you can dust for fingerprints on a (replica) handgun, read police interviews and the coroner's report, then look for clues with a magnifying glass. The twist? It appears Murant and Bisset became firm friends in prison.

The exhibition takes a more somber turn in the main foyer, where Murant's time as a Resistance fighter is documented. Among the exhibits are lists of hundreds of contacts who operated in the early days of the Resistance, along with meeting minutes, article notes, and maps with safe houses and escape routes marked out. Also, there are handfuls of five-franc notes stamped with *Vive de Gaulle* in red. Murant had secreted all these items beneath the parquetry of her Montmartre studio apartment, and they were only recently discovered by her family.

The centerpiece of the exhibition is the prison diary Joséphine Murant wrote in the margins of a paperback edition of Gaston Leroux's *Le Fantôme de l'Opéra*. The book is tucked in a Perspex box and flanked by security guards; a computer screen has been set up alongside it flicking through several pages so readers can experience the author's war in her own words. This is one of the few recorded first-person accounts of World War II by a woman and the only one that records the atrocities in the Phrix Rayon Factory in Germany, where Murant was sent during the war.

Mallory Press—Murant's long-term publishing partner—will be releasing a special edition next year, with an introduction and annotations by war historian Clément Tazi.

As you wander the grounds of Villa Sanary and examine Murant's artifacts, it is impossible not to ask: Where is the line between fiction and reality?

Murant often took inspiration from newspaper headlines, threading real events—such as kidnappings, custody disputes, and terrorist attacks—into her work.

Within the library, contained in its own Perspex box, is an item that further blurs this distinction between fact and fiction: Murant's unpublished manuscript, "The French Gift." Dr. Tazi writes in the excellent catalog accompanying the exhibition:

> *The rejection letter from Mallory Press and the events described late in "The French Gift" suggest this manuscript always remained unfinished. Like all her novels, it campaigns for social justice. But unlike the remainder of her novels, it appears this is a fictionalized biography mingled with a fictionalized memoir. It contains a shocking twist, playing with the trope of an unreliable narrator. This shows that in her youth, Murant was well ahead of her contemporaries.*

Joséphine Murant was always a fighter. She never stopped using her weapon—her writing. Her diary is charming, witty, and defiant. Though her body became weak and scarred from her time as a prisoner of the Nazis, her spirit remained strong.

The exhibition is a celebration of inspirational women, wartime friendship and sacrifice, the unsavory side of unchecked privilege, and the power of transformation, all set within a spectacular renovated villa whose walls surely rattle with ghosts and secrets.

CRIME SCENE: A RETROSPECTIVE OF JOSÉPHINE MURANT AT VILLA SANARY RUNS AT VILLA SANARY, MARSEILLE MUSEUM, EVERY WEDNESDAY IN JULY.

Epilogue

EVIE

VILLA SANARY, PRESENT DAY

Le quatorze juillet. Bastille Day. Twilight. The lavender, herbs, and roses around Villa Sanary were in bloom, and avenues of red and white oleander popped. Evie stood on the balcony overlooking the pool, so she had a clear view of the launch party for the Joséphine Murant exhibition. Men and women dressed in tuxedos and flowing dresses fanned across the terrace around the sapphire pool and out over the lawn. A DJ pumped summer beats into the air, and fairy lights illuminated all the old trees.

On this balcony, Evie, Margot, and Joséphine were linked by tragedy—but also a gift.

As a warm breeze carrying the scent of the sea and wild rosemary enveloped her, Evie thought of Madame Laurent's comment about Joséphine always keeping a pot of herbs on her desk when she wrote: *They reminded her of her childhood.* A clue in plain sight. Just like the clues in Joséphine Murant's—Margot Bisset's—novels.

For how could Joséphine have grown up with the smell of wild herbs? She was a child of Montmartre in the middle of Paris. It was *Margot* who had walked the paths along the cliffs between the village and Villa Sanary, just like her mother and grandmother before her. These cliffs were in her blood.

Instead of donating all of Joséphine's artifacts to the museum, Evie had convinced the museum to partner with her to form a permanent collection at Villa Sanary. Clément had worked miracles with the paperwork, and so the villa had been declared a *monument historique*. The local government had provided a grant. From now on, the villa would be open on Wednesdays every July for visitors. She hoped that Raph, Margot, and Joséphine would have been proud of her for organizing all of this.

The foundation had granted approval for Joséphine's diary to be published with Mallory next year. Evie was just going through the final draft, and soon it would head off to proofreading and be available for purchase with the annual exhibition.

Hugo accompanied guests around the rose garden with Madame and Monsieur Laurent. He was wearing a tux—he'd filled out this summer; his shoulders were almost as broad as his father's. She thought of his haunted face, so pale it was almost translucent, only a few years ago. Now it was tanned, framed by curls that tumbled along the edge of his collar, and his smile reached all the way to his eyes. Yesterday he'd flown in from Copenhagen.

"Surprise!" he'd said as he walked into the kitchen, fresh ink spiraling up his arm under his T-shirt. "Couldn't miss this party, could I?" He poked his finger into the batch of gazpacho Madame Laurent was straining through some muslin.

She swatted him away with a tea towel, clucking, "Just like your father."

"Is that a bird winding its way up your forearm?" Evie asked as she hugged him, trying to sound far more woke than she actually was.

"A phoenix—appropriate, don't you think?"

Their eyes met, and she smiled. "Perfect."

Evie surveyed the fake crime scene on the balcony one last time before joining the rest of the party. She thought of Margot and Joséphine curled up in their filthy lower bunk at Anrath, whispering about the murder.

It might be possible to prove that the great author Joséphine Murant was Margot Bisset. They could use the handwriting expert's testimony, or even get a DNA test for Hugo to see if he was indeed a blood relative of the late author. But Evie still wasn't sure if she wanted to try. She had agonized about what to include in the exhibition.

Right after Hugo's graduation dinner, nervous about telling her son the truth, she'd called Clément, pouring her hurt and confusion down the line. "She never spoke a word. Not once did she even try to reveal who she was."

"That's true, but she made a determined effort to change the trajectory of her life. She may have initially regretted living past the war. Survivor's guilt. But she became stronger by the day. She claimed a name and a villa that society said she had no right to, and she kept going. Kept giving."

Clément had been right, but she'd still been worried Hugo would be upset by the deception.

On the contrary, he had appeared rather delighted. "Two brilliant women. I mean, it doesn't make Joséphine any *less* brave, does it? She still recorded her diary and hid all the documents. Inspired people in prison. All of that was true. And Margot, well, she kept Joséphine's name alive. She reinvented herself when all she must have wanted to do was collapse after being in hell. She was wrongfully accused, sent to a forced-labor factory, and still she survived. She helped other women too—look at all the charities for the shelters and schools. She picked herself up again. And again and again. Like that phoenix statue we saw at Fort Mont-Valérien. Oh, and one last thing—she loved us. That wasn't a lie."

Once again, Hugo had seen the truth.

"Fucking brilliant," he'd added, "if you ask me."

"Language!"

❧

Evie needed to get back to the launch party. Over by the pool she spotted Camille, dressed head to toe in black YSL, speaking to a dazzled museum official in a white tux. Nina was crossing the lawn in an emerald cocktail dress with a flute of champagne in each hand; she'd traveled down for the night and intended to make the most of it.

Before Evie walked inside from the balcony, she touched a glossy palm leaf. Had Margot been crouched behind a pot just like this?

As Evie walked downstairs to the library, she wandered past

310

original yellowing copies of the *Liberté* newsletter in Perspex boxes, all eight issues set in a row. She wondered how she would react if she were faced with war. Would *she* write for an underground newsletter, carry messages into enemy territory, or nurse wounded soldiers back to health?

Everyone would like to think they'd be the best version of themselves during a war, but Evie wasn't so sure. She'd been tested and left keening on her knees when Raph died. Her family from Australia had visited right after he died, and that was a consolation. Hugo had helped her through; Nina, Camille, Gilles and Olivier, and the Laurents too.

"There you are!" said Clément. "You look beautiful." He kissed her on the lips and stepped back to admire the fitted navy YSL dress Camille had gotten her half price. There were huge perks to Camille's job as a stylist.

Just as Clément had envisaged the day they met, he had recreated the workspace. Much to the chagrin of Madame Laurent, the cherrywood desk was cluttered with pieces of paper, a fountain pen, and notebooks. At the last minute, Evie had added the small vase with some rosemary. The wall beside it was dotted with multicolored sticky notes, each replicating a chapter and color-coded by characters' points of view.

With its view of the pool and across the garden, it was a cheery place to work while lost in other people's worlds, voices both imagined and real.

On the far wall, Clément's BBC documentary was playing, and she found herself grinning as a younger Clément spoke to the camera and asked the central question of the documentary:

Where does fiction end and the writer's own reality begin? Around the library, he had painstakingly shown the influence of current events on each novel. A headline about three children missing from an Australian beach, never found, sat beside the first-edition hardback of *The Missing*. One about an American heiress kidnapped, only for her family to refuse to pay the ransom, sat beside a pile of international editions of *Hell's Ransom*.

Evie and Clément walked hand in hand to the last cabinet.

```
This is the only remaining unpublished manuscript
by Joséphine Murant.
```

Alongside the manuscript was a poster with newspaper clippings that covered the case of Margot Bisset.

Margot and Joséphine *would* have been proud; Evie was sure of it.

She looked at Clément, felt his steady hand in hers, and reflected on his competence, his sharp intelligence, his curious nature, and his family history of trauma. He'd reached into Evie's confusion and anxiety, holding her with gentle patience, waiting until she was ready.

Inspired by Margot, Evie had started to rearrange the pieces of her life. She'd taken on a business partner in London to help with manuscript sales, and Gilles had agreed to stay for a few more years. "What else would I do? Golf?" He'd grimaced. "Besides, Olivier would fall apart if I didn't lunch on the Left Bank every day—he needs me!"

She'd planned a hike with Hugo outside Santiago, and then

Christmas in Australia with her family—and Clément. She couldn't wait to be crammed into her father's tiny pickup together, bumping over dusty potholes.

⁓

They walked to join all the guests gathered on the sandstone terrace out by the pool. Waiters carried silver trays piled with fresh oysters and scallops, champagne flutes were filled and refilled. Jars with blush-colored roses from Monsieur Laurent's rose garden were scattered across tables laden with hors d'oeuvres.

A spoon clinked against crystal. The speeches were beginning.

Clément made opening remarks and welcomed the guests. "And now I would like to hand it over to Genevieve Black, trustee and caretaker of Joséphine Murant's legacy, including Villa Sanary."

Evie stepped up to the microphone and raised her glass. "I'd like to dedicate this exhibition not only to Joséphine Murant, but also to all the brave Resistance fighters she went to prison protecting. Also, the hundreds of women who were forced to work in the Phrix Rayon Factory at Krefeld. We owe them so much." She drew a deep breath. "Tonight, take the time to read the words Joséphine wrote in her makeshift diary. She showed us all how to be courageous. Fearless when others would cower. Funny when others drowned in bitterness.

"Afterward, look at the many names of her fellow fighters. There are many more we will never know—cannot know, because the Nazis eradicated them. They will never have their names on books or memorials.

"It seems only fitting to end with the words of Joséphine Murant: 'The stories of this factory, this war, need to be shared.' So please raise your glasses and join me in toasting Joséphine and her brave comrades: *Liberté, égalité, fraternité!*"

The jubilant audience raised their glasses and repeated, "*Liberté, égalité, fraternité!*" The DJ started to play, and the electronic bass notes lifted the murmur of the crowd into a roar as they fanned out across the terrace.

"Also, to the phoenix," said Evie, winking at Hugo as she turned off the microphone.

She looked to where dusk was throwing pink light against Villa Sanary. It seemed to absorb shadows and secrets into its stone walls, yet carry on reflecting the sun. Radiating warmth. The mistral would come along soon enough, and with it the changing of the seasons.

She stepped down from the podium, reached for Clément's hand, and pressed it to her cheek.

"Great speech. Think you could wing one about bird-hipped dinosaurs next month?"

"Consider it done!" She stood on her tiptoes and kissed him as fireworks started to whistle into the sky.

She'd come here last summer to discover Joséphine's past. But she'd been given an unexpected gift: the story of Margot Bisset. And just like these two courageous women, Evie had been given a chance to write a different story.

She was ready to take it.

Acknowledgments

Many thanks to my agent, Clare Forster, who managed to keep a professional face when I pitched her the idea of a high-society murder party gone wrong, set in the lush grounds of a villa on the Riviera, blended with the Occupation of Paris during World War II, the Resistance, and clandestine newspapers, plus the little-known horror of the Phrix Rayon Factory. We got there!

The novel would not have happened without the wisdom and kindness of Annette Barlow and Christa Munns at Allen & Unwin, Australia; Stacy Testa at Writers House; Lucy Morris of Curtis Brown, London; and the thoughtful Tessa Woodward at William Morrow.

Special mention to editor Kate Goldsworthy, who wrangled the text many times more than she probably cared to. I'm indebted to your patience, professionalism, and . . . patience. Carolyn Manning always reads my drafts on late notice (thanks, Mum!). Sue Peacock is always a superb beta reader, and Sara James is my go-to plot whisperer. Thanks for staying with me right to the end for this one. Thanks also to fellow writers Sally Hepworth, Lisa Ireland, and Jane Cockram for the laughs, Zoom virtual drinks, and ridiculous texts during lockdown. God, we needed that!

Barbara Mellor kindly read the entire manuscript and was generous with her feedback (and the correction of historical points, as well as French grammar!). I'm grateful for her time and considerable expertise.

Eternal gratitude to you, my readers. I've been overwhelmed by your touching messages and kindness as *The Song of the Jade Lily* and *The Lost Jewels* have been published in Australia and around the world. Your feedback really does propel me to keep hunting for stories, to research a little more.

Lastly, many thanks to my beautiful family: Alex, Henry, Jemima, and Charlie. They totally get that I talk to people who don't exist and walk for hours and consider it work.

So 2020 was quite the year, wasn't it? I wrote this at the dining-room table in lockdown with teenage children walking past all the time, asking me what to eat, or to listen to a school debate via Zoom, or for help with a Shakespeare essay. Or doing PE in the living room (so much jumping!). It was a strange time for our family—and the world—and I'll cherish the time we spent together . . . mostly!

Thanks for nourishing us with all the good things in life, Alex Wilcox; for the superb cooking and mealtime repartee, Henry; for the laughs, cakes, and baked treats, Jemima. And thanks for the

Acknowledgments

perpetual smiles and hugs from Charlie (and Winter). Trust me, this novel would never have gotten over the line without you lot.

Writing a book like this takes me to some of the darkest and most haunting moments of our recent history, but also to magical places that instill hope. Always, there thrums a single thought that feeds every line I write: *My family is everything.* Thank you. xx

P.S.

About the author

About the book

Insights,
Interviews
& More . . .

Meet Kirsty Manning

JK Henshaw

KIRSTY MANNING is the author of *The Song of the Jade Lily* and *The Lost Jewels*. She grew up in northern New South Wales, Australia. She has degrees in literature and communications and worked as an editor and a publishing manager in book publishing for more than a decade. A country girl with wanderlust, her travels and studies have taken her through most of Europe, along the East and West Coasts of the United States, and into pockets of Asia. Kirsty's journalism and photography specializing in lifestyle and travel regularly appear in magazines, in newspapers, and online. ~

Author's Note

The French Gift is a work of fiction. But like all my books, it is inspired by true snippets of history.

A paragraph in the excellent nonfiction book *The Riviera Set*, by Mary S. Lovell, lit my imagination. She described a decadent party arranged by a famous hostess, where one of the guests was (faux) murdered and the local police were roped in as part of the game.

What fun! I thought. *What if I write a book about a decadent murder party . . . and then it goes wrong?*

But I also wanted to write a story inspired by the ordeal of women in World War II who were forced into labor in factories and of whom so little about their history is known. I had stumbled across the memoir of Agnès Humbert, *Résistance*, which had been expertly translated into English by Barbara Mellor. Humbert was part of the Resistance, a founding member of the subterfuge group that called itself the Cercle Alain-Fournier and is now known as the Musée de l'Homme network, with whom she cofounded the clandestine newspaper *Résistance*. Betrayed and arrested, she spent a year in brutal Gestapo prisons in Paris, before a military show trial found her guilty of espionage and sentenced her to five years' hard labor for the Third Reich. Sent to ▶

3

Author's Note *(continued)*

Anrath Prison near Krefeld, she endured forced labor at the Phrix Rayon Factory.

During her trial, she managed to record her thoughts in an edition of René Descartes's *Discourse on Method*, and she herself hinted (though this was never confirmed) that "the *Résistance* file, with its 400 names and addresses," lay quietly hidden under her stair carpet throughout her arrest and interrogation by the Gestapo and subsequent incarceration. A committed socialist with a sense of justice, compassion, and the absurd that never failed her, she formed life-saving bonds of mutual support with her fellow prisoners, both in prison in Paris and at the Phrix Rayon Factory, and even elicited the admiration and support of some of her jailers.

Unlike my heroine Joséphine, Humbert was a key figure in the liberation and stayed in Germany to assist the American troops as they hunted down escaping Nazis. Her story does not end at the Phrix Rayon Factory, for at fifty-one years of age she returned to a liberated France and to work and writing. She was also a devoted mother to her young son, Pierre, who lived with her in Paris, and daughter to her elderly and ailing mother, at whose hospital bedside she was arrested by the Gestapo. Agnès did not survive her captivity.

Humbert was an extraordinary

woman. It has long been my quest in historical fiction to draw attention to forgotten pockets of history. Humbert's English translator, Barbara Mellor, captured with accuracy and visceral reality a type of reportage, a female first-person experience of the Resistance, which shines a spotlight on the forced-labor factories used in World War II that have long been overlooked in history. We are indebted to the work of Humbert and Mellor.

But make no mistake, my heroine Joséphine Murant is fictional. In no way must the reader mistake Joséphine's internal musings for those of a real person. You must go to the source (and there are many listed in Further Reading) for a true account of all these places and people.

In my heroine Joséphine I wanted to capture some of that resilience and inspiration of wartime women, and to honor the women who were forced to work in atrocious conditions and whose stories have largely been forgotten. Joséphine is young, educated, and sassy. The crux of the book is her abiding friendship with Margot and their working together to unpack the mystery at the heart of the story.

There were many clandestine newspapers in Paris during the Occupation, including *Combat, Défense* ▶

de la France, *L'Humanité*, and *Le Franc-Tireur* as well as *Résistance*, and Joséphine could have worked for any of them.

Lastly, I wanted to call attention to how women through the generations have often served as the emotional ballast for their families. Also, how trauma is passed and healed through generations.

The atrocities of the Phrix Rayon Factory and the systematized use of forced labor in wartime factories were documented and recorded in the French government report I refer to a number of times in the novel: *Collection Défense de l'Homme: Les témoins qui se firent égorger* (Editions Défense de la France, 1946).

La Maison Rustique is a real-life botanical bookshop I stumbled into quite by accident in Saint-Germain-des-Prés well over a decade ago, and it has lived in my heart ever since. My fictional version is vastly different, of course. But if ever you are in Paris . . .

Marseille Museum is fictional, but there are many fine museums on the Riviera if you care to visit.

As with all my books, I have taken some liberties with the historical record and places, shifting events and combining others to serve the story. Some war timelines have been condensed or changed.

I wrote this book in a monthslong lockdown when the COVID-19 pandemic was circling the globe. The present day

I write about is COVID-free. This was a deliberate choice, as to include it would not have served the story (Hugo and Evie in Paris lockdown? Going nowhere. Watching Netflix. Baking sourdough . . .). But mostly, I wanted to switch off for a moment when I was writing. Also, to hold a space for the reader to have a reprieve from the news. I hope this book gives you a few enjoyable COVID-19-free hours.

Any mistakes are my own. ～

Sources and Further Reading

The complete list of sources consulted for *The French Gift* is too long to include here. Below are selected sources for further research around this topic.

MUSEUMS

Fort Mont-Valérien, Suresnes

The Liberation of Paris Museum–General Leclerc Museum–Jean Moulin Museum, Paris

Marseille History Museum, Marseille

Mémorial de la France Combattante (Memorial to Fighting France), Suresnes [The quotes on the wall at Mémorial de la France Combattante are a true record. The names are fictional. See www.mont-valerien.fr.]

FILM

Sisters in Resistance, directed by Maia Wechsler (2000).

BOOKS

Chanel's Riviera: Life, Love and the Struggle for Survival on the Côte d'Azur, 1930–1944, by Anne de Courcy (London: Weidenfeld & Nicolson, 2019).

Collection Défense de l'Homme: Les témoins qui se firent égorger (Editions Défense de la France, 1946).

Côte d'Azur: Inventing the French Riviera,
by Mary Blume (London: Thames &
Hudson, 1994).

*Fake Silk: The Lethal History of
Viscose Rayon*, by Paul David Blanc
(New Haven, CT: Yale University Press,
2016).

*Occupation: The Ordeal of France,
1940–1944*, by Ian Ousby
(London: John Murray, 1997).

*Provençal Escapes: Inspirational Homes
in Provence and the Côte d'Azur*,
by Caroline Clifton-Mogg (London:
Ryland Peters & Small, 2005).

*Resistance: European Resistance to the
Nazis, 1940–1945*, by M. R. D. Foot
(London: Biteback Publishing, 2016).

*The Resistance: The French Fight Against
the Nazis*, by Matthew Cobb (London:
Simon & Schuster, 2009).

Résistance: Memoirs of Occupied France, by
Agnès Humbert, translated by Barbara
Mellor (London: Bloomsbury, 2008).

*Resistance in Vichy France: A Study of Ideas
and Motivation in the Southern Zone,
1940–1942*, by H. R. Kedward (Oxford:
Oxford University Press, 1978).

*The Riviera at War: World War II on the
Côte d'Azur*, by George G. Kundahl
(London: I.B. Tauris, 2017).

The Riviera Set, by Mary S. Lovell
(London: Little, Brown, 2016). ▶

Sources and Further Reading *(continued)*

The Secret Museum, by Molly Oldfield (Buffalo, NY: Firefly Books, 2013).

The Shameful Peace: How French Artists and Intellectuals Survived the Nazi Occupation, by Frederic Spotts (New Haven, CT: Yale University Press, 2008).

When Paris Went Dark: The City of Light Under German Occupation, 1940–1944, by Ronald C. Rosbottom (London: J. Murray, 2015).

ARTICLE

"Eyewitness to the Evil That Men Do," by Linda Grant, *Guardian*, September 27, 2008, www.theguardian.com/books /2008/sep/28/biography2.

MISCELLANEOUS

"Nacht und Nebel," from the poem "Erlkönig," by Johann Wolfgang von Goethe (1782, first performed as part of *Die Fischerin*). [The catalog explanation of Nacht und Nebel is obviously fictional, but for the full facts see the United States Holocaust Memorial Museum, Washington, DC, https://encyclopedia.ushmm.org /content/en/article/night-and-fog -decree.]

"La Marseillaise" (French national anthem), by Claude-Joseph Rouget de Lisle, April 24, 1792. ⌒